FAIR JUNO

A Selection of Recent Titles Available from Severn House by
Stephanie Laurens

THE REASONS FOR MARRIAGE
TANGLED REINS
FOUR IN HAND
IMPETUOUS INNOCENT
A COMFORTABLE WIFE
A LADY OF EXPECTATIONS
AN UNWILLING CONQUEST
FAIR JUNO

FAIR JUNO

Stephanie Laurens

This hardcover edition published 2018
in Great Britain and the USA by
SEVERN HOUSE PUBLISHERS LTD of
Eardley House, 4 Uxbridge Street, London W8 7SY
by arrangement with Harlequin Books S.A.

British Library Cataloguing in Publication Data
A CIP catalogue record for this title is available from the British Library.

ISBN-13: 978-0-7278-8825-9 (cased)

All Severn House titles are printed on acid-free paper.

Severn House Publishers support the Forest Stewardship Council™
[FSC™],
the leading international forest certification organisation.
All our titles that are printed on FSC certified paper carry the FSC logo.

MIX
Paper from
responsible sources
FSC   FSC® C013056
www.fsc.org

Typeset by Palimpsest Book Production Ltd.,
Falkirk, Stirlingshire, Scotland.
Printed and bound in Great Britain by
TJ International, Padstow, Cornwall.

Chapter One

Martin Cambden Willesden, fifth Earl of Merton, strode purposefully along the first-floor corridor of the Hermitage, his principal country residence. The scowl marring his striking features would have warned any who knew him that he was in a foul mood. A common saying among the men of the 7th Hussars had been that if any emotion showed on Major Willesden's face the portents were bad. And, thought ex-Major Willesden savagely, I've every right to feel furious.

Recalled from pleasant exile in the Bahamas, forced to leave behind the most satisfying mistress he had ever mounted, he had landed in gloomy London to face an uphill battle to extricate the family fortunes from the appalling state they had, apparently unaided, tumbled into. Matthews, the elder, of Matthews and Sons, his and his family's man of business, had warned him that the Hermitage was in need of attention and would not, in its present state, meet with his approval. He had thought that was all part of the old man's attempt to persuade him to return to England without delay. He should have recalled Matthews' habit of understatement. Martin's lips thinned. The grim look in his grey eyes deepened. The Hermitage was in even worse case than the investments he had spent the last three weeks reorganising.

As he paced the length of the corridor, the crisp clack of boot-heels penetrated his reverie. In a state bordering on shock, Martin stopped and stared down. There were no runners! Just bare wooden boards and, to his critical eye, they were not even well-polished.

Slowly, his grey gaze lifted to take in the sombre tones of decaying wallpaper framed by faded and musty hangings. A pervasive chill inhabited the gloom.

His frown now black, the Earl of Merton swore— and added yet another item to the catalogue of matters requiring immediate attention. If he was ever to visit the Hermitage again, let alone reside for more than a day, the place would have to be done up. Downstairs was bad enough—but this! Description failed him.

Setting aside his aggravation, Martin resumed his determined progress towards the Dowager Countess's rooms. Since his arrival eight hours ago, he had postponed the inevitable meeting with his mother on the grounds of dealing with the problems crippling his major estate. The excuse had not been exaggeration. But the critical decisions had been made; the reins were now firmly in his grasp.

Despite such success, his hopes for the coming interview were less than certain. Curiosity brushed shoulders with a lingering wariness he had not thought he still possessed.

His mother, Lady Catherine Willesden, the Dowager Countess of Merton, had terrorised her household for as long as Martin could recall. The only ones apparently immune from her domination had been his father and himself. His father she had excused. He had not been so favoured.

He halted outside the plain wooden door that gave access to the Dowager's apartments. Despite all that lay between them, she was his mother. A mother he had not seen for thirteen years and whom he remembered as a cold, calculating woman with no room in her heart for him. How much of the blame for the decay of his ancestral acres could be laid at her door? The question puzzled him, for he knew her pride. In fact, he had a good few questions, including how she would deal with him now; the answers lay beyond the door facing him.

Recognising the instinctive squaring of his shoulders as his habit when about to enter his colonel's domain, Martin's lips twitched. Without more ado, he raised a fist to the plain panels and knocked. Hearing a clear instruction to enter, he opened the door and complied.

He paused just beyond the threshold, his hand on the doorknob and, with a practised air of languid ease, scanned the room. What he saw answered some of his questions.

The tall, upright figure in the chair before the windows was much as he remembered, more gaunt with hair three shades greyer, perhaps, but still retaining that calm air of determination he so vividly recalled. It was the sight of the gnarled and twisted hands resting, useless, in her lap and the peculiar rigidity of her

pose that alerted him to the truth. They had told him
she kept to her room, a victim of rheumatism. He had
interpreted that as a fashionable response to a relatively minor ailment. Now, reality stared him in the
face. His mother was an invalid, bound to her chair.

Pity stabbed him, sharp and fresh. He remembered
her as an active woman, riding and dancing with the
best of them. Then his eyes locked with hers, chilly
grey, haughty as ever—and more defensive than he
had ever seen them. Instantly, he knew that pity was
the very last thing his mother would accept from him.

Despite the real shock, his face remained impassive.
Unhurriedly, he closed the door and strolled into the
room, taking a moment to acknowledge the round-
eyed stare of the only other occupant of the large
chamber—his eldest brother's relict, Melissa.

Catherine Willesden sat in her high-backed chair
and watched her third son approach, her features as
impassive as his. Her lips thinned as she took in his
long, powerful frame, and the subtle elegance that
cloaked it. The light fell on his features as he drew
nearer. Her sharp eyes were quick to detect the hardness behind the elegance, a ruthless determination, a
hedonism ill-concealed by the veneer of polite manners. It was a characteristic she was honest enough to
recognise.

Then he was before her. To her horror, he reached
for her hand. She would have stopped him if she'd
been able but the words stuck in her throat, trapped
by her pride. Warm, strong fingers closed over her
gnarled fingers. Her surprise was swamped beneath a
sudden rush of emotions as Martin's dark head bent

and she felt his lips brush her wrinkled skin. Gently, he replaced her hand in her lap and dutifully kissed her cheek.

"Mama."

The single word, uttered in a gravelly voice deeper than she recalled, jolted Lady Catherine to reality. She blinked rapidly. Her heart was beating faster. Ridiculous! She fixed her son with a frown, struggling to infuse an arctic bleakness into her grey eyes. The slight smile which played about his mouth suggested that he was well aware he had thrown her off balance. But she was determined to keep this black sheep firmly beneath her thumb. She could, and would, ensure he brought no further scandal upon the family.

"I believe, sir, that I sent instructions that you were to attend me here immediately you reached England?"

Entirely unperturbed by his mother's icy glare, Martin strolled to the empty fireplace, one black brow rising in polite surprise. "Didn't my secretary write to you?"

Indignation flared in Lady Catherine's pale eyes. "If you are referring to a note from a Mr Wetherall informing me that the Earl of Merton was occupied with taking up the reins of his inheritance and would call on me at his earliest convenience, I received it, sirrah! What I want to know is what the meaning of it is. And why, once you finally arrived, it took you an entire day to remember the way to my rooms!"

Observing the unmistakable signs of ire investing his mother's austere features, Martin resisted the temptation to remind her of his title. He had not expected to enjoy this discussion, but, somehow, his mother no longer seemed as remote nor as truly hostile as he recalled. Perhaps it was her infirmity that made her appear more human? "Suffice it to say that the Merton affairs were in a somewhat deeper tangle than I had understood." Placing one booted foot on the brass fender, Martin braced an arm against the heavily carved mantel and, with unimpaired calm, regarded his mother. "However, now that I have managed to spare you some time away from the damnable business of setting this estate to rights, perhaps you could tell me what it is you wish to see me about?"

By the conscious exercise of considerable will-power, Lady Catherine kept surprise from her face. It wasn't his words that shook her, but his voice. Gone entirely were the light, charming tones of youth. In their place, there was depth containing a great deal of hardness, harshness, with the undertones of command barely concealed beneath the fashionable drawl.

Inwardly, she shook herself. The idea of being cowed by this scapegrace son was ludicrous. He had always been impudent—but never stupid. Such languid insolence would be a thing of the past, once she made his position clear. Wrapping herself in haughty dignity, Lady Catherine embarked on her son's education. "I have much to say concerning how you should go on."

Exuding an attitude of polite attention, Martin settled his shoulders against the mantelpiece, elegantly crossing his long legs before him, and fixed his mother with a steady regard.

Frowning, Lady Catherine nodded towards a chair. "Sit down."

Martin's lips twisted in a slow smile. "I'm quite comfortable. What are these facts you needs must inform me of?"

Lady Catherine decided not to glare. His very ease was disconcerting. Much better not to let on how disturbing she found it. She forced herself to meet his unwavering gaze. "Firstly, I consider it imperative that you marry as soon as possible. To this end, I've arranged a match with a Miss Faith Wendover."

One of Martin's mobile brows rose.

Seeing it, the Dowager hurried on. "Given that the title now resides with the third of my four sons, you can hardly be surprised if, in my estimation, securing the succession is a major concern."

Her eldest son George had married to please his family but Melissa, dull, plain Melissa, had failed lamentably in satisfying expectations. Her second son Edward had died some years previously, part of the force which had successfully repelled The Monster's invasion. George had succumbed to the fever a year ago. Until then, it had never dawned on the Dowager that her impossible third son could inherit. If she had thought of it at all, she would have expected him to die, somwhere, on one of his outlandish adventures, leaving Damian, her favourite, as the next Earl.

But Martin was now the Earl; it was up to her to ensure that he toed the line.

Determined to brook no opposition, Lady Catherine fixed her son with a commanding eye. "Miss Wendover is an heiress and passably pretty. She'll make an unexceptionable Countess of Merton. Her family is well-respected and she'll bring considerable land as her dower. Now you are here and the settlements can be signed, the marriage can take place in three months' time.''

Prepared to defend her arrangements against a storm of protest, Lady Catherine tilted her chin at an imperious angle and regarded the lean figure propped by the fireplace with keen anticipation. Once again, she was struck by the changes, enveloped by a unnerving sense of dealing with a stranger who was yet no stranger. He was looking down, his expression guarded. Unexpectedly curious, Lady Catherine studied her son. Her last memories of Martin were of a twenty-two-year-old, already steeped in every form of fashionable vice—drinking, gambling and, of course, women. It was his propensity for dabbling with the opposite sex that had brought his tempestuous career to a sudden halt. Serena Monckton. The beauty had claimed Martin had seduced her. He had denied it but no one, least of all his family, had believed him. But he had steadfastly resisted all attempts to coerce him into marrying the chit. In a fury, her husband had bought off the girl's family and banished his third son to a distant relative in the colonies. John had regretted that action bitterly, regretted it to his dying day, quite literally; Martin had always been his favourite and he had died without seeing him again.

Intent on finding evidence that the son of her memories had not in truth changed, Lady Catherine acknowledged the broad shoulders and long, lean limbs with an inward snort. He still possessed the figure of Adonis, hard and well-muscled through addiction to outdoor pursuits. His long-boned hands were clean and manicured; the gold signet his father had given him on his twenty-first birthday glowed on his right hand. The hair that curled about his clear brow was as black as a raven's wing. All that she remembered. What she could not recall was the strength engraved in the chiselled features, the aura of confidence which went further than mere arrogance, the graceful movements that created an impression of harnessed power. Those she could not remember at all.

Unease growing, she waited for some show of resistance. None came.

"Have you nothing to say?"

Startled from his reverie, induced by memories of the last time his mother had insisted he marry, Martin lifted his gaze to the Dowager's face. His brows rose. "On the contrary. But I would like to hear all your plans first. Surely that's not the sum of them?"

"By no means." Lady Catherine threw him a glance that would have wilted lesser men and wished he would sit down. Towering over her, he seemed far too powerful to intimidate. But she was determined to do her duty. "My second point concerns the family estates and businesses. You say you've been acquainting yourself with them. I wish you to leave all such matters in the hands of those retainers George hired. They're doubtless better managers than you could ever be. After all, you can have no experience of running estates of such size."

A muscle at the corner of Martin's mouth quivered. He stilled it.

Lady Catherine, absorbed in ordering her arguments, missed the warning. "Lastly, once you and

Miss Wendover are married, you will reside here throughout the year.'' She paused to eye Martin speculatively. ''You may not yet realise, but it is my money that keeps the Merton estates afloat. Remember, I wasn't a nobody before I married your father. I've allowed what passed back to me through settlements on your father's death to be drawn upon for living expenses as the estates are unable to pay well enough.''

Martin remained silent.

Confident of victory despite his impassivity, Lady Catherine advanced her trump card. ''Unless you agree to my conditions, I'll withdraw my funds from the estate, which will leave you destitute.'' On the word, her eyes flickered over the long frame still negligently propped against the mantelpiece. The subtle hand of a master showed in the cut of his dark blue coat; the pristine state of his small clothes was beyond reproach. Gleaming Hessians completed the picture. Martin, his mother reflected, had never been cheap.

The object of her scrutiny was examining the toe of one boot.

Undeterred, the Dowager added a clincher. ''Should you choose to flout my wishes, I'll see you damned and will settle my fortune on Damian.''

As she made this final, all-encompassing threat, Lady Catherine smiled and settled back in her chair. Martin had always disliked Damian, jealous of the fact that the younger boy was her favourite. Knowing the battle won, she glanced up at her son.

She was unprepared for the slow smile which spread across his dark face, softening the harsh lines, imparting a devilish handsomeness to the aristocratic features. Irrelevantly, she reflected that it was hardly surprising that this son, of the four, had never had the slightest trouble winning the ladies to his side.

"If that's all you have to say, ma'am, I have a few comments of my own."

Lady Catherine blinked, then inclined her head regally, prepared to be gracious in victory.

Nonchalantly, Martin straightened and strolled towards the windows. "Firstly, as regards my marriage, I will marry whom I please, when I please. And, incidentally, if I please."

The stunned silence behind him spoke volumes. Martin's gaze skimmed the tops of the trees in the Home Wood. His mother's suggestions were outrageous, but entirely expected. However, while her machinations were unwelcome, he understood and respected the devotion to family duty that prompted her to them. Even more to the point, they confirmed his supposition that she had had no hand in the decline of the Merton fortunes. As she was tied to her room, her household under the sway of an unscrupulous factor he had derived great satisfaction from verbally flaying before evicting him in the time-honoured way, he doubted his mother had any idea of the state of the rest of the house. Her chambers were in reasonable condition, better than any others in the rambling mansion. The factor had succeeded in intimidating the rest of the staff and, very likely, had gulled Melissa and possibly even George into believing that the decay was unavoidable. And if the section of gardens he could now see was the only fragment of the grounds still deserving of the title, how could his mother know the rest was wilderness? Martin paused by the window, his fingers drumming lightly on the wide ledge. "Apropos of Damian, I should point out that he will hardly thank you for rushing me to the altar. He is, after all, my heir until such time as I father a legitimate son. Considering his current pecuniary embarrassments, he's unlikely to appreciate your motives in assisting me to accomplish that deed, and in such haste."

Lady Catherine stiffened. Martin spared a glance for his sister-in-law, huddled back in her chair, listening intently to the exchange between mother and son while ostensibly absorbed with her embroidery. One brow rising cynically, Martin turned to his mother's fury.

"How *dare* you!" For a moment, rage held the Dowager speechless. Then the dam broke. "You will marry *as I say!* To think of any other course is out of the question! The arrangements have been made."

"Naturally," Martin replied, his voice cool and precise, "I regret any inconvenience your actions may cause others. However," he continued, on a sterner note, "I am at a loss to understand what gave you the impression that you were empowered to speak for me in this matter. I find it hard to believe that Miss Wendover's parents were so ill-advised as to imagine you did. If they have, in truth, done so, their discomfiture is the result of their own folly. I suggest you inform them without delay that no alliance will occur between Miss Wendover and myself."

Stunned, Lady Catherine blinked. "You're mad! I would be mortified to do so!" She sat bolt upright, her hands twisting in her lap, her expression one of dawning dismay.

Martin quelled an unexpected urge to comfort her. She would have to learn that the youth who left this house thirteen years before was no more. "I hesitate to point out that any embarrassment you might feel has been accrued through your own machinations. It would be well if you could bring yourself to understand that I will not be manipulated, ma'am."

Unable to meet his stern gaze, Lady Catherine glanced down at her crabbed fingers, conscious for the first time in years of an urge to fuss with her skirts. Suddenly, Martin looked very like—sounded very like—his father.

When his mother remained silent, Martin continued calmly, his tone dry. "As for your second point, I can inform you that, having become thoroughly acquainted with my inheritance, I've rescinded all the appointments made by George. Matthews and Sons and Bromleys, our brokers, together with our bankers, Blanchards, remain. They date from my father's time. But my people are now in charge of this estate and the smaller estates in Dorset, Leicestershire and Northamptonshire. The men George hired were bleeding the estate dry. It's beyond my comprehension, ma'am, why even you did not question the story that estates of the size of the Merton holdings were, within two years of my father's death, mysteriously no longer able to support the family."

Martin paused, tamping down the anger simmering beneath his calm. Just thinking of the state of his patrimony was enough to summon his demons. Surmising from his mother's stunned expression that she needed a few minutes to adjust to his revelations, he let his gaze wander the room.

Lady Catherine's mind was indeed reeling. A niggling memory of the odd look old Matthews had given her when, angry at Martin's inheriting, she had given vent to her frustrations in a long catalogue of his shortcomings, returned with a thump. She had been taken aback by the man's quietly tendered opinion that Mr Martin was just what the Merton estates needed. Martin, expensive profligate that he was, was hardly the sort she had expected Matthews to support. Later, she had learned that Martin had engaged the same firm his family had long used to represent him in his business dealings. It had come as something of a shock to realise that Martin had the sort of dealings with which a firm such as Matthews and Sons would assist. Matthews' comment had bothered her. Now she knew what he had meant. Damn him—why had he not explained more fully? Why had she not asked?

After gazing at Melissa's bent head, pale blonde flecked with grey, and recalling his conclusion of years before that nothing much actually went on inside it, Martin turned back to his mother. As he guessed rather more of her thoughts than she would have wished, his lips twisted wryly. "You're quite right in saying that I've little experience in running estates of this size—my own are considerably more extensive."

Confirming as they did that her third son had changed in more ways than met the eye, his words seriously undermined Lady Catherine's composure. They more than undermined her plans.

At her thunderstruck look, Martin's grin converted to a not ungentle smile. "Did you think your prodigal son was returning from a life of deprivation to hang on your sleeve?"

The glance she threw him was answer enough. Martin leant back against the window-ledge, long legs stretched before him. "I'm desolated to disappoint you, ma'am, but I'm in no need of your funds. On my return to London, I'll instruct Matthews to call on you here, to assist in redrafting your will. I pray you hold to your threat to disown me. Damian will never forgive you if you don't. Besides," he added, grey eyes gleaming with irrepressible candour, "he needs the support that the news that he's your beneficiary will bring. If nothing else, it should relieve me of the necessity of repeatedly rescuing him from the River Tick. As far as I'm concerned, he may go to the devil in whatever way he chooses. If he uses your money to do it, I'll be even better pleased. However, regardless of what you may choose to do, no further monies from your settlements will be used for the Merton estates, in any way whatever."

Martin examined his mother's face, sensitive to the encroachments of age on past beauty. After her initial shock, she had drawn herself up, her eyes grey stone, her lips compressed as if to hold back her incredulity. Despite her ailment, there was a deal of strength and determination still descernible in the gaunt frame. To his surprise, he no longer felt the need to strike back at her, to impress her with his successes, to demonstrate how worthy of her love he was. That, too, had died with the years.

"And now to your last stipulation." He pushed away from the window-ledge, glancing down to re-settle his sleeves. "I will, of course, be residing for part of the year in London. Beyond that, I anticipate travelling to my various estates as well as visiting those of my friends, as one might expect. I also antic-ipate inviting guests to stay here. As I recall, during my father's day, the Hermitage was renowned for its hospitality." He looked at his mother; she was staring past him, plainly struggling to bring this new image of him into focus.

"Of course, such visits will have to wait until the place is refurbished."

"*What?*" The unladylike exclamation burst from Lady Catherine's lips. Startled, her gaze flew to Mar-tin's face, her question in her eyes.

"You needn't concern yourself about that." Martin frowned. There was no need for her to know how bad it really was; she would be mortified. "I'm sending a firm of decorators down once they've finished with Merton House." He paused but his mother's gaze was again far-away. When she made no further comment, Martin straightened. "I'm returning to London within the hour. So, if there's nothing further you wish to discuss, I'll bid you goodbye."

"Am I to assume these decorators will, on *your* instruction, redo these rooms as well?" The sarcasm in Lady Catherine's voice would have cut glass.

Martin smothered his smile. Rapidly, he reviewed his options. "If you wish, I'll tell them to consult with you—over the rooms that are peculiarly yours, of course."

He could not, in all conscience, saddle her with the task of overseeing such a major reconstruction, and, if truth be known, he intended to use this opportunity to stamp his own personality on this, the seat of his fore-bears.

His mother's glare relieved him of any worry that she would react to his independence by going into a decline. Reassured, Martin raised an expectant brow.

With every evidence of reluctance, Lady Catherine nodded a curt dismissal.

With a graceful bow to her, and a nod for Melissa, Martin left the room.

Lady Catherine watched him go, then sought counsel in silence. Long after the door had clicked shut, she remained, her gaze fixed, unseeing, on the un-lighted fire. Eventually shaking free of her recollections, she could not help wondering if, in her most secret of hearts, despite the attendant difficulties, she was not just a little bit relieved to have a man, a real man, in charge again.

Downstairs, Martin briskly descended the steep steps of the portico to where his curricle awaited, his prize match bays stamping impatiently. A heavy hacking cough greeted him, coming from beyond the off-side horse. Frowning, Martin ignored the reins looped over the brake and, patting the velvety noses of his favourite pair, rounded them to find his groom-cum-valet and ex-batman Joshua Carruthers propped against the carriage, eyes streaming above a large handkerchief.

"What the devil's the matter?" Even as Martin asked the question, he realised the answer.

"Nuthing more'n a cold," Joshua mumbled thickly, waving one gnarled hand dismissively. He gulped and stuffed the handkerchief in his breeches pocket, revealing a shiny red nose to his master's sharp eyes. "Best get on our way, then."

Martin did not move. "You're not going anywhere."

"But I distin'ly 'eard you say nuthin' on earth woul' induce you to spen' the night in this ramshackle "ole."

"As always, your memory is accurate, your hearing less so. I'm going on."

"No' without me, you're not."

Exasperated, hands on hips, Martin watched as the old soldier half staggered to the back of the curricle. When he had to brace himself against the curricle side as another bout of coughing shook him, Martin swore. Spotting two stable boys gazing in awe, whether at the equipage or its owner Martin was not at all sure, he beckoned them up. "Hold 'em."

Once assured they had the restless horses secured, Martin grasped Joshua by the elbow and steered him remorselessly towards the house. "Consider yourself ordered back to barracks. Dammit, man—we wouldn't get around the first bend before you fell off."

In vain, Joshua tried to hang back. "But—"

"I know the place is in a state," Martin countered, sweeping his reluctant henchman back up the steps. "But now I've got rid of that wretched factor, the rest of the staff will doubtless remember how things should be done. At least," he added, stopping in the gloomy front hall, "I hope they will."

He had given orders that the household should conduct itself as it had previously, in his father's day. Enough of the staff remained for him to expect a reasonable outcome. All locals, many from generations of Merton servitors, they had been overwhelmed by the outsider George had installed over them. Freed from the tyrannical factor, they seemed eager to return the Hermitage to its proper state.

Joshua sniffed. "What about the horses?"

Martin's lips twitched but he suppressed the urge to smile, assuming instead a repressively haughty attitude. His brows rose to chilling heights. "You aren't about to suggest I don't know how to take care of my cattle, are you?"

Muttering, Joshua threw him a darkling glance.

"Get off to bed, you old curmudgeon. When you're well enough to ride, you may take a horse from the stables and come on to London. It'll have to be that hack of George's; it's the only animal remaining with sufficient resemblance to the equine species to meet your high standards."

Not at all mollified, Joshua humphed. But he knew better than to argue. Contenting himself with a last warning—"There's rain on the way, so's you'd best take heed"—he stumped down the hall towards the faded baize-covered door at its rear.

Smiling, Martin returned to his curricle. Dismissing the wide-eyed lads, he climbed to the box seat and clicked the reins. The carriage swept down the weed-choked drive. Martin did not glance back.

As he passed through the gateposts marking the main entry, through the heavy iron gates, half off their hinges, Martin heaved a heartfelt sigh. For thirteen years, his home had glowed in his memory, a place of charm and grace, an Elysian paradise he had longed to regain. Fate had granted him his wish but, as fickle as ever, had denied him his dream. The charm and grace had vanished, victim to the neglect of the years since his father had had it in his care.

He would restore it—bring back the gracious beauty, the calming sense of peace. On that he was determined. Martin's jaw set, his eyes glinted, grey steel in the afternoon sun. In truth, he was glad to leave behind the travesty of his dream. He would remain in London until the work was done. When next he saw his home, it would once again be the place he had carried in his heart through all the years of his roaming. His particular paradise.

The road to Taunton loomed ahead. Checking his team for the turn, Martin cast a quick glance to the west. Joshua had been right—there was rain on the way. Pursing his lips, Martin considered his options. If he stopped at Taunton, London the next day would be a tough order. He would make for Ilchester—he and Joshua had passed the previous night at the Fox in tolerable comfort. Decision made, Martin dropped his hands, letting the horses stretch their legs. From memory, there was a short cut, just south of Taunton, which would see him in Ilchester before the coming storm.

Two hours later, the curricle swayed perilously as the wheels hit yet another rut. Martin swore roundly. He reined in his team to peer ahead into the gathering gloom. The short cut, dimly remembered as a fair road, had not lived up to expectations. A low mutter came from the west. Martin scanned the horizons, barely visible beneath the low-lying cloud. He doubted he could even make the London road before the storm struck.

He was gently urging the horses over the rutted stretch, dredging his memory in an effort to recall any nearby shelter, when a scream rent the air. The horses plunged. Rapidly bringing them under control, Martin leapt from his perch and ran to their heads. He caught hold of their bits just in time to prevent them rearing as a second scream sliced through the night. No doubt about it, a woman's scream, coming from the woods just ahead. Swiftly, Martin tied the team securely to a nearby gate and, grabbing the pair of loaded pistols from beneath the seat, made for the trees. Once in their shadow, he took care to move silently, thanking the years of his misspent youth, when he had often gone poaching on his father's preserves with young Johnny Hobbs from the village.

Some distance into the wood, he froze. Before him lay a small clearing, a track leading into it from the opposite direction. Sounds of a struggle came from an ill-assorted trio, waltzing in the shadows in the centre.

"Keep still, you little...!"

"*Ow!* Gawd! She bit my finger, the doxy!"

As one man pulled away, the group resolved into two burly men dressed in unkempt frieze and a lady, unquestionably a lady, in a silk gown which shimmered in the twilight. The larger of the men succeeded in grabbing the woman from behind, trapping her arms by her sides. Despite her efforts to kick him, he managed to hold her.

"Listen, missus. The master said to hold you 'ere and not to harm a single hair of your head. Now how's we to do that if'n you don't stop still?"

The exasperation in the man's voice brought a sympathetic smile to Martin's face. The clearing was too large to allow him to creep up on them. Quietly, he worked his way around so that the man holding the woman would have his back to him.

"You fools!" The woman and her captor teetered perilously. "Don't you know the price for kidnapping? If you let me go, I'll pay you double what your master will!"

Martin's brows rose. The woman's voice was unexpectedly mature. Clearly, she had not lost her head.

"Maybe so, lady," growled the man nursing his finger. "But the master's gentry and they're mean when crossed. No—I don't rightly see as how we can oblige."

Holding both pistols fully cocked, Martin stepped from the trees. "Dear me. Haven't you been taught to always oblige a lady?"

The man holding the woman let her go and swung to face Martin. In the same moment, Martin saw the second man draw a knife. He had a clear shot and took it, the ball passing into the man's elbow. The man dropped the knife and howled. His comrade turned to the source of the sound and so missed the pretty sight of ex-Major Martin Willesden, soldier of fortune and experienced man at arms, being laid low by a right to the jaw, delivered by a very small fist. Martin, his attention on the man he had shot, did not see the blow coming. His head jerked back from the contact and struck a low branch. Stunned, he crumpled slowly to the ground.

Helen Walford stared at the long form stretched somnolent at her feet. God in heaven! It wasn't Hedley Swayne after all! The discharged pistol, still smoking, was clutched in the man's left hand. His right hand held a second pistol, cocked and ready. She darted forward and grabbed it. Catching her skirts in one hand, she leapt over the sprawled form and swung to train the pistol on her captor, hampered in his efforts to reach her by the body between. "Keep your distance!" she warned. "I know how to use this."

Noting the steadiness of the pistol pointed at his chest, the man who had held her decided to accept her word. He glanced back at his accomplice, now on his knees, moaning in pain. He threw Helen a malevolent glance. "Blast!"

He eyed her menacingly, then turned and stumped over to his mate. Helping him up, he growled, "Let's get out of this. The master's bound to be along shortly. To my mind, he can sort this lot out hisself."

His words carried to Helen. Her eyes widened in shock. "You mean this man isn't your master?" She spared a glance for the still form at her feet. Heavens! What had she done?

The men looked at the crumpled figure. "That swell? Never set eyes on him afore, missus."

"Whoever he be, he's goin' to be none too pleased with you when he wakes up," added the second man with relish.

Helen swallowed and gestured with the gun. Grumbling, the two rogues made their way to the edge of the clearing where stood a disreputable gig pulled by a single broken-down nag. They clambered aboard and, whistling up the horse, departed down the rough track.

Left alone in the gloom with her unconscious rescuer, Helen stood and stared at the recumbent form. "Oh, lord!"

Thus far, her day had been a resounding disaster. Kidnapped in the small hours, bundled up in a distinctly odoriferous blanket, bustled from one carriage to another until the sounds of London had been left far behind, she had spent the day being battered and jostled, tied and gagged, trussed and trapped in a worn-out chaise. Her head was still pounding. And now she had been rescued, only to lay her rescuer low.

With a groan, Helen pressed a hand to her temple.

Fate was having a field day.

Chapter Two

The back of his head hurt. Martin's first thought on regaining consciousness convinced him he was still alive. But, when his lids fluttered open, he realised his error. He had to be dead. There was an angel hanging over him, her golden hair lit by an unearthly radiance. A sudden twinge forced his eyes shut.

He could not be dead. His head hurt too much, even though it was cradled in the softest lap imaginable. A delicate hand brushed his brow. He trapped it in one of his. No spectre, his angel, but flesh and blood.

"What happened?" He winced, pain stabbing behind his eyes.

Helen, bending over him, winced in sympathy. "I'm dreadfully afraid that I hit you. On the jaw. You stumbled back and hit a branch."

When a spasm of pain—or was it irritation?—passed over her rescuer's strong features, Helen's guilt increased. As soon as the rattle of the gig had receded, she had fallen on her knees beside her victim. Quelling all maidenly hesitation—she was hardly a maiden, after all—she had bent her mind to ministering to the injuries she had caused. His shoulders were abominably heavy, but, eventually, she had managed to lift his head on to her lap, gently stroking back the raven locks that had fallen across his brow.

Martin held on to her hand, reluctant to let his anchor to reality slip. It was a small hand, the bones delicate between his fingers. Gradually, the pounding in his head subsided, leaving a dull ache. He put up his free hand to feel the bruise on his chin. Just in time, he remembered not to try and feel the bump on his head. It was, after all, resting on her lap and she sounded like a lady.

"Do you always attack your rescuers?" Martin struggled to sit up.

Helen helped him, then sat back on her heels to look at him, open concern in her eyes. "I really must apologise. I thought you were Hedley Swayne."

Gingerly, Martin examined the lump rising on the back of his skull. Her voice, if nothing else, confirmed his angel's station. The soft, rounded tones slid into his consciousness like warmed honey. He frowned. "Who's Hedley Swayne? The master who arranged your abduction?"

Helen nodded. "So I believe." She should have guessed this man wasn't Hedley—his voice was far too deep, far too gravelly. Feeling at a distinct disadvantage due to the unfortunate circumstance of their meeting, she studied her hands, clasped in her lap, and wondered what her rescuer was thinking. She had had ample opportunity to admire his length as he had lain stretched out beside her. A most impressive length. The single comprehensive glance she had had, before his head had hit the branch, had left a highly favourable impression. Despite her predicament, Helen's lips twitched. She could not recall being quite so impressed in years. Reality intruded. She had hit him and knocked him out. *He,* doubtless, was not impressed at all.

Surreptitiously observing his damsel in distress as she knelt beside him in the shadowy twilight, Martin could understand his earlier conviction that she was an angel. Thick golden curls rioted around her head, spilling in chaotic confusion on to her shoulders. Very nicely turned shoulders, too. A silk evening gown which he thought would be apricot under normal light clung to her shapely curves. He could not guess how tall she was but all the rest of her was constructed on generous lines. He glanced at her face. In the poor light, her features were indistinct. An unexpectedly strong desire to see more, in better light, possessed him. "I take it this same Hedley Swayne is expected here at any moment?"

"That's what the two men said." Helen spoke dismissively. In truth, she could summon little interest in her abductor; her rescuer was far more fascinating.

Slowly, Martin got to his feet, grateful for his angel's steadying hand. His faculties were a trifle unsettled, his senses distracted by her nearness. "Why did they leave?" She was quite tall; her curls would tickle his nose if she were closer, her forehead level with his lips. Just the right height for a tall man. Her legs, glorious legs, were deliciously long. He resisted the urge to examine them more closely.

"I held the second pistol on them." Sensing his

distraction and worried that she might have caused him serious injury, Helen frowned, trying to study his expression through the gloom. Reminded of his pistols, she bent to retrieve them, her silk skirts clinging to her shapely derrière.

Martin looked away, shaking his head to dislodge the fantasies crowding in. Damn it! The situation was potentially dangerous! Definitely not the time for idle dalliance. He cleared his throat. "In my present condition, I feel it might be wise to leave before Mr Swayne arrives. Unless you think it preferable to stay and face him?"

Helen shook her head. "Heavens, no! He'll have a coach and men with him. He never travels without outriders." Her contempt for her abductor rang in her tone. A sudden thought struck her. "Where are we?"

"South of Taunton."

"Taunton?" Helen stood, the pistols hanging from her hands, and frowned. "Hedley mentioned estates somewhere in Cornwall. I suppose he was going to take me there."

Martin nodded; the explanation was likely, given their present location. He glanced around to reorientate himself, then reached for his pistols. "If he's likely to come with friends, I suggest we depart forthwith. My curricle's in a lane beyond the wood. I was passing when I heard your screams."

"Thank heaven you did." Belatedly, Helen shook out her skirts. "I held very little hope we would be near any main road."

She glanced up at her rescuer, to find he was studying her, the shadows concealing his expression.

Martin smiled, a little wryly. His angel was not out of the woods yet. "I hesitate to disabuse you of such a comforting thought, but we're some way from any main road. I was taking a short cut through the lanes in the hope of reaching the London road before the storm."

"You're going to London?"

"Eventually," Martin conceded. The branches above obscured too much of the sky to let him judge the approach of the rainclouds. "But first we'll have to find shelter for the night."

With a last glance about, Martin offered her his arm.

Quelling a rush of uncharacteristic nervousness, Helen placed her hand on his sleeve. She had no choice but to trust him, yet her trust in gentlemen was not presently high.

"Was it from London you were taken?"

"Yes," Helen felt no constraint in revealing that much but the question reminded her to be wary until she knew more of her rescuer, fascinating though he might be.

Absorbed in negotiating the numerous hurdles in the congested path through the trees without further damaging her gown, Helen felt the calm certainty with which she normally faced her world return. Her rescuer's strong arm assisted her over the blockages. The subtle deference in his attitude effectively dispelled her fears, settling a cloak of protectiveness about her. Relieved to find his behaviour as gentlemanly as his elegance, she relaxed.

Martin waited until they were some distance from the clearing before appeasing his burgeoning curiosity.

The question burning his tongue was who she was. But that, doubtless, would be best left for later. He contented himself with, "Who is Hedley Swayne?"

"A fop," came the uncompromising reply.

"You mistook *me* for a *fop?*" Despite the potential seriousness of their plight, Martin's latent tendencies were too strong to repress. When she turned her head his way, eyes wide, her lips parted in confusion, his eyes wickedly quizzed her.

Helen caught her breath. For an instant, her eyes locked with her rescuer's. Three heartbeats passed before, with a desperate effort, she wrenched her gaze free and snatched back her wandering wits. "I didn't see you, remember."

At the sound of her soft and slightly husky disclaimer, Martin chuckled. "Ah, yes!"

A fallen tree blocked their path. He released her to step over it, then turned and held out his hands. From beneath her lashes, Helen glanced up at his face. A strong, intriguing face, rather more tanned and harsh-featured than one was wont to see. She wondered what colour his eyes were. With a calm she was not entirely sure she possessed, she put her hands into his. His strong fingers closed over hers; a peculiar constriction tightened about her chest. Helen glanced down, ostensibly to negotiate the fallen tree, in reality to hide her sudden frown at the ridiculous skitterishness that had attacked her. Surely she was too old for such girlish reactions?

Resuming his place by her side, Martin glanced down at her bent head, perfectly sure, now, that the tremor he had felt in her fingers had not been a figment of his over-active imagination. Highly experienced in the subtleties of this particular form of play, he sought for some topic to get her mind off him. "I trust you've suffered no harm from your ordeal with those ruffians?"

Determined not to let her ridiculous nervousness show, Helen shook her head. "No—none at all. But they were under orders to take care of me."

"So I heard. Nevertheless, I dare say you've had your wits quite addled by fright."

Despite an unnerving awareness of the presence by her side, Helen laughed. "Oh, no! I assure you I'm not such a poor creature as all that." She risked a glance upwards and saw her rescuer's dark brows rise. The look he bent on her was patently disbelieving. Her smile grew. "Very well," she conceded, "I'll admit to a qualm or two, but when they were plainly being as gentle as they knew how I could hardly quake for fear of my life."

"I've rescued an Amazon."

The bland statement floated above her curls. Helen chuckled and shook her head, but refused to be further drawn.

As the trees thinned, she resolutely turned her mind to her present predicament. With the uncertainty of her abduction receding, she was conscious of an oddly light-hearted response to this new set of circumstances. Twilight was drawing in; she was walking through woods, very much alone, with an unknown gentleman. While she was quite convinced of his quality, she was not nearly so sure it was safe to approve of his style, much less his propensities. Nevertheless, trepidation was not what she felt. Unbidden, a smile curved her lips. Not since childhood had such a whimsical, adventurous mood claimed her; the same buoyant exuberance had whirled her through her most outrageous childhood exploits. Why on earth it should surface now, in response, she was sure, to the stranger by her side, she had no idea. But the thrill of exhilaration tripping along her nerves was too marked to ignore. In truth, she had no wish to ignore it—life had been too serious, too mundane, for too long. A little adventure would lighten the dim prospect of her lonely future.

They emerged from the trees. In the narrow lane, a fashionable curricle was outlined against the gathering gloom, a pair of high-stepping bays restlessly shifting between the shafts. Impulsively, Helen gasped, "What beauties!"

The lines of both equipage and horses spoke volumes. Clearly, her rescuer was a man of means. Smiling, he released her beside the carriage, going to the horses' heads to run a soothing hand over their noses.

Helen eyed the curricle, wondering if, in her slim evening gown, it was possible to gain the box seat perched high above the axle with reasonable decorum. She was about to attempt the difficult climb when a pair of strong hands fastened about her waist and she was lifted, effortlessly, upwards.

"Oh!" Her eyes widened; she bit back a most unladylike squeal. Deposited gently on the seat, she blushed rosy red. "Er...thank you." The smile on her rescuer's face was decidedly wicked. Abruptly, Helen busied herself with settling her skirts, while, under her lashes, she watched him untie the reins.

It wasn't just the fact that she knew she was no lightweight, nor that no man before had ever lifted her like that, making her feel ridiculously delicate. It wasn't even the impression of remarkable strength that lingered with the memory of his hands gripping her waist. No. It was her quite shocking response to that perfectly mundane little intimacy that was tying her nerves in knots. Never in her life had she felt so odd, so thoroughly witless. What on earth was the matter with her?

Her rescuer swung up beside her. He moved with the ease of a born athlete, compounding the impression of leashed power created by the combination of understated elegance and sheer size. A deliciously fascinating impression, Helen was only too willing to admit. Then he glanced at her.

"Comfortable?"

She nodded, the simple question dispelling any lingering fears. In her estimation, no blackguard would ask if his victim was comfortable. Her rescuer might make her nervous; he did not frighten her.

A drop of rain fell on Martin's hand as he clicked the reins. The sensation drew his mind from contemplation of the woman beside him and focused it on more practical matters. Night was closing in and, with it, the weather.

He levelled a measuring glance at his companion. When he had lifted her to the box seat, getting a good glimpse of a pair of shapely ankles in the process, he had confirmed the fact that her dress was indeed silk, fine and delicate. Furthermore, his experienced assessment told him her fashionable standing extended to wearing no more than a fine silk chemise beneath. In the wood, the warmth of the afternoon had been trapped beneath the trees but now they were in the open and the temperature was dropping. The neckline of her gown was cut remarkably low, a fact which met with his unqualified approval; the tiny puffed sleeves, badly crushed, were set off her shoulders. Even in the poor light, her skin glowed translucently pale. She was not yet shivering, but it could only be a question of time. "If you'll forgive my impertinence, why are you gallivanting about without even a cloak?"

Helen frowned, considering. How much was it safe to reveal? Then, unconsciously lifting her chin, she took the plunge. "I was at Chatham House, at a ball given for Lady Chatham's birthday. A footman brought a note asking me to meet...a friend on the portico."

In retrospect, she should have been more careful. "There were...circumstances that made that seem quite reasonable at the time," she explained. "But there was no one about—at least, that's what I thought. I waited for a moment or two, then, just as I was about to go back inside, someone—one of those two ruffians, I think—threw a coat over my head."

Helen shivered slightly, whether from the cold or the memory of her sudden fright she was not sure. "They bundled me into a waiting carriage—it was still early and there were no other coaches in the drive." She drew a deep breath. "So that's why no cloak."

"I see." Martin trapped the reins under his boot and

reached behind the seat to drag his greatcoat from where it was neatly stowed. He shook it out and flung it about his companion's distracting shoulders, then calmly picked up the reins. "What makes you think it was this Hedley Swayne behind your abduction?"

Helen frowned. In reality, now that she considered the matter more closely, there was no firm evidence to connect Hedley with the kidnap attempt.

Observing her pensive face, Martin's brows rose. "No real reason—just a feeling?"

At the superior tone rippling beneath the raspy surface of his deep voice, Helen drew herself up. "If you knew how Hedley's been behaving recently, you wouldn't doubt it."

Martin grinned at her prickly rejoinder and infused a degree of sympathy into his, "How has he been behaving?"

"He's forever at me to marry him—heaven only knows why."

Pressing his lips together to suppress the spontaneous retort that had leapt to his tongue, Martin waited until his voice was steady before asking, "Not the obvious?"

Absorbed in cogitations on the vagaries of Hedley Swayne, Helen shook her head. "Definitely not the obvious." Suddenly recalling to whom she was speaking, she blushed. Praying that the poor light would conceal the fact, she hurried on. "Hedley's not the marrying kind, if you know what I mean."

Martin's lips twitched but he made no comment.

Helen considered the iniquitous Mr Swayne, a slight frown puckering her delicate brows. "Unfortunately,

I've no idea why he wants to marry me. No idea at all.''

They proceeded in silence, Martin intent on the bad road, Helen lost in thought. The land about was open pastures, separated by occasional hedgerows, with not even a farmhouse to be seen. A stray thought took hold in Martin's mind. "Did you say you were at a ball when they grabbed you? Have you been missing since last night?''

Helen nodded. "But I went in my own carriage — not many of my friends have returned to town yet.''

"So your coachman would have raised the alarm?''

Slowly, Helen shook her head. "Not immediately. I might have gone home in some acquaintance's carriage and my message to John got lost in the fuss. That's happened before. My people wouldn't have been certain I was truly missing until this morning.'' Her brows knit, she considered the possibilities. "I wonder what they'll do?''

For his own reasons, Martin also wondered. The possibility of being mistaken for a kidnapper, and the consequent explanations, was not the sort of imbroglio he wished to be landed in just at present — not when he had barely set foot in England and had yet to establish his bona fides. "You'll certainly cause a stir when you reappear.''

"Mm.'' Helen's mind had drifted from the shadowy possibilities of happenings in London, drawn to more immediate concerns by the presence beside her. Her rescuer had yet to ask her name, nor had he volunteered his. But her adventurous mood had her firmly in its grip; their state of being mutually incognito seemed perfectly appropriate. She felt comfortably secure; appellations, she was sure, were unnecessary.

Absorbed in the increasingly difficult task of managing his team over the severely rutted track, Martin racked his brains for some acceptable avenue to learn his companion's name. Their situation was an odd one—not having been formally introduced, he did not expect her to volunteer the information. He balked at simply asking, not wanting her to feel impelled to reveal it out of gratitude for her rescue. Yet, without it, could he be sure of finding her in London? He ought, of course, to introduce himself, but, until he was more certain of her, was reluctant to do so.

Another drop of rain and a low mutter from the west jerked his mind back to practicalities. Skittish, the horses tossed their heads. He settled them, carefully edging them about a sharp corner. The dark shape of a barn loomed on the left, set back in a field and screened on the west by a stand of chesnuts. The mutter turned into a growl; lightning split the sky.

With a grimace, Martin checked the horses for the turn into the rough cart track leading to the barn. He glanced at his companion, still lost in thought. ''I'm afraid, my dear, that before you you see our abode for the night. We're miles from the nearest shelter and the horses won't stand a thunderstorm.''

Startled from her reverie, Helen peered ahead. Seeing the dark structure before her, she considered the proposition of spending the night in a barn with her rescuer and found it strangely attractive. ''Don't mind me,'' she replied airly. ''If I'm to have an adventure then it might as well be complete with a night in a disused barn. Is it disused, do you think?''

"In this area? Unlikely. Hopefully there'll be a loft full of fresh straw.''

There was. Martin unharnessed the horses and rubbed them down, then made them as secure as possible in the rude stalls. By now very grateful for the warmth of his thick greatcoat, Helen clutched it about her. She wandered around the outside of the barn and discovered a well, clearly in use, by one side. Before the rain set in, she hurried to draw water, filling all the pails she could find. After supplying the horses, she splashed water over her face, washing away the dust of the day. Refreshed, she belatedly remembered she had no towel. Eyes closed, she all but jumped when a deep chuckle came from behind her, reverberating through her bones, sending peculiar shivers flickering over her skin. Strong fingers caught her hand; a linen square was pushed into it. Hurriedly, Helen mopped her face and turned.

He stood a yard or so behind her, a subtle smile twisting his firm lips. He had found a lantern and hung it from the loft steps. The soft light fell on his black hair, glossing the curls where they formed over his ears and by the side of his neck. Hooded grey eyes— she was sure they were grey—lazily regarded her. Helen's diaphragm seized; her eyes widened. He was handsome. Disgustingly handsome. Even more handsome than Hazelmere. She felt her throat constrict. Damn it! No man had the right to be so handsome. With an effort, she masked her reactions and swept him an elegant curtsy. "Thank you most kindly, sir—for your handkerchief and for rescuing me."

The subtle smile deepened, infusing the harshly handsome face with a wholly sensual promise. "My pleasure, fair Juno."

This time, his voice sent tingling quivers down her spine. Fair Juno? Shaken, Helen held out the handkerchief, hoping the action would cover her momentary fluster.

Taking back the linen square, Martin let his eyes roam, then abruptly hauled back on the reins. Dammit—he was supposed to be a gentleman and she was very clearly a lady. But if she kept looking at him like that he was apt to forget such niceties.

Smoothly, he turned to a rough bin against one wall. "There's corn here. If we grind some up, we'll be able to have pancakes for supper."

Helen eyed the blue-suited back a touch nervously, then turned her gaze, even more dubiously, on the corn bin. Were pancakes made of corn? "I'm afraid..." she began, forced to admit to ignorance.

Her rescuer threw her a dazzling smile. "Don't worry. I know how. Come and help."

Thus adjured, Helen willingly went forward to render what assistance she could. They hunted about and found two suitable rocks, a large flat one for the grinding base and a smaller, round one to crush the corn. After a demonstration of the accepted technique, Helen settled to the task of producing the cornmeal, while her mentor started a small fire, just outside the barn door, where the lee of the barn gave protection from the steady rain.

Every now and then, a crack of lightning presaged a heavy roll of thunder. The horses shifted restively, but they settled. Inside the barn, all was snug and dry.

"That should be sufficent."

Seated on a pile of straw, Helen looked up to find her mentor towering beside her, a pail of water in one hand.

"Now we add water to make a paste."

Struggling to keep his eyes on his task, Martin knelt opposite his assistant and, dipping his fingers in the water, sprinkled the pile of meal. Helen caught the idea. Soon, a satisfyingly large mound of soft dough had been formed. Helen carried the dough to the fire in her hands, while Martin brought up the heavy rock.

She had seen him wash an old piece of iron and scrub it down with straw. He had placed it across the fire. She watched as he brought up the water pail and let a drop fall to the heated surface. Critically, he watched it sizzle into steam.

Martin smiled. "Just right. The trick is not to let it get too hot."

Confidently, he set two pieces of dough on to the metal surface and quickly flattened them with his palm.

Helen pulled an old crate closer to the fire. "How do you know all this?"

A slow grin twisted Martin's lips. "Among my many and varied past lives, I was a soldier."

"In the Peninsula?"

Martin nodded. While they cooked and ate their pancakes, he entertained her with a colourful if cen- sored account of his campaigning days. These had necessarily culminated with Waterloo. "After that, I returned to...my business affairs."

He rose and stretched. The night was deepest black about them. It was as if they were the only souls for miles. His lips twisted in a wry grin. Stranded in a barn with fair Juno—what an opportunity for one of his propensities. Unfortunately, fair Juno was unquestionably gently bred and was under his protection. His grin turned to a grimace, then was wiped from his face before she could see it. He held out a hand to help her to her feet.

"Time for bed." Resolutely, he quelled his fantasies, insistently knocking on the door of his consciousness. He inclined his head towards the ladder. "There are piles of fresh straw up there. We should be snug enough for the night."

Helen went with him readily, any fears she had possessed entirely allayed by the past hours. She felt perfectly safe with him, perfectly confident of his behaving as he ought. They were friends of sorts, engaged in an adventure.

Her transparent confidence was not lost on Martin. He found her trust oddly touching, not something he was usually gifted with, not something he had any wish to damage. Reaching the foot of the ladder, he unhooked the lantern. "I'll go up first." He smiled. "Can you climb the ladder alone?"

The idea of being carried up the ladder, thrown over his shoulder like a sack of potatoes, was not to be borne. Helen considered the ascent, then shrugged out of his greatcoat. "If you'll take that up, I think I can manage."

Briskly, Martin went up, taking the coat and the lantern with him. Then he held the lantern out to light her way. Helen twisted her skirts to one side and, guarding against any mis-step, carefully negotiated the climb.

Above her, Martin swallowed his curses. He had thought coming up first was the right thing to do, relieving her of the potential embarassment of accidentally exposing her calves and ankles to his view. But the view he now had—of a remarkable expanse of creamy breasts, barely concealed by the low neckline of her gown—was equally scandalous. And equally tempting. And he was going to have to spend a whole night with her within reach?

He gritted his teeth and forced his features to behave.

After drawing her to safety, he crossed to the hay door and propped it ajar, admitting the cool night air and fitful streaks of moonlight, shafting through breaks in the storm clouds. He extinguished the lantern and placed it safely on a beam. Earlier in the evening, he had brought up the carriage blanket from the curricle. Spreading his greatcoat in the straw, he picked up the blanket and handed it to her. "You can sleep there. Wrap yourself up well or you'll be cold."

The air in the loft was warmer than below but the night boded ill for anyone dressed only in two layers of silk. Gratefully, Helen took the blanket and shook it out, then realised there was only one. "But what about you? Won't you be cold, too?"

In the safety of the dark, Martin grimaced. He was hoping the night air would cool his imagination, already feverish. Only too aware of the direction of his thoughts, and their likely effect on his tone, he forced his voice to a lighter pitch. "Sleeping in a dry loft full of straw is nothing to the rigours of campaigning." So saying, he threw himself down, full-length in the straw, a good three yards from his coat.

In the dim light, Helen saw him grin at her. She smiled, then wrapped the blanket around her before snuggling down into his still warm coat. "Goodnight."

"Goodnight."

For ten full minutes, silence reigned. Martin, far from sleep, watched the clouds cross the moon. Then the thunder returned in full measure. The horses whinnied but settled again. He heard his companion shift restlessly. "What's the matter? Afraid of mice?"

"Mice?" On the rising note, Helen sat bolt upright.

Silently, Martin cursed his loose tongue. "Don't worry about them."

"Don't...! You must be joking!"

Helen shivered, an action Martin saw clearly as a shaft of moonlight glanced through the hay door and fell full on her. God, she was an armful!

Hugging the greatcoat about her, Helen struggled to subdue her burgeoning panic. She sat still, breathing deeply, until another crack of thunder rent the night. "If you must know, I'm frightened of storms." The admission, forced through her chattering teeth, came out at least an octave too high. "And I'm cold."

Martin heard the querulous note in her voice. She truly was frightened. Hell! The storm had yet to unleash its full fury—if he did nothing to calm her she might well end up hysterical. Revising his estimate on which was the safer—spending an innocent night with fair Juno or campaigning in Spain—he sighed deeply and stood up, wondering if what he was about to do qualified as masochism. It was certainly going to make sleep difficult, if not impossible. He crossed to where she sat, huddled rigid beneath the blanket. Sitting beside her, on his coat, he put his arm about her and gave her a quick hug. Then, ignoring her confused reluctance, he drew her down to lie beside him, her head resting on his shoulder, her curls tickling his chin. "Now go to sleep," he said sternly. "The mice won't get you and you're safe from the storm and you should be warm enough."

Rigid with panic, Helen held herself stiffly within his encircling arms. Heaven help her, she did not know which frightened her most—the storm, or the tempest of emotions shattering her confidence. Nothing in her extensive experience had prepared her for spending a night in a stranger's arms but, with the storm raging outside, she could not have forced herself from her safe haven if the stars had fallen. And she was safe. Safe from the elements outside. Gradually, it dawned that she was also safe from any nearer threat.

Reassurance slowly penetrated the mists of panicky confusion assailing her reason. Her locked muscles eased; the tension left her limbs. The man in whose arms she lay was still and silent. His breathing was deep and even, his heart a steady thud muffled beneath her cheek. She had nothing to fear.

Helen relaxed.

When she melted against him, Martin stifled a curse, willing his muscles to perfect stillness.

"Goodnight." Helen sighed sleepily.

"Goodnight," Martin replied, his accents clipped.

But Helen was still some way from sleep. The storm lashed the countryside. Inside the barn, all was quiet. Martin, very conscious of the warm and infinitely tempting body beside him, felt her flinch at the thunderclaps. In the aftermath of a particularly violent report, she murmured, "I've just realised I don't even know your name."

Helen excused her lie on the grounds of social nicety; she had been wondering for hours how to approach the subject. Their unexpected intimacy gave her an opening she felt justified in taking. It was part of the adventure for him not to know her name, but she definitely wanted to know his.

"Martin Willesden, at your service." Despite his agony, Martin grinned into the darkness. He was only too willing to serve her in any number of ways.

"Willesden," Helen repeated, yawning. Then, her eyes flew wide. "Oh heavens! Not *the* Martin Willesden? The new Earl of Merton?" Helen twisted to look up into his face.

Martin was entertained by her tone. "'Fraid so," he answered. He glanced down, but her expression was hidden by the dark. "I presume my reputation has gone before me?"

"Your reputation?" Helen drew breath. "You, dear sir, have been the sole topic of conversation among the tabbies for the last fortnight. They're all dying for you to show your face! Is the black sheep, now raised

to the title, going to join polite society or give us all
the go-by?''

Martin chuckled.

Helen felt the sound reverberate through his chest.
The temptation to stretch her hands over the expanse
of hard muscle was all but overwhelming. Resolutely,
she quelled it, settling her head once more into his
shoulder.

''I've no taste for the melodramatic.'' Martin shifted
his hold, adjusting to her position. ''Since landing I've
been too busy setting things to rights to make my presence known. I'm returning from inspecting my principal seat. I'll be joining in all the normal pastimes
once I get back to London.''

'''All the normal pastimes'?'' Helen echoed. ''Yes,
I can just imagine.''

''Can you?'' Unable to resist, Martin squinted down
at her but could not see her face. He could remember
it, though—green-flecked amber eyes under perfectly
arched brown brows, a straight little nose and wide,
full lips, very kissable. ''What do you know of the
pastimes of rakes?''

Helen resisted the temptation to reply that she had
been married to one. ''Too much,'' she countered, reflecting that that, also, was true. Then the oddity of
the conversation struck her. She giggled sleepily. ''I
feel I should point out to you that this is a most *improper* conversation.'' Her tone was light, as light-
hearted as she felt. She was perfectly aware that their
present situation was scandalous in the extreme, yet it
seemed oddly right, and she was quite content.

Martin's views on their situation were considerably

more pungent. Sheer madness designed to make his head hurt more than it already did. First she had hit him on the jaw, and caused him to crack his skull. Now this. What more grievous torture could she visit on him?

With a soft sigh, Helen snuggled against him.

Martin's jaw clenched with the effort to remain passive. A chuckle he could only describe as siren-like escaped her. "I've just thought. I escaped from the clutches of a fop only to spend the night in the arms of one of the most notorious rakehells London ever produced. Presumably there is a moral in this somewhere." She giggled again and, to Martin's profound astonishment, as innocently and completely as a child, fell asleep.

Martin lay still, staring at the rough beams overhead. Her admission to a knowledge of rakes and their activities struck him as distinctly odd. Also distinctly distracting. Before his imagination, only too willing to slip its leash, could bring him undone, he put the peculiar statement aside for inspection at a later date — a safer date. Given fair Juno's apparent quality, taking her declaration at face value and acting accordingly might not be wise.

With an effort, he concentrated on falling asleep. First, he tried to pretend there was no woman in his arms. That proved impossible. Then he tried thinking of Erica, the mullato mistress he had left behind. That did not work either. Somehow Erica's dark ringlets and coffee-coloured skin kept transforming to golden curls and luscious white curves. Instead of Erica's small, dark-tipped breasts, he saw fuller white breasts with dusky pink aureoles. His experienced imagination had no difficulty in filling in what the apricot silk gown hid—a subtle form of mental torture. Finally, after making a vow to learn fair Juno's name and track her down once she was restored to her family and no longer under his protection, Martin forced himself to think of nothing at all.

After an hour, he drifted into an unsettled doze.

Chapter Three

Early morning sunlight tickled Martin's consciousness awake. Luckily, he opened his eyes before he moved, not something he always did. What he saw stopped him from reacting on impulse to the warm softness in his arms. Biting back his curses, he extricated himself from the clasp of silken limbs and, without disturbing fair Juno, got down from the loft as fast as he was able.

He greeted the horses, then went outside. The sky was clear, the air fresh and clean. The storm had drenched the countryside but the sun now shone bright. A good day for travelling. After stretching his legs, he was about to go inside and wake his companion in adventure when he bethought himself of the state of the roads.

A few paces down the cart track saw his plans revised. Used to travelling on gravel or the hard-surfaced highways, he had forgotten they were on byways not much more than cattle tracks. The track from the barn turned to a quagmire before it reached the road. The road itself was little better. Closer inspection suggested a few hours would suffice to render it passable, at least as far as he could see.

Resigned to the wait, he returned to the barn.

He climbed to the loft and found fair Juno still asleep. The morning sunlight spilled through the hay door, gilding the curls that escaped in random profusion from the simple knot on the top of her head. Her lips were slightly parted in sleep, her breathing shallow. A delicate blush tinted her perfect complexion. An ivory and gold goddess, or so she seemed to him. He stared long and hard at the vision, drinking in the symmetry of her features, the arch of her brows and the warm glow of full lips. Most of the rest of her was concealed by the folds of the carriage blanket, much to his relief. Only one arm, nicely rounded in a distinctively feminine mould, showed bare, ivory-sheathed, nestling on the straw where he had laid it down.

Who was she? Quietly, Martin descended the ladder. Let her sleep—after the storm, she probably needed the rest.

Once more on firm ground, he rubbed his hands over his face. In truth, he could do with a few hours of extra sleep, but he was not fool enough to try relaxing in the straw by fair Juno's side.

The morning was far advanced before Helen awoke. For a full minute, she lay, confused and disorientated, before recollections of the previous evening returned her to full understanding.

She was alone in the loft. Abruptly, she sat up. Then she heard his voice, dimmed by distance. After a moment, she realised he was outside, talking to the horses. Hurriedly, she scrambled out of the carriage blanket. She shook it and folded it neatly before laying it, along with his coat, on the edge of the loft by the ladder. Then, with a last glance to make sure he was still outside, she gingerly descended the ladder, her skirts hiked to her knees.

Relieved to have reached the ground undetected, she let her skirts down, brushing ineffectually at the creases. She pulled a wisp of straw from her hair, grimacing at the thought of how she must look. There was a pail of fresh water beside the ladder, the linen handkerchief she had used the day before draped over the side. Quickly, she splashed her face and rinsed her hands. She was patting her face dry when she heard his step behind her.

"Ah! Fair Juno awakes. I was just about to roust you out."

Helen turned. In daylight, her rescuer was even more distressingly handsome than in lamplight. The broad shoulders seemed broader than ever; his height was no dream. Small wonder he had made her feel weak and small. The aquiline features held a touch of harshness, but the impression might be due to his tan. Helen blinked and found his grey eyes laughingly quizzing her. She prayed her blush was not detectable. "I'm so sorry. You should have woken me earlier."

"No matter." Martin reached for the harness he had left on the wall of the stall. He had wondered what colour her eyes would prove to be in daylight. Pools of amber and limpid green highlighted with gold, they were the most striking features of a remarkably striking package. He thanked his stars he had not seen her in daylight before being forced to spend a night by her side. Her blush suggested she felt much the same. Martin knew for a certainty that relaxing with rakes was much easier in the dark but he did not want her to retreat behind a correct façade. He smiled and was relieved when she smiled back. "The roads are only just dry enough to attempt the curricle."

Helen followed him outside, pausing to breathe deeply of the fresh morning air. She saw him struggling to harness the restive horses and went forward to help, approaching steadily so as not to spook the highly strung beasts. Catching hold of the bit of the nearside horse, she crooned sweet nothings and stroked the velvet nose.

Martin nodded his approval, pleasantly surprised by her practical assistance. Together, they efficiently hitched the pair to the curricle.

Holding the reins, he went to her side, intending to lift her to the box seat.

"Er—I left the blanket and your coat in the loft." The words tumbled out. Helen prayed that he would not notice her fluster. Panic had risen to claim her at the mere thought of him touching her again. After the past ten minutes' surreptitious observation, she could not understand how she had had the nerve to survive the night.

One black brow rose; the grey eyes rested thoughtfully on her face. Then he handed her the reins. "I'll get them. Don't try to move 'em."

He was back in two minutes, but by then she had steeled herself for the ordeal. He stowed the blanket and coat behind the seat, then reached for the reins. Helen relinquished them. An instant later, his hands fastened about her waist. A moment of weightlessness followed, before she was deposited, gently, on the seat.

As she fussed about, settling her skirts, Helen reflected that new experiences were always unsettling. Just what it was she felt every time he touched her she could not have said—but she had no doubt it was scandalous. And delicious. And very likely addictive, as well. Doubtless, it was one of those tricks rakes had at their fingertips, to make susceptible women their slaves. Not that her late and wholly unlamented husband had had the facility. Then again, she amended, giving the devil his due, Arthur had never had much time for her, the gawky sixteen-year old he had wed for her fortune and supplanted within weeks with a more experienced courtesan. However, none of the countless admirers she had had since her return to social acceptability had ever affected her as Martin Willesden did.

The curricle jerked into motion. Her eyes fell to his hands, long, strong fingers managing the reins. His ability probably owed more to his undeniable experience—the experience that glowed in the smouldering depths of those grey eyes. Whatever it was, wherever its origin, he was dangerous—a fact she should strive to remember.

The sun found her face; Helen tilted her head up and breathed in the fresh scent of rain-washed greenery. Her mental homily was undoubtedly apt, but, try as she might, she could not take the threat seriously.

This was an adventure, her first in years. She was reluctant to allow strictures, however appropriate, to mar the joy. The situation was, after all, beyond outrageous; decorum and social niceties had necessarily been set aside. Why shouldn't she enjoy the freedom of the moment?

"We should reach Ilchester for a late breakfast."

Helen wished he had not mentioned food. Determined to keep her mind from dwelling on her empty stomach, she cast about for some suitably innocuous topic. "You said you'd been visiting your home. Is it near here?"

"The other side of Taunton."

"You've been away for some time, haven't you? Was it much changed?"

Martin grimaced. "Thirteen years of mismanagement have unfortunately taken their toll." The silence following this pronouncement suggested that his anger at the fact had shown in his tone. He sought to soften the effect. "My mother lives there, but she's been an invalid for some years. My sister-in-law acts as her companion but unfortunately she's a nonentity— hardly the sort to raise a dust when the runners disappeared."

"Disappeared?" Shocked incredulity showed in fair Juno's eyes, echoed in her tone.

Reluctantly, Martin grinned. "I'm afraid the place, beyond my mother's rooms, is barely habitable. That's why I was so set on heading back to London without delay." Reflecting that had this not been the case he would not have had the honour of rescuing fair Juno, Martin began to look on the Hermitage's shortcomings with a slightly less jaundiced eye. Considering the matter dispassionately, something he had yet to do, he shrugged. "It's not seriously damaged—the fabric's sound enough. I've a team of decorators at work on my town house. When they've finished there, I'll send them to the Hermitage."

Intrigued by the distant look in his eyes, Helen gently prompted, "Tell me what it's like."

Martin grinned. His eyes on his horses, and on the ruts in the road, he obliged with a thumbnail sketch of the Hermitage, not as he had found it, but as he remembered it. "In my father's day, it was a gracious place," he concluded. "Whenever I think of it, I remember it as being full of guests. Hopefully, now I've returned, I'll be able to restore it to its previous state."

Helen listened intently, struck by the fervour rippling in the undercurrents of his deep voice. "It's your favourite estate?" she asked, trying to find the reason.

Martin considered the question, trying to find words to convey his feelings. "I suppose it's the place I call home. The place I most associate with my father. And happier memories."

The tone of his last sentence prevented further enquiry. Helen mulled over what little she knew of the new Earl of Merton and realised it was little indeed. He had clearly been out of the country, but why and where she had no idea. She had heard talk of a scandal, unspecified, in his past, but, given the anticipation of the hostesses of the *ton,* it was clearly of insufficient import to exclude him from their ballrooms and dinners.

While he conversed, one part of Martin's mind puz-

zled over the conundrum of his companion. Fair Juno
was not that young, nor yet that old. Mid-twenties was
his experienced guess. What did not seem right was
the absence of a ring on her left hand. She was undeniably beautiful, attractive in a wholly sensual way,
and the sort of lady who was invited to Chatham
House. The possibility that she was a lady of a different hue occurred only to be dismissed. Fair Juno was
well-bred enough to recognise his potential and be
flustered by it—hardly the hallmark of a barque of
frailty. All in all, fair Juno was an enigma.

"And now," he said, bringing their companionable
silence to an end, "we should put our minds to deciding how best to return you to your home." He glanced
at the fair face beside him. "Say the word, and I'll
drive you to your door." Entirely unintentionally, his
voice had dropped several tones. Which, he thought,
catching Juno's wide-eyed look, merely indicated how
much she affected him.

"I don't really think that would be altogether
wise," Helen returned, suppressing her scandalous inclinations. He was teasing her, she was sure.

"Perhaps not. I had hoped London starchiness had
abated somewhat, but clearly the passing of the years
has yet to turn that particular stone to dust." Martin
smiled down into her large eyes, infusing his expression with as much innocence as he was capable.
"How, then?"

Helen narrowed her eyes and stared hard at him. "I
had expected, my lord, that one of your reputation
would have no difficulty in overcoming such a minor

obstacle. If you put your mind to it, I'm sure you'll think of something.''

It was a decidedly impertinent speech and provoked a decidedly audacious reply. The gleam in the grey eyes gave her warning.

"I'm afraid, my dear, that if you consult my reputation more closely you'll realise I've never been one for placating the proprieties.''

Realising her tactical error, Helen retreated to innocence. How silly to try to deflate a rake with outrageousness. "Don't you really know? I confess, I'd thought you would.''

For an instant, the grey eyes held hers, suspicion in their depths. Then their quality subtly altered. She was conscious of a stilling of time, of her surroundings dimming into blankness. His grey eyes, and him, filled her senses. Then his lips twisted in a gently mocking smile and he looked away.

"As you say, fair Juno, my experience is extensive.'' Martin slanted another glance her way, and saw a slight frown pucker her brow. "I suspect it might be best if we try for one of the minor inns, just before Hounslow. I'll hire a chaise and escort for you there.'' When the frown did not immediately lift, he smiled. "You may give the coachman instructions once you reach the outskirts of London.''

"Yes,'' said Helen, struggling to preserve her calm in the face of the discovery that grey eyes of his particular shade seemed to possess a strange power over her. For a moment, she had been mesmerised, deprived of all will, totally at his mercy. And it had felt quite delicious. "I suppose that will do.''

Her tone of reluctant acceptance brought a smirk to Martin's lips, quickly suppressed. What a very responsive yet oddly innocent goddess she was. His interest in her, already marked, was growing by the minute. Just as well that they had agreed to part that evening. "We should reach Hounslow before dark," he said, eager to settle that point.

They journeyed on in silence. Martin pondered how to broach the subject of her name; Helen pondered him. He was, without doubt, the most attractive man she had ever met. It was not just his physical attributes, though there was no fault to be found with those. Neither could his manners, polished and assured though they were, account for the effect. It was, she decided, something far more fundamental, like the raspy growl of his deep voice and the fire banked like coals in the smoky grey eyes.

"Do you spend much of your year in the country, fair maid?"

The question jolted Helen back to reality. "I often visit at—" She broke off, then continued smoothly, "At friends' houses."

"Ah."

The quality of the glance that rested fleetingly upon her face confirmed her suspicion. He was trying to learn more of her.

"So you spend most of your year in London?"

"Other than my visits."

Conversation rapidly degenerated to a game of quiz and answer, he trying to glean snippets of information, she trying to avoid revealing any identifying fact while politely answering all his queries.

"Do you attend the opera?"

"During the season."

"In friends' boxes?"

Helen threw him a haughty look. "I have my own box."

"Then no doubt I'll see you there." Martin smiled, pleased to have scored a hit.

Realising her slip, Helen had no choice but to be gracious. She inclined her head. "Countess Lieven often joins me. I'm sure she'll be only too pleased to meet you."

"Oh." Stymied by the mention of the most censorious of the patronesses of Almack's, Martin looked suitably chagrined. Then his brow cleared. "A capital notion. I can sue for permission to waltz in Almack's. With you."

At the thought, Helen had to laugh. The vision of Martin Willesden stalking the hallowed boards, an eagle among the lambs, setting all the mother ewes in a flap, was intensely appealing.

It was Martin's turn to look haughty. "Do you think I won't?"

Abruptly, Helen found herself drowning in smouldering grey, warmed and shaken to the core. Dragging her eyes from his, she looked ahead. "I...hadn't imagined you would be attracted to the mild entertainments of the Marriage Mart."

"I'm not. Only the promise of all manner of earthly pleasures could get me over its threshold."

Helen was not game to try to cap that. She rapidly became absorbed in the scenery.

A slow smile curved Martin's lips before he gave

his attention to his horses. He could not recall ever
enjoying thirty minutes of conversation with a female
half as much. In fact, he could not recall any other
woman he had ever favoured with half an hour of ver-
bal discourse. Fair Juno was a novelty, her mind quick
and adroit. Innocent though the information he had
gained was, it confirmed his suspicion that she had
attained a position in the *ton* normally reserved for
older matrons. Or widows.

At the thought, he let his eyes roam in leisurely
appraisal over the curvaceous form beside him. She
felt his gaze and glanced up, a slightly nervous smile
hovering on her rosy lips.

Helen saw the predatory gleam in the grey eyes and
accurately read their message. Dragging her dignity
about her, the only protection she possessed, she
arched one brow in spirited defence, perfectly ready
to continue their banter. But the reprobate by her side
merely smiled in a thoroughly seductive way and gave
his attention to his horses. Helen transferred her gaze
to the scenery, her lips irrepressively curving in appreciation. Conversing with a rake while free of the
normal strictures, protected from any physical consequences by the fact he had both hands full of high-
tempered horseflesh, was every bit as scandalously exciting as she had ever, as a green girl, imagined it
would be. It was all deliciously dangerous but, in this
case, completely safe. She had realised as much some
miles back. It was a game that, in this particular instance, she could play with impunity. She was in his
care and, instinctively, she knew he would honour that

charge. While she remained under his protection, she was safe from him.

Heaven help her later.

But, of course, there would be no later. Helen stifled a sigh as reality intruded, impossible to deny. The future, for them both, was fixed. When he reached London, he would be the focus of the matchmaking mamas—with good reason. He was titled, wealthy and hideously handsome to boot. Their darling daughters would make cakes of themselves trying to catch his grey eyes. And, inevitably, he would choose one of them as his wife. Some well-dowered, biddable miss with an immaculate reputation. A widow, with no pretensions to property, with a murky marriage to a social outcast behind her and nothing more than her connections to recommend her, was a poor bargain.

Inwardly, Helen shook herself. Reality began in London. There was no need to cloud her day of adventure with such dismal forebodings. She tried to force the image of Martin Willesden paying court to a sweet young thing from her mind. In truth, the tableau was somewhat hazy. It was hard to believe that a man of his tastes, as demonstrated by their dalliance of the past half-hour, would settle to marriage with a sweet young thing. Doubtless, he would be the sort who kept a mistress or two on the side. Well, who was she to complain? Her husband had done the same, with her blessing. Not that her blessing would have been forthcoming had Martin Willesden been her husband.

With a determined effort, Helen redirected her thoughts. He wanted to know her name. She could tell him, but her anonymity was a comforting sop to her conscience. Besides which, when he reached London and learned who she was, he would realise such a connection was unsuitable, for no one would ever believe it innocent. If she refused to tell him her name, he would not feel obliged to acknowledge her when he met her again. Then, too, many men felt widows were fair game and she would hate him to consider her a potential candidate for his extramarital vacancy. All in all, she decided, he did not need to know her name.

Martin wondered what thoughts held his goddess so silent. But the peace of the morning was soothing about them and he made no move to interrupt her reverie. Despite not knowing her name, he felt confident of finding her in the capital. London might be the teeming hub of the nation, but its hallowed halls were trod by few. A gold and ivory goddess would be easy to trace.

The road widened then dipped. A ford lay ahead. Engrossed in contemplation of the predictable delights of waltzing with fair Juno, Martin automatically checked his pair, then sent them into the shallow water at a smart trot.

The horses' hooves clopped on the gravelly surface of the opposite bank; they slowed, then leaned into the traces and strained. The carriage wheels stuck fast, rocking the occupants of the box seat to full awareness of their predicament.

Helen clutched the side of the seat, then turned a wide-eyed look on her rescuer as a muttered expletive was belatedly smothered.

Martin shut his eyes in frustration. He had forgotten

that minor fords were often not paved. The heavy rain had washed silt into the ford; his wheels felt as if they were six inches deep.

With a heavy sigh, he opened his eyes. "We're stuck."

Helen glanced around at the swiftly moving stream. "So we are," she agreed helpfully.

Martin cast her a warning look. She met it with unlikely innocence. Grimacing, he lifted his gaze to scan their surroundings. About them, the silence of woods and fields lay unbroken by human discord. No smoke rose above the trees to give hint of a nearby cottage. Memory suggested they were still some miles from the London road.

With a groan, Martin shortened the reins. "I'll have to get down and find some stones. Can you hold them, do you think?"

A mischievous grin lit Helen's face. "I was under the impression that no out-and-outer would ever entrust his cattle to a mere woman."

Martin grimaced. "*Touché*. I wouldn't—except that I wouldn't give a farthing for their behaviour if I simply tied the reins to the rail. The devils would sense the absence of a master and they'd be off as soon as the stones were in place." He glanced down into the large green eyes. "All they need is a light touch on the reins for reassurance—and you seem to know your way about horses."

Helen reached for the reins. "I do. But if you spook them by throwing stones, I'll drive off and leave you to your fate. So be warned!"

Martin laughed at her melodramatic tone and relinquished the reins. He stood carefully and removed his coat, placing it over the seat before jumping down from the carriage. The water covered his ankles. With an inward sigh for his gleaming Hessians, he splashed to the bank and cast about for stones to place beneath and before the wheels.

Helen watched, the reins held gently in both hands. Every now and then, she felt a tug as the horses lived up to their owner's expectations and tested their freedom. They were clearly unhappy to be standing stockstill, half in and half out of the stream, rather than stretching their legs along the highway. As the minutes ticked by, Helen became infected with their impatience. Martin had to go further and further afield to find stones to lay in the mud before the wheels. She had no idea of the time, but thought it close to noon. How far were they from London?

Then her reckless self emerged and shouldered aside her worries. This was adventure and in adventure important things took care of themselves. Things would turn out all right; she need not concern herself—fate was in charge.

Determinedly light-hearted, she started to hum, then, as Martin had disappeared upstream, lifted her voice in the refrain from an old country air.

Martin heard the lilting melody as he returned with yet more rocks. He paused for a moment, out of sight, and let her gentle contralto wash over him, waves of song lapping his consciousness. The sound was close to a caress. With a chuckle, Martin moved forward. A siren's song, no less.

She checked when she saw him, but when he raised

one brow in question she raised one back and, tilting her chin, resumed her song.

With a broad smile, Martin settled the stones he carried to best effect and headed back for more. In truth, he found fair Juno's fortitude somewhat remarkable, he who would have sworn he knew all there was to know of women. But this woman had not whined at the delay, nor raised peevish quibbles about the consequences. Consequences neither he nor she could do anything to avoid. Had she realised yet?

An interesting question. Yet, he reflected, fair Juno was no one's fool.

Three more trips and there were enough rocks to attempt to break free of the cloying mud. Hands on hips, Martin stood by the side of the carriage and looked up at his assistant. "I'll have to push the carriage from behind. Do you think you can hold them, once they gain the bank?"

A look of supercilious condescension was bestowed upon him. "Of course," Helen said, then deserted the high ground to ask, "Do you think they'll bolt?"

With a half-smile, Martin shook his head. "Not if you keep the reins short." He moved to the back of the curricle, praying that that was so. "When I say so, give 'em the office."

On her mettle, Helen obediently waited for his call before clicking the reins. The horses heaved, the curricle slowly edged forward. Then the wheels gained firm purchase and the carriage abruptly left the water. The horses pulled hard. Suppressing her sudden fear, stirred to life by the strength of the great beasts sensed through the reins, she determinedly hauled back, struggling to hold them. She applied the brake to lock the wheels, and the carriage skidded slightly.

Then Martin was beside her, taking the reins from her suddenly weak fingers.

"Good girl!"

The approval in his voice warmed her; the glow in his eyes raised her temperature even more. To her annoyance, Helen felt herself blushing. An odd sensation of weakness, not quite faintness but surely an allied affliction, bloomed within. She shifted along the seat, making room for him, supremely conscious of the large body when it settled once more by her side.

To her relief, Martin seemed content to resume their journey without further delay, leaving her to the task of shackling her wayward thoughts. Never before had they been so astray. And, if she was any judge at all of the matter, Martin Willesden was the type of man who could sense a wayward feminine thought at ten paces. Her present safety might be ensured, but she did not need to lay snares for her future.

Having learned his lesson somewhat belatedly, Martin devoted as much of his attention as he could summon to driving. The London road was gained without further mishap. Soon, they were bowling along at a spanking pace. Even so, it was past two o'clock when, accepting the inevitable, Martin checked and turned into the yard of the Frog and Duck at Wincanton.

He turned to smile into Juno's questioning eyes. "Lunch. I'm famished, even if, being a fashionable woman, you are not."

Helen's eyes widened slightly. "I'm not that fashionable."

Martin laughed and jumped down. He reached up to lift fair Juno to the ground, noting her slight hesitation before, without fuss, she drew nearer and let him grasp her waist.

Flustered again but determined not to show it, Helen accepted Martin's proffered arm. He led her up the steps to the inn door, then stood aside to allow her to enter. As she did so, the head groom, having laid eyes on the horses his ostlers had taken in charge, came hurrying to ask Martin's orders.

Alone, Helen crossed the threshold, thankful for the cool dimness within. She was feeling unduly warm. The door gave directly on to the taproom, a large chamber, low-ceilinged and cosy with a huge fireplace at one end. Alerted by the noise outside, the landlord was coming forward from his domain on the other side of the room. Seeing her, he stopped. And stared. Helen became aware that all the other occupants of the tap, six in all and all male, were likewise transfixed. Then, to her discomfort, a leering grin suffused the landlord's face. Faint echoes appeared on his patrons' faces, too.

Simultaneously realising what a sight she must present, and the likely conclusion the landlord had drawn, Helen drew herself up, ready to defend her status.

There was no need. Martin came through the door and stopped by her side. One comprehensive glance was all it took for him to grasp the conclusion the inhabitants of the Frog and Duck had jumped to. He scowled at the landlord. "A private parlour, host, where my wife can be at ease."

The growled command wiped the leer from the

landlord's face so fast, he had no expression ready to cover the ensuing blankness.

Helen was not sure whether to laugh or gasp. *Wife?* In the end, she covered her left hand with her right and, tipping up her chin, looked down her nose at the landlord, a feat assisted by the fact that she was taller than he. The man shrank as obsequiousness took hold.

"Yes, m'lord! Certainly, m'lord. If madam would step this way?"

Bowing every two paces, he led them to a neat little parlour. While Martin gave orders for a substantial meal, Helen sank, with a little sigh of thankfulness, into a well-padded armchair by the hearth, carefully avoiding the mirror above the mantelpiece. She had little real idea how bad her state was, but could not imagine knowing would help.

Martin heard her sigh. He glanced at her, then said to the landlord, "We had an accident with our chaise. Our servants are following behind, with our luggage. Perhaps," he continued, raising his voice and turning to address a weary Juno, "you'd like to refresh yourself above stairs, my dear?"

Helen blinked, then readily agreed. Led to a small chamber and supplied with warm water, she washed the dust of the road from her face and hands, then steeled herself to examine the damage her adventures had wrought in her appearance. It was not as bad as she had feared. Her eyes were sparkling clear and the wind had whipped colour into her cheeks. Clearly, driving about the countryside with Martin Willesden agreed with her constitution. In the end, she undid her hair and reformed the mass of curls into a simpler knot. Her dress, the apricot silk marred by a host of creases, was beyond her ability to change. Other than shaking and straightening her skirts, there was little else she could do.

Returning to the parlour, she found their repast laid out upon the table. Martin rose with a smile and held a chair for her.

"Wine?"

At her nod, he filled her glass. Then, without more ado, they applied themselves to the task of demolishing the food before them.

Finally satisfied, Martin sat back in his chair and put aside contemplation of their problems the better to savour his wine while quietly studying fair Juno, absorbed in peeling a plum. His eyes slid over her generous curves—generous, ample—such words came readily to mind. Along with luscious, ripe and other, less acceptable terms. Martin hid a smile behind his goblet. All in all, he had no fault to find in the arrangement of fair Juno's dispositions.

"We won't reach London tonight, will we?"

The question drew Martin's gaze to her lips, full and richly curved and presently stained with plum juice. A driving urge to taste them seared through him. Abruptly, he refocused his mind on their problem. He raised his eyes to Juno's, troubled green and concerned. He smiled reassuringly. "No."

Helen felt justified in ignoring the smile. "No", he said, and smiled. Did he have any idea of the panic she was holding at bay by dint of sheer determination?

Apparently, he did, for he continued, more seriously, "Getting stuck in that ford has delayed us too much. However, I draw the line at driving my horses through the night, not that that would avail us, for I can't see arriving in London at dawn to be much improvement over our current state.''

Helen frowned, forced to acknowledge the truth of that remark. He would not be able to hire a chaise for her if they passed by Hounslow in the middle of the night.

''And, before you suggest it, I refuse to be a party to any scheme to hire a chaise for you to travel alone through the night.''

Helen's frown deepened. She opened her mouth to argue.

''*Even* with outriders.''

Helen shut her mouth and glared. But his tone and the set of his jaw warned her that no argument would shift him. And, in truth, she had no wish to spend the night jolting over the roads, a prey to fears of highwaymen and worse. ''What, then?'' she asked in her most reasonable tone.

She was rewarded with a brilliant smile which quite took her breath away. Luckily, he did not expect her to speak.

''I had wondered,'' Martin began diffidently, unsure how his plan would be received, ''if we could find an inn where neither of us is known, to put up in for the night.''

Helen considered the suggestion. She could see no alternative. Raising her napkin to wipe her lips, she raised her eyes to his. ''How will we explain our disreputable state—and our lack of servants and luggage?''

The instant she asked the question, she knew the answer. Deliciously wicked, but, she reasoned, it was all part of her adventure and thus could be viewed with a lenient eye.

Pleased by her tacit acceptance of the only viable plan he had, Martin relaxed. "We can tell the same story I edified our host with—that we've had an accident and our retainers are following behind with the luggage."

Still a little nervous of the idea, Helen nodded. Did he intend to claim they were wed?

"Which reminds me," said Martin, sliding the gold signet from his right hand. "You had better wear this for the duration." He held the heavy ring out and dropped it into her palm.

Helen studied the ring, still warm from his hand. Obviously, they were to appear married. She slipped it on to the third finger of her left hand. To her surprise, its weight, in that remembered place, did not evoke the expected horror. Instead, it was strangely reassuring, a source of strength, a pledge of protection.

"Very well," she said. She drew a deep breath and purposefully added, "But we'll have to have separate rooms." Determined to be clear on that point, she raised her eyes to his darkly handsome face and beheld a haughty expression.

"Naturally," returned Martin repressively. It would undoubtedly be safer that way. Aside from anything else, he would need to get some sleep. He studied Juno's fair countenance and the need to know her real name grew. Given that they were to masquerade cloaked in wedded bliss, he felt that their increasing intimacy justified a request for enlightenment. "I rather think, my dear, that, given our new relationship, it might be appropriate if I knew your name."

Engrossed in fantasies revolving around their new relationship, Helen gave a start. "Oh." She thought once more of the matter, inwardly acknowledging her reluctance and her reasons for it. Eyeing the handsome face, the strangely compelling eyes fixed on hers, she admitted to an urge to tell him, to confide in a man so transparently at ease in her world. But hard on the heels of that feeling came a premonition of how he would look when he heard her name. He would know of her husband; they would likely have met. What would he feel—pity? Revulsion, albeit carefully cloaked? Doing anything to damage the closeness she sensed between them was repugnant.

Letting her gaze fall, she picked up her napkin, creasing the folds between her fingers. "I...really..." Her words trailed away. How to explain what she felt?

Martin smiled a little crookedly. He would have liked her to confide in him but the point was not worth disturbing her over. "You really feel you shouldn't?"

Helen threw him a grateful look. "It's just that the adventure seems more...complete—and," she added, determined at least to have some of the truth, "my behaviour more excusable if I continue incognito."

Smiling more broadly, Martin inclined his head in acceptance. "Very well. But what should I call you?"

With a gentle smile that, unbeknown to her, held an element of sweet shyness quite at odds with her years, Helen said, "You choose. I'm sure you can invent something appropriate."

Her smile very nearly overset Martin's much tried control. He had thought it strengthened by the years, but fair Juno was temptation beyond any he had ever faced. Invent something? His mind was seething with invention, did she but know it. But, as knowledge of his thoughts would hardly be conducive to allowing her to continue with reasonable calm in his company, he could only be thankful that they did not show in his face.

They did show in his eyes. Even with the table between them, Helen saw the smoke rise and cloud the grey. Stormy heat caressed her. Mesmerised, she sat and waited, breathless and trying to hide it. Heaven forbid that he ever realise how much he affected her!

"Juno," Martin said, just managing to keep his voice within acceptable range. "Fair Juno." His smile was entirely beyond his control, laced with wicked thoughts and scandalous suggestion.

Helen lifted one brow, trying to pour cold water on the flames she could feel flickering around them. "I hardly think, my lord, that such an allusion is appropriate."

His smile only gained in intensity. "On the contrary, my dear. I feel it entirely appropriate."

Helen tried to frown. Juno—queen of the goddesses. How could she argue with that?

"And now, having settled our immediate future, I suggest we get on our way." Martin rose and stretched, letting languid grace cloak his haste. If he did not get out of here soon, and back to the relative safety of the curricle's box seat, he would not answer for the consequences. Exposure to fair Juno was sapping all will to resist his rakish inclinations. And he had dinner with her, alone, to look forward to. He had need to recoup what strength he could.

He went around the table and helped her to her feet. Tucking her small hand into the crook of his arm, he led her to the door. "Come, my lady. Your carriage awaits."

Chapter Four

They had chosen the Bells at Cholderton as their overnight stop. The small town nestled just south of the London road, the major traffic passing by without pause. The Bells was an old house, less frequented in these days of rapid travel but still in sufficiently good state to hold promise of a comfortable night.

Shown into a private parlour, Helen glanced about at the faded elegance. She nodded in approval, her haughty demeanour supporting their fiction. Martin had told their story, his natural arrogance wiping out any possibility of disbelief. Lord and Lady Willesden required rooms for the night. The landlord found nothing amiss with the request; he was, in fact, only too pleased to see them.

"My good wife will have your supper ready directly, m'lord. There's duck and partridge, with lamb's-foot jelly and a wine syllabub to follow."

Languidly superior, Martin nodded. "That should do admirably."

When the door closed behind the little man, Martin glanced her way, laughter lurking in his grey eyes.

"Just so," he said, his smile warming her every bit as much as the fire in the grate.

Feeling her nervousness increase as he drew nearer, Helen turned to hold out her chilled fingers to the blaze. When the sun had slipped beneath the horizon, he had insisted she don his greatcoat. Her fingers went to the heavy garment to ease it from her shoulders. Instantly, he was beside her. His fingers brushed hers.

"Here, let me."

She had to, for she could not have moved if the ceiling had fallen. His gentle touch, so simple but almost a caress, and the velvety quality cloaking his rumbling growl, drowned her senses in dizzying distraction. The effect he had on her was intensifying with time. How on earth was she to survive the evening?

As soon as he stepped away from her to drop the coat over a chair, Helen sank into the armchair by the fire. She drew a deep breath, forcing herself to meet his intent gaze when he turned once more to face her.

Martin studied the vision before him, reading her unease with accomplished certainty. If circumstances had been different, she would have every reason to feel threatened. As things stood, she was safe. Or at least, he amended, safe enough. He knew she could sense his attraction and was hourly more entertained by her efforts to hide her consciousness of him. Entertained and intrigued. Clearly, fair Juno, if widow she was, was not one of those who dispensed her favours with gay abandon.

As he watched, a small frown creased Juno's brow.

"Why aren't you travelling with a groom or tiger?"

Elegantly disposing his long limbs in the chair opposite hers, Martin smiled, perfectly ready to converse on such innocent topics. "My groom fell victim to a severe head cold. I left him at the Hermitage." Considering that fact, privately Martin owned to some relief that Joshua had not been perched behind, cramping his style.

"Does the Hermitage have many farms attached?"

"Six. They're all leased to long-term tenants."

Succeeding questions, which Martin was shrewd enough to know were far from artless, led them to a discussion of farming and the care of estates. He could appreciate Juno's desire to avoid questions on town pursuits; such topics were likely to give him more clues to her identity. Yet her opinions on the organisation of farm labour and the problems faced by tenant farmers were equally revealing. Her knowledge of the subject could not have been acquired other than through first-hand experience. All of which added to his mental picture of fair Juno. She had spent a goodly portion of her life on a large and well-run estate.

A brisk knock on the door heralded the landlord. "Your dinner, m'lord." Carrying a heavily laden tray, he entered, closely followed by a buxom woman with tablecloth and cutlery. Together, they efficiently laid the table, then bowed and withdrew.

Rising, Martin held out his hand. "Shall we?"

Placing her hand in his, Helen ruthlessly stifled the thrill that shot through her at his touch, assuming her most regal manner as she allowed him to lead her to the table and seat her at one end. The slight smile which played about his lips suggested he was not deceived by her worldly air.

Thankfully, the food gave her a safe topic for discussion.

"I have to admit to ignorance of the latest fads. Thirteen years is a long time away from the boards of the fashionable."

Encouraged by this admission, Helen ignored the laughing understanding lighting his grey eyes and launched into a catalogue of the latest culinary delights.

When the landlord re-entered to draw the covers, Helen grasped the opportunity to retreat to the chair by the fire. She heard the door shut behind their host and wondered, a little frantically, how she was to manage for the next two hours.

"Brandy?"

Turning to see Martin at the sideboard, decanter in hand, she shook her head. Did he but know it, he did not need any assistance to befuddle her wits.

Helping himself to a large dose, undoubtedly required if he was to sleep with Juno, alone, next door, Martin came to stand by the fire, one booted foot on the fender, his shoulders propped against the mantelpiece.

"Your man is not going to be impressed with your boots."

Martin followed her glance and grimaced. "I'll have to entrust them to the boots here. Joshua will, in all probability, never forgive me."

Helen smiled at his nonsense. Despite the tingling of her nerves, due entirely to her company, she felt relaxed and at peace, not a state she had had much experience of over her life. Content, she thought, searching for the right word. Engaged in a most scandalous escapade and I feel content. How odd.

Catching Martin's gaze as it rested lightly upon her, she smiled. He smiled back, a slow, pensive smile, and she felt the heat rise inside her. Her eyes locked with his, smoky grey and intent, and she felt her will start to slip from its moorings.

Sounds of an arrival disrupted their silent communion. Martin turned to stare at the door. The noise beyond rose until it resolved into the clamour of many voices. An invasion had found the Bells.

Helen frowned. "What could it be?"

Equally at sea, Martin shook his head. "Too late for a scheduled stop, I would have thought." Inwardly, he hoped that whatever company had sought shelter at the inn did not include any who might recognise either Juno or himself. If it ever became known, there was no possibility that their escapade would be viewed as innocent.

The noise outside subsided to a steady hum. Almost immediately, the landlord arrived to satisfy their curiosity.

"Excuse me, m'lord, but it seems a night for accidents. The night coach for Plymouth's lost a wheel just up the road. The smith says as it can't be fixed 'til the morrow, so's we're having to put up all the passengers here. If it be all the same to you and her ladyship," he said, ducking his head in Helen's direction, "I've put you in the main chamber. It's got a huge bed, m'lord—you won't be disappointed. But there's more people than we have beds as 'tis, so I didn't think as how you'd mind.''

The man looked hopefully at Martin. Martin looked back, wondering how Juno was taking the news. From his point of view, the disaster was a damned nuisance. But if he insisted on separate rooms, they would probably end up sharing with some less suitable bedfellows—the sort who travelled on the night coach. And, all in all, with the extra men in the house, he would much rather Juno was safe by his side, even if he got no sleep as a result. "Very well," he replied in his most languid voice. He heard the hiss of Juno's indrawn breath and suppressed a smile. "In the circumstances, your best chamber will have to do."

Obviously relieved, the landlord bobbed his head and departed.

Martin turned to meet Juno's reproving gaze. One black brow rose. "In truth, my dear, you'll be far safer with me than alone this night."

There was no answer to that. Helen dragged her gaze from his face and fastened it on the flames leaping and dancing about the large log in the grate. The prospect of sleeping in the same bed as Martin Willesden left her feeling numb. It was shock, she supposed. She had slept in his arms in the loft last night, but a loft was not the same as a bed. Her adventure was taking a decidedly dangerous turn. No—it was impossible. She would have to think of some alternative.

But she had still to discover another way from the impasse when, at Martin's suggestion, they went upstairs to their room, the largest chamber as promised.

A welcoming fire burned in the grate, a bed which was every bit as huge as her fevered imagination had anticipated stood against one wall. The room was comfortably furnished, the age of the hangings disguised by the soft candlelight. Martin held the door for her, then followed her in.

The click of the latch jolted Helen to action. She swung to face him, clasping her hands firmly before her. "My lord, this is impossible."

He smiled and moved past her to the window. "Martin," he said, throwing a mild glance over his shoulder. "You'd better stop 'my lording' me if we're supposed to be married."

Martin checked the window, opening it a crack to let in some air, then rearranged the heavy drapes. He strolled back to the middle of the room, pausing to shrug out of his coat. He draped it over the back of a chair, then smiled at Juno, still standing, uncertain and nervous, near the door. "It's not impossible," he said, beckoning her forward. "Come here by the fire and let me unlace your gown." He ignored the alarm flaring in her eyes. "Then you can wrap yourself in the sheet and be as modestly garbed as a nun."

Helen considered his words, her nerves in knots, her mind incapable of finding any way out. When his hand beckoned again, with increasing imperiousness, she walked hesitantly forward, her eyes reflecting her troubled state.

With a reassuring smile, Martin took her hand and drew her to face the fire. Behind her, he found the lacings of her silk gown. His practised fingers made short work of the closures. He resisted the temptation to part the sides of the garment and run a fingertip down her spine, clad only, as he had suspected, in a fine silk chemise. "Stay there a moment. I'll fetch the sheet."

Helen stared at the flames, her cheeks rosy red. So far, his behaviour had been as reassuringly unthreatening as his words. It was her own inclinations that were undermining her confidence. She was perfectly well aware of how close she stood to having an illicit affair with one of the most notorious rakes in England. All she needed to do was to give him a sign that she would welcome his advances and she would learn what it was that made rakes so sought after as lovers. Martin Willesden was temptation incarnate. But her common sense stood firmly in her way, prosaically pointing out that the last thing she needed was a fling, an affair of the moment, based on nothing more than a passing attraction. That had never been her style.

The sheet descended over her shoulders.

"I'll look the other way. I promise not to peek."

Helen did not dare look to see just where he was or if he complied. Hurriedly, she slipped the silk dress down, letting it puddle about her ankles while she wrapped the sheet around and about her, tucking the ends in to secure it. She stepped out of her dress and bent to pick it up.

The sheet rustled as she moved and Martin turned around, just in time to see her pick up her dress. He admired the view before she straightened, shooting him an uncertain look. The firelight gilded her curls, sheening softly on the exposed ivory shoulders and arms. The ache in his loins, a niggling pain for the past twenty-four hours, intensified. Determined to ignore it, he grinned at her. "If you get into bed, I'll tuck you in."

Discovering the teasing glint inhabiting his grey eyes, Helen glared, but obediently moved to the bed. "Where are you going to sleep?" There was no armchair in the room.

Martin's grin grew. "As the landlord said, it's a large bed." He unbuttoned his waistcoat then started on the laces of his shirt.

Helen stopped and stared. "What are you doing?"

His control under strain, Martin grimaced. "Getting ready for bed. I'll be damned if I sleep another night in these clothes." At the look on fair Juno's face, a picture of scandalised horror, he growled, "For God's sake, woman! Get into bed and turn the other way. You know you're perfectly safe."

Which was more than he knew, but the longer she stood there, wide green eyes on him, the more danger she courted. When she blinked, then climbed rapidly on to the bed, curling up on one side and pulling the covers about her ears, Martin let out a sigh of relief.

Nerves skittering uncontrollably, Helen lay and stared at the wall. The candles were snuffed, but the flames from the fire shed enough light to see by. She heard his Hessians hit the floor, then the door opened as he stood them in the corridor for the boots to attend to. He closed the door and she heard the muffled sounds of him undressing. She wished she could stop listening, but her nerves, at full stretch, would not let her. Then the bed at her back sagged. With a small

squeak, she clutched the side of the mattress to stop
herself from rolling into him.

In spite of his pain, Martin chuckled. He had not
anticipated that difficulty. "Don't worry. You have my
word as a gentleman that I won't take advantage."

That's not what I'm worried about! Helen kept the
thought to herself. She was scandalised, tantalised, ter-
rified by the possibilities. It had been a long time since
she had been in bed with a man, and that never innocently. Last night in the straw did not count—that
had been quite different—that had not been a bed. This
was definitely a bed. To her horror, her thoughts kept
sliding to how easy it would be to relax, to let herself
drift back in the bed, until she met the hard, heavy
body indenting the mattress behind her.

In the dark, Martin mentally gritted his teeth. His
loins were as girded as they could get. But the warm
perfume of her hair tickled his senses; his body was
alive to her nearness. If last night had been difficult,
tonight would be torture. As the firelight faded, leaving them in comforting darkness, he realised she was
stiff and rigid beside him, definitely not asleep.

"You needn't worry I'll move in the night. I sleep
very soundly." Once I sleep, he added silently. "I
suspect it's something to do with having been in the
army. One slept when one could, usually in far from
comfortable surroundings."

"How long were you in the Peninsula?"

Her question, muffled by the bedclothes, reminded
Martin of an ascerbic comment made by some high-
ranking hostess, to the effect that there was nothing so
boring as hearing of men's military exploits. He seized

the idea. Within ten minutes, the woman's astuteness was confirmed. He paused in the middle of a detailed description of his second major battle. No sound beyond the crackle of the fire disturbed the stillness of the chamber. Then his straining ears caught the soft huff of Juno's breathing, shallow and even. She was asleep.

He smiled into the darkness, oddly elated, as if he had succeeded in winning another battle. Knowing she was asleep allowed him to relax. As he slipped into slumber, he sternly reminded himself to make sure he woke properly—before he moved.

The reminder was needed. He awoke to find that, as he had expected, he had passed the night without stirring. He was no nearer to where Juno had laid her head than before. Unfortunately, Juno herself had moved. A lot closer. She had somehow insinuated herself into his arms, her head comfortably settled on his chest. One naked arm lay about his waist.

And her sheet had ridden up in the night. He could feel her silken limbs entwined with his.

Martin clenched every muscle he possessed and willed his body to compliance. Carefully, excruciatingly slowly, he disentangled their limbs, trying not to glance at her legs, too worried about waking her to draw the sheet down. He was naked; if she woke now, she was going to get a shock.

It was a relief to leave the warmth of the bed. Quickly, he dressed and escaped downstairs.

He found the landlord in the taproom, serving some of the male passengers from the coach. There were others still asleep on some of the benches. After greeting the man and asking after the weather, Martin casually asked, "Have our servants by any chance appeared?"

The landlord shook his head. "No, m'lord. No one's been by this morning."

Frowning direfully, Martin swore. "In that case, I'll hire one of your carriages. My wife can go on to town while I back-track to find out what's become of our people."

The landlord was all sympathetic help. He assured Martin of the quality of his carriage and that the coachman and groom could be trusted to see her ladyship safe into London.

"Very well," said Martin, tossing a small purse to the man. "Have the carriage ready. I'll want her ladyship on her way immediately after we breakfast." Martin glanced about the taproom and remembered the sensation Juno had caused the previous day. "Perhaps you could send a tray upstairs?"

"Certainly, m'lord. I'll send my missus up directly."

Martin returned upstairs, pausing to gather his strength before tapping lightly on the door and entering. To his relief, Juno, fair as ever, was out of bed and fully dressed.

Helen was seated before the small dressing-table, setting her hair once more into a neat knot. She turned when Martin entered, returning his smile as calmly as she could. She had woken to find him gone, but had found herself in the middle of the bed, her protective sheet twisted high on her thighs. The coverlet had been over the top, but she could not begin to think of where he had been when he had awoken. "Good morning."

Her pulse accelerating, she turned back to the mirror.

"A fair morning it is." Martin came to stand beside the dressing-table, propping his shoulders against the wall.

To Helen's sensitised senses, he exuded an overwhelming aura of potent masculinity. Struggling to keep her wits focused, she listened as he told her of his arrangements.

"With luck, you'll be home shortly after midday."

Despite the fact that home was where she wished to be, Helen was acutely aware of a dull, shrinking feeling as he pronounced the end to their adventure. Suddenly, the morning seemed less bright.

Their breakfast arrived and was laid out on the small table by the window. Bidden to attend, Helen tried to shake off her attack of the dismals and respond to his banter as she should. He had been a knight in shining armour, in truth, and she owed him a great deal. So she put a brave face on her irrational despondency and replied brightly to his comments.

She would have been mortified to know the ease with which Martin read her thoughts. Clearly, Juno had never mastered the art of prevarication. Her expression was open, her eyes a direct reflection of her mood. He accurately sensed her feelings, and her desire to keep them hidden. Wisely, he made no reference to his knowledge, but was inordinately pleased that she should feel saddened at having her time in his company brought to an end. It would make it so much easier to draw her to him when next they met.

Breakfast over, he escorted her downstairs. The day was fine; Juno did not need his coat. He paused, holding her beside him on the steps of the inn. The carriage which was to convey her to London stood ready before them, as neat and clean as the landlord had said. The coachman and groom were burly fellows, both with the open honesty of countrymen. Juno would be safe in their care. He looked down into her clear green eyes. A wry smile twisted his lips. "I've told them they should take you to London but that you'll make up your mind where you wish to go when you get there. I've paid them fully, so you don't need to worry about that."

Helen felt breathless. "I don't know how to thank you, my lord," she began, her voice soft and low so that none would hear them. "You've been of inestimable help."

Martin's smile broadened. "The pleasure was entirely mine, fair Juno." He lifted her hand from his sleeve and placed a kiss on her trembling fingertips.

"Your ring," Helen whispered.

Smoothly, reluctantly, Martin drew the heavy signet from her finger and replaced it on his. He raised his eyes to gaze deeply into hers. "Until next we meet."

Helen smiled tremulously, aware of a desire to lean into his warmth, to clutch at his hand.

Quite where the idea sprang from Martin could not later have said. But it suddenly occurred to him that he was masquerading as her husband. And being her husband gave him certain rights. Furthermore, being a rake, he would be mad not to take advantage of those rights. His lips lifted in a wholly devilish smile.

Helen saw the smile. Her eyes widened. But she got no chance to do anything at all. One strong arm slipped about her, pulling her firmly against him, while the fingers of his other hand tipped her face up. His lips closed over hers, confidently, possessively. And time stood still.

For an instant, she held firm against that too knowledgeable kiss, but the subtle invitation to greater intimacy was too compelling to resist. Her lips parted; he took immediate advantage, tasting her, teasing her, languidly, expertly exploring her, sending her mind whirling into fathomless sensation. She was dimly aware of the tightening of his arms about her. She melted against him, seeking to press herself against his muscled length. It was utterly delicious, this invitation to delight. The heady taste of him filled her senses; she was oblivious to all else but him.

Reluctantly, Martin brought the kiss to an end, wishing he could take their interaction further but knowing that was, for the moment, impossible. But at least he had left her with something to remember him by, until he found her in London and continued her seduction.

Looking down into her dazed eyes, he smiled and, too wise to attempt conversation, led her to the carriage. The groom, studiously straight-faced, jumped down and opened the door. Martin helped his goddess into the coach and saw her settled comfortably. He raised her hand to his lips. "Farewell, fair Juno. 'Till next we meet."

Helen blinked. The message in his eyes was clear. Then the door was shut. A minute later the carriage lurched into motion. She resisted the urge to scramble to the window, to stare back at him until he was out of sight. There was no need. "'Till next we meet," he had said. She had no doubt he meant it.

Still shaken, Helen drew a ragged breath. If only dreams could come true.

In the inn yard, Martin stood and watched the carriage until it disappeared along the road to London. His impulse was to order his curricle and follow as fast as he was able. But she could not escape. He would find her in London, of that he was sure.

She was one goddess he had every intention of worshipping.

Chapter Five

Three weeks later, Helen was in her chamber, studying the contents of her wardrobe to determine what could, and could not, be used for the upcoming Little Season, when her maid, Janet, put her head around the door.

"You've a visitor, m'lady."

Before Helen could extricate herself from the silks and satins and ask who, Janet had gone.

"Bother!" Helen sat on her heels and wondered who it was. The familiar excitement that had simmered just below her surface ever since she had returned to town blossomed. But it could not be him, she reasoned, not at eleven in the morning. With a sigh, she stood and shook out her primrose morning gown, before seating herself before her dressing-table to straighten her curls.

Her reappearance in the capital had caused a minor sensation among her friends but, luckily, thanks to the discretion of her servants, her disappearance had not been broadcast throughout the *ton*. Hence, while she had had to sustain a somewhat strained interview with

Ferdie Acheson-Smythe, who had read her a lecture on the ills likely to befall women of her class who kept scandalous secrets, and a much more rigorous cross-examination from Tony Fanshawe, the entire episode had passed off without major catastrophe. Throughout her explanations, she had managed to keep the names of her abductor—for she had no evidence that it had really been Hedley Swayne—and her rescuer—who was far too scandalous to be acknowledged—to herself. In this, she had been lucky. Circumstances, in the form of the birth of his son and heir, had kept her self-appointed guardian, Marc Henry, Marquis of Hazelmere, at home in Surrey. If she had had to face his sharp hazel eyes, she was sure she would have been forced to the truth—the whole truth. Thankfully, fate had spared her.

Descending the stairs, she was conscious of anticipation still pulsing her veins despite the sure knowledge that she would not meet a pair of stormy grey eyes in her small drawing-room. Those eyes, and their warmth, had haunted her; the memory of his lips on hers lay, a jewel enshrined in her memories. But if he looked for her, he would learn her name. And then he would know. Her silly dreams could never come true.

Startling eyes did indeed meet her when she entered her drawing-room, but they were emerald-green and belonged to Dorothea, Marchioness of Hazelmere.

"Helen!" Dorothea jumped to her feet, elegantly gowned as always, her face alight with a happiness so radiant that Helen's breath caught in her throat.

"Thea—what on earth are you doing here? I thought you'd be fixed at Hazelmere for months."

Helen returned the younger woman's warm embrace. They had become firm friends since Dorothea's marriage to Hazelmere, just over a year ago. Helen's connection with Hazelmere dated from her childhood; she was distantly connected with the Henrys and had spent many of her summers with Hazelmere's younger sister in Surrey.

Helen held Dorothea at arm's length, conscious of a pang of dismal jealousy that she would never experience the joy that shone from Dorothea's face. "How's my godson?" she asked, smiling determinedly.

"Darcy's fine." Dorothea smiled back, linking her arm in Helen's. Together, they strolled through the open French windows and into the small courtyard.

An ironwork seat with a padded cushion stood facing the bank of flowerbeds, the sun-warmed house wall at its back. As they sank on to the cushions, Dorothea explained, "I've installed him on the second floor of Hazelmere House. Mytton doesn't know how to react. As for Murgatroyd—he's torn between pride and handing in his notice."

Helen grinned. Hazelmere's butler and his valet were well-known to her. "But how did you convince Marc you were well enough to come to town? I was sure he would keep you in semi-permanent seclusion until Darcy was in leading strings, at the very least."

"Quite simple, really," explained Dorothea airily. "I merely pointed out that if I was well enough to share his bed I was certainly well enough to endure the rigours of the Season."

Helen's laughter pealed forth. "Oh, gracious!" she

gasped, once she was able. "What I would have given to have been able to see his face."

"Yes," agreed Dorothea, emerald eyes twinkling. "It really was quite something." She turned to study Helen. "But enough of my managing husband. What's this I hear of a disappearance?"

With practised ease, Helen told her tale. Dorothea did not press her for the details she omitted, merely remarking at the end of the story, "Hazelmere hasn't heard and I don't see any reason to tell him." With a quick smile, she continued, "What I came here to do was invite you to dinner on Thursday. Just the family, those who are in town. It's too early yet for anything formal and we'll have enough of that once the Season begins. You will come, won't you?"

"Of course," said Helen. Then she grimaced. "Mind you, by then Hazelmere will have heard about my escapade. You may tell him from me that there's no reason for him to concern himself over it and I won't take kindly to being interrogated over the dinner-table."

Dorothea laughed and squeezed her hand. "I'll make sure he behaves."

Reflecting that she had perfect confidence in her friend's ability on that score, Helen smiled at the thought of the mighty Hazelmere being managed, on however small a scale, by his elegant wife.

Dorothea rose. "I have to hurry for I've yet to catch Cecily."

Helen escorted her guest to the door.

"Come early, if you can," Dorothea urged. "Darcy's always so good with you." With an affectionate hug and a cheery wave, Dorothea went down the steps to the street and was handed into the waiting coach by her footman.

Helen watched her depart, then, smiling, went back upstairs to see which of her gowns would do for Thursday.

Martin strolled down St James's oblivious of the noise and bustle that surrounded him. He had yet to learn fair Juno's name, an aberration he had every intention of rectifying with all possible speed. Returning to town in her wake, he had expected to be able to make enquiries the next day. Fate, however, had stepped in and engineered a crisis on his Leicestershire estate. His presence had been necessary; the ensuing wrangle had forced him to post down to London in search of documents, then back to the country to see his orders executed. When the dust had finally settled, three weeks had flown.

He had woken this morning determined to make up for lost time. White's seemed the obvious place to start. He had never let his membership lapse, despite the years spent far afield. Consequently, when challenged, he felt perfectly confident in directing the porter to the membership lists. All proved in order. From the man's change in manner, Martin assumed his ascension to the title was common knowledge. He was bowed into the rooms with all due deference.

He strolled through the interconnecting chambers, pausing to scan the scattered groups for signs of familiar faces. As it transpired, it was they who recognised him.

"Martin?"

The question had him turning to meet hazel eyes on a level with his own. Delighted, Martin grinned. "Marc!"

They shook hands warmly. After they had exchanged their news, and Martin had duly exclaimed over his friend's recent marriage, Hazelmere gestured to the rooms ahead.

"Tony's here somewhere. He's married too. To Dorothea's sister, as it happens."

Martin turned laughing eyes on him. "That must have caused comment. How did Tony take the ribbing about always following your lead?"

"Strangely, this time, I don't think he cared."

They found Anthony, Lord Fanshawe, and various other members of what had once been Martin's set, ensconced in one of the back rooms. Martin's entrance caused a mild sensation. He was bombarded with questions, which he answered with good grace, picking up the threads of long-ago friendships, and, to his surprise, gradually relaxing into what had once been his milieu. With so many present, he put aside his questions on fair Juno. To Hazelmere or Fanshawe, his oldest friends, he might admit to an interest in an unknown widow. But to raise speculation in so many minds was not his present aim.

Leaving the club some hours later, still in company with Hazelmere and Fanshawe, he wryly reflected that at least he had made a start at re-establishing himself socially.

They were about to part, when Hazelmere stayed him. "I've just remembered. Come to dinner tomorrow—we're having an informal affair, just family. Tony's coming, so you can meet both our wives." He smiled proudly. "And my heir."

"God, yes!" said Fanshawe. "Come and add to the mood. It'll be chaos anyway."

Martin could not help his laugh. "Very well. I have to confess I'm dying to meet your paragons."

"Six, then. We still dine early at present."

With a nod and a wave, they parted. Striding along the pavement in the direction of his newly refurbished home in Grosvenor Square, Martin mused that the new Lady Hazelmere might well be one who could assist him in discovering fair Juno's identity.

Letting himself into his front hall, he surrendered his cane and gloves to his butler, Hillthorpe, who had instantly materialised from beyond the green baize door. Strolling the corridor to his library, Martin was struck again by the silence of the large house. In his memories, there had always been people around— children, friends of his brothers, friends of his parents. All gone now. Only his mother, tied to her room in Somerset, and his younger brother Damian remained. And God knew where Damian was, nor yet how long he was likely to remain. Martin's expression hardened, then he shrugged aside all thought of his younger brother. Damian could take care of himself.

Sinking into a newly upholstered chair, a glass of the finest French brandy in his hand, Martin considered his house. It was empty—indubitably empty. He needed to fill it—with life, with laughter. That was what was still missing. He had rectified the damp and the decay and had cast forth the unscrupulous. The structure was now sound. It was time to turn his mind, and energies, to rebuilding a family—his family.

Hazelmere's transparent pride in his wife and son had impressed him. He knew Marc, and a few hours had sufficed to assure him that the bonds of similarity that had drawn them to each other in earlier years still persisted.

Perhaps that was why fate had thrown fair Juno at his head?

Martin's lips twisted in a self-deprecatory smile. Why could he not just admit that he was besotted with the woman? There was no need to invoke fate or any such infernal agency. Juno was very real and, to him, wholly desirable. And, for the first time in his life, he was not contemplating a temporary relationship, limited by his interest. He was quite sure his interest in Juno would never die.

With a grin, Martin raised his glass in a silent toast. To his goddess. He tossed off the brandy, then, laying down the glass, left the room.

Thursday evening was mild and clear. Martin walked the few blocks to Cavendish Square. He was admitted to Hazelmere House by the butler, Mytton, whom he recognised and who, to his amazement, recognised him.

"Welcome back, my lord."

"Er—thank you, Mytton."

Hazelmere strolled into the hall. "Thought it was you."

Martin shook hands but his eyes were drawn to the woman who had followed his host into the hall. Fair-skinned and slender, a wealth of auburn hair crowned a classically featured face. Martin glanced at Hazelmere, his brows lifting in question.

The smile on the Marquis's face was answer enough. "Permit me to introduce you to my wife. Dorothea, Marchioness of Hazelmere — Martin Willesden, Earl of Merton."

Martin bowed over the slim hand that was bestowed on him; Dorothea curtsied, then, rising, looked up at him frankly, green eyes twinkling. "Welcome, my lord. We've heard so much about you. You see me positively preening, such is the cachet of being the first hostess to entertain you."

The low voice invited him to laugh with her at society's vagaries. Martin smiled. "The pleasure is entirely mine, my lady." She was, he thought, entirely enchanting, just right for Hazelmere. His gaze shifted to his friend's face. Hazelmere was watching his wife, the proprietorial gleam in his hazel eyes pronounced.

"But do come in and meet the others." Dorothea took his arm and led him towards the drawing-room.

Hazelmere fell in on his other side. "You have to exclaim over the heir, too," he murmured, hazel eyes dancing with laughter.

They paused on the threshold of the large drawing-room. A babble of gay voices, unaffected by polite restraint, filled the air. Martin scanned those present, noting Fanshawe, with a pretty blonde chit at his side, talking to an older woman whom he recognised as Marc's mother, the Dowager Marchioness. Martin remembered her with affection; she was one of the few who had not condemned him over the Monckton affair. By her side was an even older woman in a purple turban. She looked vaguely familiar but he could not place her.

His gaze travelled on to a group before the fireplace— And froze. A woman stood before the hearth, a baby balanced on one hip, cradled in one cruvaceous arm. The light from the wall sconce glittered over her golden curls. Her ample charms were exquisitely sheathed in topaz silk; pearls sheened about her throat. She was taller than the dandy she had been talking to, a slim, slight figure with pale blond hair. But his entrance had brought an abrupt halt to their discourse. Eyes of pale green, wide with shock, were fixed on him.

With a slow, infinitely wicked smile, Martin made straight for fair Juno.

As he crossed the large room, he was aware of Dorothea by his side, chattering animatedly. Her comments led him to understand that she thought he was interested in seeing her son. Martin's smile deepened; his eyes locked with fair Juno's. The sight of her, with a baby on her hip, affected him more strongly than he wished to admit. No desire, in a life strewn with desire, had ever been so strong. He wanted to see her standing before his fireplace, with his son in her arms. It was that simple.

Helen couldn't breathe. The sight of Martin in the doorway had quite literally scattered her wits. In the middle of a sentence, in reply to a question of Ferdie's, her voice had simply suspended, stopped, her mind totally focused on the rake across the room. And now he was coming to her side! With an effort, she drew breath, and panic rushed in. Her gaze lifted to his and was trapped in clouds of grey. The quality of his smile registered. It was devilish. Repressing a shiver of pure anticipation, Helen dragged her mind free of his spell. Heavens! She was going to have to do better than this—where had her years of experience flown to?

Then Dorothea was there, reaching for her son. "Let me introduce Lord Darcy Henry."

Helen handed Darcy over, desperately struggling to find her mental feet. Dorothea held Darcy for Martin to admire. The Earl of Merton barely glanced at Hazelmere's heir.

"He's nearly two months old." Dorothea looked up to find that her husband's old friend was not even looking at her son. She stared at Martin, then realised he was staring at Helen. Dorothea followed his gaze and beheld her usually impervious friend mesmerised, bedazzled, wholly hypnotised by Lord Merton's grey gaze.

Fascinated, Dorothea was glancing from Martin to Helen and back again when her husband appeared by her side. Ex-rake that he was, Hazelmere took in the scene in one, comprehensive glance.

"Martin, Lord Merton, allow me to introduce Helen, Lady Walford, Darcy's godmother." Hazelmere turned to his wife. "Perhaps, my dear, you'd better take Darcy back to the nursery." With an innocent air, the hazel gaze returned to Helen. "And perhaps, Helen, you could introduce the others—or at least those Martin can't recall?"

With a benedictory smile, Hazelmere moved off, firmly removing his by now intrigued wife.

Finding his field clear, Martin allowed a rakish smile to surface. He moved to Helen's side, one black brow rising quizzically. "Revealed by the hand of fate, fair Juno."

The softly spoken words caressed Helen's ear, sending a delicious shiver down her spine. "Helen," she whispered back urgently, searching for some semblance of equilibrium. She dared not look at him until she had found it.

"You'll always be fair Juno to me," came the outrageous reply. "What man of flesh and blood could let that image go? Just think of the memories."

Helen decided she had better not—her composure was rattled enough already.

Calmly, Martin appropriated her hand and dropped a light kiss on her fingers, smiling at the tremor of awareness the action provoked.

Wide-eyed, Helen glanced up at him, only to glance away rapidly. The glow in his eyes suggested he was going to be outrageous; his smile was a declaration of devilish intent.

Indignation came to her rescue. "I take it you're acquainted with Hazelmere?"

Martin's eyes danced. "We're old friends—very old friends."

Of that Helen had not a doubt. For years, Marc had sternly protected her from the advances of the rakes of the *ton;* now, in his own drawing-room, he had all but handed her into Martin Willesden's arms. Typical! Helen repressed a most unladylike snort.

With his usual good manners, Ferdie had drifted away when Martin had approached so purposefully.

With a warning glance for the reprobate beside her, Helen raised her voice. "Ferdie—have you and Lord Merton met?"

It transpired that they had not. Helen performed the introductions, adding for Martin's benefit, "Ferdie is Hazelmere's cousin."

Martin frowned slightly. "The one who rode his father's stallion?"

To Helen's amusement, Ferdie blushed. "Didn't think anyone would remember that."

"I've a particularly good memory," Martin averred, his eyes seeking Helen's. Trapping her gaze, he added, his voice low, "Particularly vivid."

It was Helen's turn to blush. Studiously avoiding Ferdie's interested eye, she placed a hand on Martin's sleeve, risking the contact in the pursuit of greater safety. "Have you met Dorothea's grandmother, my lord?" With a nod for Ferdie, she purposefully steered Martin in the direction of the dowagers, hoping that in their presence he would get little opportunity to exercise his facility for unnerving innuendo.

To her relief, as they circulated among Hazelmere's guests, Martin behaved in a manner which when she later had time to consider it, only confirmed her assessment of his experience and expertise. He chatted easily with whoever she introduced him to, the ready charm she had always associated with the most dangerous species of rake very apparent. However, at no time did he give any indication of wishing to leave her side. In fact, his attitude declared that, had it been permissible, he would unhesitatingly have monopolised her time.

He made his preference so clear that both the Dowager, Marc's mother, and Lady Merion, Dorothea's grandmother, took great delight in twitting them both over it.

"I gather you've been in the colonies for some years, my lord. I dare say it takes time to remember our ways?"

The pointed look Lady Merion bent on Martin should, by rights, have flustered even him. Yet, to her horror, Helen heard his deep voice reply, "Having but recently laid claim to an exceptionable memory, I can hardly now advance forgetfulness as my excuse, ma'am."

For the life of her, Helen could not resist glancing his way. The grey eyes were glowing and fixed on her face.

"Perhaps, my lord, you should seek guidance in achieving your re-entry to society?" The Dowager Marchioness's eyes were even more innocent than her son's. "Perhaps Lady Walford would be willing to assist?"

Helen blushed furiously.

"A capital notion, ma'am." With a smile for the delighted dowagers that relieved Helen of any need to speak, Martin drew her from their questionable safety.

Her composure severely compromised, Helen tried to act calmly, tried to convince herself that, in the present circumstances, it was she who should be in control, not he, but in that she failed miserably. As the evening progressed, and they went into dinner, she was not even surprised to find that Martin had somehow arranged things so that it seemed natural for him to lead her in and sit on her right.

Under cover of an uproarious discussion on the latest of the Prince Regent's peccadilloes, Martin leaned closer and asked, ''Will you consent to a drive with me in the Park, fair Juno?''

Helen sent him a glittering glance, intended to convey her disapproval of his continued use of that name. He received it with an unrepentant smile.

''Good. I'll call for you at eleven tomorrow.''

Before she could do more than gasp at his effrontery, he was offering her a dish of crab. Helen drew a determined breath. ''My lord...'' she began.

''My lady?'' he promptly replied, grey eyes intent.

Frantically searching for some means of bringing him to a sense of his shortcomings in respect of accepted procedures, Helen looked deep into his eyes, saw them calmly predatory, and knew she stood no chance of turning him from his purpose. His gaze held hers and the fire shrouded by the grey glowed bright. One brow rose. Abruptly, Helen looked down at her plate.

Smoothly, Martin turned back to the company, a confident smile curving his lips.

Nerves aflutter, Helen decided she would do well to regroup before she took on an opponent of Martin Willesden's calibre.

When they adjourned to the drawing-room, the men eschewing their port in favour of joining the ladies, a different light was cast on Martin's propensities. It was Cecily, Lady Fanshawe, who opened Helen's eyes to what had, until that moment, escaped her notice, pre-

occupied as she had been with Lord Merton's potential
for outrageousness. The youthful Cecily, just seven-
teen, had bubbled about the company in her usual
fashion, but had missed being introduced to Martin
earlier. Helen performed the introduction and was
slightly startled by Cecily's reaction. The big pansy
brown eyes opened wide; Lady Fanshawe simply
stared.

"*Ohh,*" she finally breathed, her round eyes taking
in as much of Martin as she could.

Tony Fanshawe came up in time to witness his
wife's response. With a deep sigh, he took her arm.

"Go away, Martin," he said, and, with a long-
suffering look, drew Cecily around. About to lead her
off, he paused and glanced back, wicked lights gleaming in his blue eyes. "On second thoughts, why not
take Helen away, too?"

Helen glared. They were *insufferable,* the lot of
them! A gaggle of unrepentant rakes.

Martin's chuckle brought her around to face him.
"What a very good idea." The nuance he managed to
infuse into the words sent her eyes flying wide. Somehow, his fingers had trapped her hand. Held by the
glow in his grey eyes, smoky now with an emotion
she was coming to recognise, Helen could only stare
as he raised her hand to his lips. The gesture was so
simple, yet heavy with meaning. The lingering touch
of his lips, a warm caress on her fingertips, sent a
succession of shivers through her.

In desperation, Helen blinked—and saw him
through Cecily's eyes. She was used to men being the
same height as she, but Martin was a good half-head

taller. His dark hair curled lightly; there was the faintest trace of silver at his temples. The grey eyes, so mesmeric, were watching her from under arched and hooded lids. The lines at their corners suggested that laughter came easily to their owner. His cheeks were lean and tanned, his lips fine-drawn and firm. One glance at his jaw gave warning of his temper.

With a little sigh, Helen acknowledged the face and moved on to the figure. She was a large woman, junoesque in truth, but he made her feel small. His shoulders were wide, his chest broad, leaving an impression of lean muscle cloaking a large and powerful frame. She knew he moved gracefully, as an athlete would; the idea of waltzing with him was more than just attractive.

As she realised, with a jolt, just how long she had stood staring, her eyes flew to his. Heightened consciousness, of him, of her susceptibility, of how much he could see, threatened to overwhelm her. Her breath caught in her throat. She looked away, nervous, confused and more at sea than she had ever been. ''Can you see Ferdie anywhere?''

Martin heard the panic in her tone. Smiling, he dutifully scanned the room. Her response was encouraging but now was not the time to press her further. With consummate ease, he took charge. ''He's by the fireplace.'' Tucking her hand into the crook of his arm, he strolled back into the fray of conversation.

Grateful for his understanding, for she knew it was that, Helen took the opportunity he gave her to reassemble her faculties and get her feet back on the ground. As they circulated about the big room, she recalled a comment of Dorothea's that being in Marc's care often felt like being caught in a web, with him, the spider, in the centre. That was exactly how she now felt, except that it was Martin at the centre of her web. It was a protective web; the bonds did not hurt. But they were there, inescapable, unbreakable.

Her relief was very real when Hazelmere approached them, saying to Martin, "Tony and I are for White's. Gisborne—" he waved in the direction of his brother-in-law " — is coming, too. Are you for the tables?"

Martin smiled. "Lead the way."

Hazelmere laughed. "I didn't think you'd have changed." With a nod for Helen, he left them.

Martin had taken possession of her hand. Helen glanced up and discovered that the expression in his eyes went far beyond the acceptable, a warm and distinctly intimate caress. He raised her fingers to his lips.

"Until tomorrow, fair Juno."

It was all she could do to nod her farewell.

Much later, in the privacy of her chamber, Helen stared at her reflection in the mirror, and wondered when such madness would end.

Chapter Six

Not soon, was Helen's conclusion when, the next day, Martin called as promised to take her for a drive in the Park. Bowling along beneath the trees, their leaves just beginning to turn, perched in her familiar spot beside him on the box seat, she discovered that he intended to give her no chance to ponder the wisdom of the outing. Instead, he seemed intent on following the Dowager Marchioness of Hazelmere's advice and enlisting her aid.

"Who is that quiz in the shocking purple toque?"

Helen followed his glance. "That's Lady Havelock. She's a bit of a dragon."

"And looks it. Does she still hold sway with the Melbourne House set?"

"Not so much these days, now that Lady Melbourne lives so retired." Helen raised her hand in acknowledgement of a bow from a painted fop.

"And who's he?"

At the possessive growl, Helen's lips twitched. "Shiffy? Sir Lumley Sheffington."

"Oh." Martin glanced again at the white-painted

face above an outrageous apricot silk bow. "I remember now. I'd forgotten about him—entirely understandable."

Helen giggled. Shiffy was one of the more memorable figures among the *ton*.

Martin kept up a steady stream of questions—on the other occupants of the Park, on the happenings in town and whether certain personages were as he remembered them. Engrossed with her answers, Helen did not notice the passage of time. Their hour together vanished more swiftly, and with greater ease, than she had expected.

Descending the steps of Helen's small house in Half Moon Street, having seen his goddess safely inside, Martin startled Joshua, standing at the bays' heads, with an exceedingly broad grin. Gaining the box seat and retrieving the reins, Martin waved Joshua to his perch. "The day bodes fair, my projects proceed apace—what more could a man ask for?"

Scrambling up behind, Joshua rolled his eyes heavenwards. "No mystery what's come over you," he muttered, *sotto voce,* making a mental note to learn more of Lady Walford. In blissful ignorance of his henchman's deductions, Martin gave his horses the office, well-pleased with his beginning.

As the week progressed, he had even more reason for satisfaction. His re-entry to the *ton* was accomplished more easily than he had hoped. A visit to the theatre, escorting fair Juno to view the latest of Mrs Siddons' dramatic flights, had brought him to the notice of the major hostesses. The pile of white cards stacked upon his mantelpiece grew day by day. Eschewing all subtlety, he determined which of the parties his delight intended to grace by dint of the simple expedient of asking. Thus forearmed, he felt assured of enjoying those assemblies he deigned to attend.

Climbing the stairs to Lady Burlington's ballroom for the first of the larger gatherings on his list, Martin spared a moment to contemplate how the *ton* would receive him. Invitations were one thing, but how would they treat the black sheep in the flesh? If he was to marry Helen, the *ton's* approbation was a hurdle he would have to clear.

He need not have worried.

"Lord Merton!" Lady Burlington positively pounced on him. "I'm so thrilled you could find time to attend my little party."

Replying all but automatically to his hostess's gushing comments, Martin reflected that, from what he could see, her "little party" numbered over one hundred.

"Pleased you could come."

The gruff accents of Lord Burlington were a welcome release. After shaking hands, Martin moved into the room, only to find himself surrounded. By women.

Blonde hair in ringlets, black hair in curls, every shade and hue pressed in on every side. A medley of perfumes washed over him, light fractured in their gems. "Lord Merton!" was on each pair of lips. The hostesses of the *ton,* many the very women who had, thirteen years before, closed their doors in his face, all but fell over themselves in their eagerness to impress him with their credentials. Manfully quelling an unnerving impulse to laugh in their powdered faces, Martin drew on his experience, cloaking his antipathy with just the right degree of patronising superiority, and accepted their admiration as became one who knew how their games were played.

"I do hope you'll find time to call."

Martin allowed a black brow to rise at the tone of that particular invitation, coming from a blonde whose eyes vied with her diamonds in hardness. He could hardly be unaware of the heated glances some of the younger matrons were flinging his way. Cynically, he wondered if, had he returned as plain Martin Willesden, unadorned with an earldom and colossal wealth, he would have been welcomed quite so enthusiastically.

Due to the importunities of the more clinging mesdames, it was late before Martin saw Helen. Instantly, he knew she was aware of him, but, unsure of whether he would notice her, she was making every effort not to notice him. With a devilish smile, he nodded a brief but determined farewell to his court and escaped across the ballroom to his goddess's side.

Helen knew he was approaching long before he reached her. It was not simply that the majority of female eyes in the vicinity had suddenly found a common target, nor that Mrs Hitchin, with whom she was conversing, had stopped, slack-jawed, in the middle of a sentence, her eyes fixed on a point beyond Helen's left shoulder. Her flickering nerves would have told her he was near and getting nearer even had she been blindfold.

Quelling her traitorous senses, ignoring her increasing pulse, Helen turned and, smoothly, surrendered her hand into his. "My lord." His fingers closed about hers in a warm, possessive clasp. Determined not to fluster, Helen curtsied.

Martin raised her, then, slowly, deliberately, holding her gaze with is, he carried her fingers to his lips.

For an instant, Helen could have sworn that the entire host held its breath. Kissing ladies' hands was a gallantry no longer common; pray heaven that they put it down to his years away. She, of course, knew better. The glow in his eyes warmed her, the smouldering grey igniting a familiar warmth within.

To her relief, years of ballroom etiquette came to her rescue. "My lord, pray allow me to present Mrs Hitchin."

Martin had no interest in Mrs Hitchin. He bestowed a civil nod upon the lady, and a comforting smile. But he did not let go of Juno's hand. Instead, he tucked it into his arm. "My dear Lady Walford, there's a waltz about to start. I do hope Mrs Hitchin will excuse us?"

Helen blinked. How *dared* he simply walk up and appropriate her? Then full understanding of what he was suggesting broke upon her. A waltz? Held in his arms—and she could imagine just how. Heaven help her—how was she to manage? Just the thought made her feel weak.

In panic, she looked about for assistance. Mrs Hitchin was no use; the woman was positively basking in the glow of Martin's smile. But before she could find a lifeline to cling to, Martin was moving towards the area of the room given over to the dancers.

"I promise not to bite."

His words, gentle in her ear, stiffened her resolve.

She was being silly—missish, she who did not know the meaning of the word. He would not do anything truly outrageous in the middle of a ballroom, would he?

And then he was drawing her into his arms, holding her every bit as close as she had feared. They joined the whirling couples on the floor. A host of emotions she had never experienced before being exposed to Martin Willesden threatened to overcome her. Helen struggled to quell them. She could not—must not—let him get away with this...this commandeering of her senses.

"My lord," she said firmly, raising her eyes to his.

"My lady," he replied, his tone investing the term with meaning far beyond the mundane, his eyes confirming his intent.

Helen felt her eyes grow round. Great heavens! He was seducing her. In the middle of Lady Burlington's ballroom, with half the *ton* looking on. Rapidly revising her estimates of his potential, she allowed her lids to veil her eyes and sought for a lighter note. "Does polite society thus far meet with your approval?"

Martin smiled. "I hardly know. I've had so little in recent years to compare it with." He felt her relax, and took the opportunity provided by negotiating the tight turn at the bottom of the room to draw her more firmly against him. "But, as far as the company goes, I've some reservations."

"Oh?" Thankful that he was prepared to converse reasonably, Helen decided to overlook the almost imperceptible tightening of his arm about her. "Why is that?"

"Well," said Martin, frowning as if considering his words, "it's the female element I have most trouble with."

Suspicion bloomed in Helen's mind. What did a rake consider reasonable conversation? She felt compelled to give him the benefit of her doubt and asked, "What is it that particularly troubles you?"

The concerned look he threw her almost had her believing his, "It's their predatory tendencies that worry me." When she looked sceptical, he added defensively, "It's most unnerving to a fully licenced rake to find himself the pursued rather than the pursuer. Just imagine it, if you can."

"Strange," said Helen, green eyes glinting. "I could almost believe I know just how you feel."

At that he smiled, a dazzling smile that overloaded her senses and sent them spinning. By the time she had collected them, the music had ceased. "Perhaps I should return to—" In confusion, Helen bit her lip. Heavens, she was no débutante to be returning to a chaperon's side! What was she thinking of—what was it the man by her side made her think of?

Martin chuckled, following her thoughts easily. "Fear not, fair Juno. Your reputation is safe with me." He paused then added in a pensive tone, "As for the rest of you, though…" The shocked glance she sent him had him chuckling again.

When, a few minutes later, he relinquished her to Lord Alvanley, still flustered but recovered enough to throw him a speaking glance, he reflected that he had spoken no more than the truth throughout their exchanges. Which was odd enough. But he did, in fact,

find the cloying interest of the unmarried females re-
pelling and suspected his feeling sprang, as he had told
her, from his liking to be the driving force behind his
relationships. Her far more natural response to him
was gratifying; her attempts to hide it, believing, correctly, that it gave him far more influence over her
than she would like, made her irresistibly attractive to
a man of his ilk. Given his long-term plans for her, he
had no intention that her reputation should suffer at
his or anyone else's hands. And he felt positively righ-
teous that he had gone so far as to give her clear warning of his intent.

Halo glowing, he strolled about the room, waiting
for the time to claim her for supper.

Dancing with friends and acquaintances who demanded no more from her than polite conversation
gave Helen time to consider Martin Willesden's
words. Not for the life of her could she fathom what
he meant. If it had not been for the fact that he knew
she was a connection of Hazelmere's, she might have
suspected he intended to set her up as his mistress.
But she knew enough of the peculiar code of the rake
to know that Hazelmere's protection would not be
challenged by a friend. But, if not that, then his words
could only mean he was on the lookout for a wife and
believed she would suit.

Inwardly, Helen sighed, and wished it were so. But
he was wrong—and the sooner he learned his error the
better. He was going to break her heart if he did not
desist from his determined pursuit. None knew better
than she that, while her birth was perfectly acceptable
and her connections beyond reproach, being the relict

of a social outcast would not be considered a suitable background for the new Countess of Merton. That position should rightly be reserved for one of the *incomparables,* or, at the very least, a richly dowered débutante. She had never been one of the former, though she had, for a bare month before her marriage, been one of the latter.

The cotillion came to an end. Lord Peterborough, whom she had known forever, bowed elegantly over her hand. "Thank you, Gerry," she said, smiling. "You're always such an eligible *parti.*"

His lordship laughed and offered her his arm. Supper was being served downstairs. Helen raised her hand to place it on his sleeve but, to her surprise, warm fingers closed about hers.

"Ah, Gerry. I have to tell you Lady Birchfield is looking for you."

Lord Peterborough glared. "Dammit, Martin! Lady Birchfield can look all she likes. The woman's old enough to be m'mother."

"Really? I'd no idea you were so young." Martin's eyes gleamed. "It's just as well I've arrived to escort Lady Walford to supper. It wouldn't do for her to be thought a cradle-snatcher."

Having deprived both Lord Peterborough and fair Juno of the power of speech, Martin smoothly drew Helen's hand through his arm and, with a genial nod to his friend, steered her in the direction of the supper-room.

By the time Helen found her tongue, she was seated at a small table in an alcove of the supper-room, a plate of delicacies before her. Fixing the reprobate opposite with a steely glare, her bosom swelled. "Lord Merton..." she began.

"Martin, remember?" Martin grinned at her. "You didn't really believe I'd let you go into supper with anyone else, did you?"

Staring into teasing grey eyes, Helen felt totally befuddled. Should she answer yes or no? If she said yes, he would only take the opportunity to tell her she should have known better—which was true. And saying no was out of the question. In the end, she glared. "You're impossible."

Martin smiled. "Have a lobster patty."

Helen gave up. It was simply too easy for him to pull the rug from beneath her feet in private. She had yet, she reflected, to learn how to keep him at a proper distance. If she did not master the art soon, it would be entirely too late. Already, she had noticed a few curious looks cast their way. Still, as far as the *ton* knew, he could merely be looking her over, seeking congenial company until the Little Season got into full swing and he set about the serious task of finding a suitable wife.

Pleased by her capitulation, Martin devoted his considerable talents to distracting her, in which endeavour he was so successful that, by the time he returned her to the ballroom, she was thoroughly flustered. In the circumstances, he forbore to claim another dance, contenting himself with placing a most improper kiss in her palm before leaving her to less threatening cavaliers.

The Burlington ball marked the beginning of Martin's campaign. He was assiduous in attending whatever ball or party Helen Walford graced, paying her such marked attention as could not be misconstrued. He took great delight in teasing her, knowing that she, of all who watched him, was the furtherest from divining his purpose. Many had marked his predilection for her company; he did not, in truth, give a damn. He fully intended to go a great deal further than mere predilection.

Everything he learned of her confirmed his certainty that she was the one woman he wanted before his fireplace. She was accepted and respected, unquestionably good *ton*. Her maturity was transparent, but, while she clearly understood the rules of the game, she had never, to anyone's knowledge, played. Not the closest scrutiny uncovered any degree of partiality for the numerous gentlemen who claimed her as friend. She was much admired, by the women as well as the men—no mean feat in these days of cut-throat beauty.

It was a week into the Little Season when his pursuit of her took him to the dim portals of Almack's. The Marriage Mart had never been one of his favourite venues. As a youth, he had labelled it the Temple of Doom—forswear happiness, all ye who enter here. With a grimace, he gathered his resolution and trod up the steps. Helen was within and he had determined to conquer not only her, but this last bastion of the *ton*.

The porter admitted him to the hall, but, not being a regular, there he had to wait for one or other of the patronesses to grant him permission to enter the rooms. As luck would have it, it was Sally Jersey who swept out in response to the porter's summons, her large eyes wide and incredulous.

"Good God! It *is* you!"

Martin grinned wryly and bowed. "Me, myself and I, alone." He smiled winningly. "Will you allow me to enter, dear Sally?"

Lady Jersey was no more immune to rakish charm than the next woman. But she knew Martin Willesden, and knew of the scandal in his past. She was also one of those who had never believed it. She eyed the tower of potent masculinity before her and frowned. "Will you promise not to cause any undue flutter?"

Martin put back his head and laughed. "Sally, oh, Sally. What an impossible stipulation."

When he eyed her wickedly, Lady Jersey was forced to acknowledge the truth of his words. "Oh—very well! I never believed that Monckton chit anyway," she muttered.

Martin captured her hand and bowed low. "My thanks, Sally."

"Oh, go on with you!" said Lady Jersey. "You make me feel old."

"Never *old,* Sally." With one last wicked grin, Martin headed for the ballroom.

He had hoped to slip unnoticed to the side of the room, from which vantage point, being so tall, he would have been able to locate Helen. Instead, to his horror, he was mobbed but feet from the door. While he had been speaking to Sally, word of his arrival had gone the rounds. To his incredulous gaze, it appeared that every fond mama with an insipid daughter in tow had gathered near the entrance for the express purpose of accosting him.

"My dear Lord Merton—I'm Lady Dalgleish—a very old friend of your mama's. Pray allow me to present…"

"Such an exciting career as you've had, my lord. You must take the time to tell my dear Annabelle all about it—she just *adores* tales of foreign places."

Never in his life had Martin faced such a trial. It quickly transpired that, as virtually none could claim acquaintance due to his prolonged sojourn overseas, they had all decided to ignore such niceties and introduce themselves. The reason for his thirteen-year absence was entirely overlooked.

"You must come to my soirée next week. Just a *very* select few. You'll be able to converse with Julia so much more easily without such a horde about."

Even Martin blinked at that. They were shameless, the lot of them. The temptation to tell them all to go to hell was strong, but Sally would never forgive him. And he wanted to see Helen, who was undoubtedly one of the many enjoying the unexpected entertainment.

In the end, Martin simply stood stock still and let them come at him, steadfastly refusing to ask any young lady to dance, nor to accept any invitation to look over a chit's finer points during a stroll around the rooms. He knew that none of the hostesses would be so bold as to suggest he dance with any of the young things, regardless of their parents' wishes. It was the first time he had ever had reason to be thankful for his past.

Finally, the attack faltered. In between deflecting the none too subtle invitations, he had managed to locate Helen in a small knot of ladies at the far end of the room. Sensing a hiatus, he made a bid for freedom before his besiegers had a chance to regroup.

Gracefully, Martin bowed to the stalwart matron planted plumb in front of him, her two freckle-faced daughters flanking her. "Your pardon, ma'am. I fear I must leave you. So pleasant to have met your daughters." With a vague smile, he beat a hasty retreat.

Helen had certainly noticed the crowd by the door and recognised the dark head at its centre. It was no more than she had expected—his due, nothing more. With an inward sigh, she made an effort to immerse herself in her friends' discussion. Lord Merton would have his hands full with the debs from now on.

"My dear—my *very* dear Lady Walford." Martin did not try to keep the relief from his voice. "What a pleasure it is to see you—at last."

Helen jumped and turned, knowing who she would see before she did. No one else had a voice that could frazzle her senses. "My lord." She curtsied. As usual, he raised her and appropriated her hand, as if she had made him a present of it. She had come to accept that particular trick as inevitable, knowing no way of stopping him. But she had yet to come to grips with the warmth in his eyes as they rested on her, and the promise that glowed in their depths.

Breathlessly, she introduced the three ladies in her circle. To her surprise, Martin did not try to remove her but stayed by her side, chatting politely, charming her friends utterly.

When Helen's friends moved away, to talk to other acquaintances among the growing crowd, Martin dropped the reserve he employed in such social situations. He glanced down into Helen's green eyes, his own entirely devoid of guile. "You'll have to be my mentor in this particular theatre of war. Where else can we go to be safe?"

Helen looked her astonishment. "Safe?"

Martin smiled a little ruefully. "I'm claiming your protection." When she still looked bemused, he added, "In return for my earlier efforts on your behalf."

A slight blush staining her cheeks, Helen let her eyes slide over his impressive length. "However could *I* protect *you?* You're bamming me."

"No such thing—rake's honour." Hand over his heart, Martin grinned. "The matchmaking mamas are out to leg-shackle me, I do assure you. They're hunting in packs, what's more. If I'm to retain any degree of freedom, I'll need all the help I can get."

Helen smothered a giggle. "You can't just not take any notice. You'll have to choose a wife some time."

The grey eyes holding hers suddenly became intent. But his voice was still even when he asked, "You don't seriously suppose I'd marry any of the delicate debs?"

"But...it's what's expected of men of your position." Helen coloured, then abruptly glanced away. Not only was this a most improper conversation, but she had nearly blurted out that hers had been such a conventional marriage. That, she was the first to admit, was hardly a recommendation.

To her unease, the grey eyes were still trained on

her face. She could feel them, compelling her to return his regard. Unable to withstand the subtle pressure, she glanced up. Her eyes locked with his.

Martin smiled gently, and raised her hand to his lips, his eyes holding hers steadily. "I'll never marry one of the debs, my dear. My tastes run to women of more…voluptuous charms."

If Helen had had any doubts over what he intended her to understand by that, the look in his eyes would have dispelled them. For good measure, when she blushed, his eyes dropped to caress the ripe swell of her breasts, more revealed than concealed by the current craze for low necklines. Helen felt her cheeks flame.

"Martin!"

His eyes returned to her face, gentle laughter in the grey depths. "Mmm?"

What could she say? She should talk to him of reality, of all the reasons she was ineligible. Now was the time. Determined to halt his mad schemes before they went any further, before her heart was totally torn in two, Helen raised her eyes to his. "My lord, you cannot marry me. My husband was Arthur Walford— you must have known him. He committed suicide, but only after being hounded from the *ton*. He gambled away everything he owned, including my settlements. With such a background, I'm no suitable wife for you."

All Martin's levity had flown. The expression in his eyes, intent yet infinitely gentle, did not waver; his thumb moved caressingly over the back of her hand.

"My dear, I know all this. Did you think I would care?"

The room was whirling. Helen could not breathe. "But..."

Martin's smile grew. Confidently, he drew her to stroll beside him. If they remained stationary for much longer, someone would stop to talk. "My dear Helen, I've never been one to act in accordance with society's dictates. I've been a rake and a gamester for as long as anyone here can recall. I assure you, none will think it the least odd that I, of all men, should choose to marry a more mature woman rather than saddle myself with some mindless flibbertigibbet."

A nervous giggle assured him that she had accepted the truth of that. "Now enough of your quibbles. If this is merely a ploy to deny me your protection, I take leave to tell you 'tis a shabby trick."

"As if you need my protection." Helen followed his lead in moving from the topic of marriage, trying to regain their usual, lightly bantering tone. Her mind was in a whirl. What he had suggested was beyond her wildest dreams; she would need time to consider the possibilities. Her brain was too overloaded to make much sense of it now, particularly not with him by her side. "I'm quite sure you could rout all the matchmaking mamas without difficulty."

"Unquestionably," agreed the rake by her side. "But, having done so, I'd be cast out from these hallowed halls, bidden never to return, and thus would be unable to see you on Wednesday nights. Not a prospect I relish. So, in the interests of your Wednesday nights, madam, will you consent to act as my protector?''

Helen could only laugh. "Very well. But only within strict limits."

Martin frowned. "What limits?"

"You must not misbehave with me." She glanced up, trying for stern implacability. "No dancing more than two waltzes, and never two together. In fact," she added, recalling his ability to think up new and ever more disturbing ways of dealing with her, "no going beyond the line in any way whatever."

"Unfair! How do you imagine I'll control my rakish tendencies? Have pity, fair Juno. I can't reform in an instant."

But Helen stood firm. "That's my best offer, my lord." When his brows rose, she added, her own brows rising, "You'd hardly ask me to place my own position here in jeopardy?"

Martin sighed in mock-defeat. "You drive a hard bargain, sweetheart. I capitulate. In the interests of my own skin, I accept your conditions."

It was a full minute before Helen registered the ineligible epithet and by then it was too late to gasp.

To her considerable relief, Martin did behave impeccably for the rest of the evening. She had no illusions as to how outrageous he could be if he put his mind to it. His "rakish tendencies", as he called them, were remarkably strong. But not even the highest stickler could have faulted his performance—beyond the fact that he remained anchored to her side.

After the excitement of Almack's, Helen had expected to endure a sleepless night. Instead, drugged with unaccustomed happiness, she had slept the sleep of the innocent. Unheralded but sure of his welcome, Martin had called to take her driving at eleven. What with entertaining a small procession of afternoon visitors, all agog to hear anything she might have to say about the Earl of Merton, and then dressing for dinner at Hatcham House, Helen found herself once more in Martin Willesden's arms, waltzing down a ballroom, without having had more than a moment to spend in consideration of his words of the previous night.

"Tell me, fairest Juno, is it normal for such affairs as this to be so refreshingly free of the *jeunes filles?*"

Martin's voice in her ear summoned her wits from besotted contemplation of how very strong he was and how helpless he made her feel. Helen blinked. "Well," she temporised, glancing about at the crowd and noticing he was right, "I suppose it's because the Hatchams are rather out of the deb set—their own children are all married. And Lord Pomeroy is giving a ball for his daughter tonight, too, so many of the younger folk will be there, I expect."

Martin frowned slightly. "I don't suppose I can convince you to eschew the larger balls—at least for this year?"

Helen returned his mock-frown with one of her own. "After avoiding the *ton* and the matchmaking mamas for the past thirteen years, the least you can do is allow them a try at you."

"But just think how pointless such an undertaking on their parts will be." His expression became earnest. "Shouldn't I, in the interests of the social good, and the matchmaking mamas' constitutions, simply give them all the go-by?''

The music ceased and they whirled to a halt. Taking his arm all but automatically, Helen fell to strolling by his side. ''By no means!'' She could not yet see where his conversation was taking them. ''It's your duty to be seen at the major functions.''

Martin grimaced. ''You're absolutely sure?''

Warily, Helen nodded.

''Ah, well.'' He sighed. ''In that case, just as long as you're there to protect me, I suppose I'll have to attend.''

''My lord, I cannot be forever at your side.'' She could see where he was headed now.

''Why not?''

The grey eyes, impossibly candid, held hers.

''Because...'' Helen struggled to assemble her reasons—her rational, sensible reasons. But, under the power of his grey gaze, they went winging from her head. They had halted by the side of the ballroom and she had turned, the better to look into his face. The eyes holding hers seemed to look deeper, reach deeper, to touch some chord within her and make it sing. Then, as she watched, he was distracted. His eyes left hers, focusing on some vision a few feet behind her.

''Speaking of protection...'' Martin drew her hand through his arm, securing her by his side.

''Martin—*darling!* How positively *thrilling* to see you again—after all these years!''

Helen stifled a wince at the arch tones. Small wonder that Martin wished to avoid the mesdames if that was the treatment they accorded him. She felt the muscles of his arm tense beneath her fingers. Helen shifted slightly, to stand more definitely by his side, where she sensed he wanted her, and found herself staring at blonde curls much paler than her own, arranged about a face rather older than her own. But not old enough to be a matchmaking mama. The woman cast the barest of icy smiles in her direction before turning big, pale blue eyes on the new Earl of Merton.

The new Earl remained stubbornly silent.

The lady continued unabashed. "*Such* a surprise, my dear. You should have called." A look of unlikely ingenuousness suffused the pale face. "Oh! Of *course*. You wouldn't know! I'm Lady Rochester now."

For Helen, the penny dropped with the name. She stifled the urge to look up at Martin, to see what he was making of her ladyship's performance. Lady Rochester was a widow of some years standing, one of those who, while credited with birth sufficient to enter the *ton* and title sufficient to open most doors, was nevertheless on the outer circle of polite society. No scandal had ever touched her name, but consistent rumour still tarnished it.

Martin's silence was beginning to strain her ladyship's smile. But her voice was determinedly conspiratorial when she said, "My dear Martin, I've so much to tell you. Perhaps, such old friends as we are, we should repair to some place rather more private to review our histories? If Lady Walford will excuse us?"

The last was said with a dismissive smile. Her ladyship reached for Martin's other arm. Helen stiffened, and would have drawn her hand from Martin's sleeve except that his hand, covering hers, tightened, strong fingers gripping hers.

"I think not."

Helen blinked, very glad that Martin did not use that particular tone to her. Shafts of ice and arctic winds would have been warmer. Intrigued by this by-play, for it was transparently obvious that there was more to the exchange than she yet knew, she watched Lady Rochester's face pale to blank-white.

"But—"

"As it happens," Martin continued, repressive cold-ness in every syllable, "Lady Walford and I were about to take a stroll on the terrace. If you'll excuse us, Lady Rochester?"

With a distant nod, Martin steered Helen past the importunate Lady Rochester, leaving her ladyship to stare, dumbfounded, at their backs.

Within minutes, they were strolling on the long ter-race in relative isolation. Helen felt the tension ease from Martin's long frame. Who was Lady Rochester that she should draw such a violent, albeit suppressed reaction from Martin? Out of the blue, the answer flew into Helen's head.

"Oh! Is she the one who—?" Abruptly, she cut off her words; embarrassment rose to smother her.

Beside her, she felt rather than heard Martin's sigh.

"She's the one who engineered the little drama that saw me exiled from England."

Engineered? What drama? Helen wished she had the nerve to ask.

Martin stared out over the darkly shadowed gardens, seeing the shadows from his past. He did not want them to cloud his future. There was no one within earshot. "When I was twenty-two, Serena Monckton, now Lady Rochester, was a débutante. She quite literally threw herself at my head." He glanced down at Helen's face, and saw the little frown of concentration that dragged at her brows. He smiled. "As I told you, I have a constitutional dislike of being pursued. In this case, however, I underestimated the opposition. Serena engineered a compromising situation—and then cried rape."

Helen's brows flew but she said nothing.

"Unfortunately, that little contretemps came on top of the discovery by my father of a rash of gambling debts—nothing overly outrageous, only what was to be expected from a youth such as I was. But my father was determined to keep me in line. Serena's little ploy was the last straw. He issued an ultimatum."

Despite his clipped tones, and the effort he was making to tell his story without emotion, Helen heard the pain, dulled by the years but still there, an undercurrent that had sprung to life immediately he had mentioned his father.

"Either I married the chit or he'd send me to the colonies. I chose the colonies." Martin raised his brows, considering his life in brief. "All in all, that was the luckiest decision of my life." His lips curled. "Perhaps I should thank Serena. Without her efforts, I doubt I would be worth quite as much as I am today."

Helen threw him a soft smile. Hesitantly, and only because she was desperate to know, she asked, "Did your father learn the truth later?"

There was a distinct pause before the answer came. "No. I never saw him again. He died two years after the event, while I was still in Jamaica."

Helen did not need to ask herself if she had heard the truth. Every particle of her being knew that she had. No matter how accomplished an actor, no man, she felt sure, could manufacture the emptiness, the intense loss, that vibrated in the deep, gravelly voice. She had heard vague murmurings of the scandal in his past. She was pleased that he had told her of it—now she could disregard it.

They paced the length of the terrace to where a series of shallow steps led down to a fountain surrounded by an area of parterre. A number of couples were strolling in the fresh night air, seeking relief from the closeness of the ballroom.

Glancing at the serious face beside him, Martin smiled. She was so easy to read. He felt curiously honoured that she should concern herself with his long-ago hurts. But it was time she smiled again. "Can I tempt you from the terrace, fair Juno? I promise not to abduct you."

Helen looked up and smiled as the implication of his words registered. A disavowal of any negative response to being abducted by him had almost reached her lips before, horrified, she stilled the words. Fancy admitting to a desire to be kidnapped—by a rake, no less! Her wits were becoming thoroughly untrustworthy when he was by her side. She covered her confusion by drawing away and sweeping him a curtsy. "Why, thank you, my lord. A brisk turn about the fountain will doubtless clear my head."

Martin's brows rose. "Does it need clearing? What's it full of?"

You, was her thought. But his eyes were quizzing her. Determined not to be jockeyed into making any revealing disclosures, Helen put her nose in the air and her hand on his arm. "The fountain, my lord."

His soft laugh set every nerve tingling.

"As you command, fair Juno."

Chapter Seven

The Little Season progressed and, with it, Martin's campaign. By the time the first flurry of balls had faded into memory, and the trees in the Park had begun to shed their leaves, he felt it was time to re-evaluate his position. Helen Walford was his—that was quite clear to him. Hopefully, it would, by now, also be quite clear to the *ton* at large. Watching his fair Juno from the side of Lady Winchester's ballroom, his shoulders propped against the panelled wall, he spared a moment in fond amazement that she, alone, was still uncertain on the matter, unsure that the future he had planned for her would ever come true.

He had taken great delight in conveying, by every subtle means at his disposal, just how exciting her future would be. She was fascinated. Her insecurity stemmed, he surmised, from her unhappy marriage—a fact he had no difficulty believing. Arthur Walford must have been all of fifteen years her senior.

"I wonder…is it possible to tempt you to the card-room?"

At the familiar languid tones, Martin smiled and

shifted his gaze sideways to the Marquis of Hazel-mere's face. "Unlikely."

Hazelmere sighed. "I thought not. I'll have to hunt up Tony." He clapped Martin on the shoulder and was turning away when he paused to add, "Just remember—the sooner you resolve this matter, the sooner you can join us. It doesn't do to forget your friends." With a smile of the most complete understanding, Hazelmere moved on.

Turning back to the ballroom in time to see Helen throw a laughing smile at her partner—Alvanley and therefore perfectly safe—Martin smiled wryly. He had only just arrived, yet the urge to monopolise Lady Walford's company was growing stronger by the minute. He would resist the tug yet awhile; there was a limit to all things—even the leniency of the *ton* towards one who they were now convinced had been wrongfully slighted. Martin's smile grew. In truth, the past no longer haunted him. His only concern was for the future. But the approbation of the *ton* would be important to the future Countess of Merton, so he was pleased to have secured that elusive cachet.

As to the future itself, he had no doubts. In fact, if he was forced to the truth, he would have to admit that he had made up his mind to wed Helen Walford the instant he had seen her standing before the Hazelmeres' fireplace. The only consideration that had kept him from a declaration was a desire not to startle her—or the *ton*. The *ton* was now taken care of. She was still slightly nervous over what she knew would shortly be her fate, but, if anything, that touch of the wide-eyed innocent only made him more eager to make her his.

The music came to an end and the guests milled across the floor. Conversation rose to cloak the scene lit by the heavy chandeliers. The curls in the ladies' artfully arranged coiffures sheened; jewels winked about their throats. Their gowns swirled, the colours of spring flowers about the trunks of the darker-garbed males.

Juno had her own little court. Over the heads of the throng, Martin watched as she smiled and traded quips. Her gown of palest amber became her fair charms to admiration. With an inward glow, he noted the way her eyes lifted every now and then to scan the company. She had yet to see him. Then, as he watched, waiting for the right moment to make his presence known, a fop in a coat of a peculiar shade of green insinuated himself at Helen's side.

Martin came away from the wall. He started across the floor, automatically smiling and nodding at those he knew, his attention focused on the man beside Helen. He had noticed him, and his interest in Lady Walford, before. Discreet enquiry had elicited the information that he was one Hedley Swayne, Esquire, of a small but prosperous estate in Cornwall. Despite the lack of firm evidence, it was entirely possible that Hedley Swayne had indeed been behind Helen's kidnapping. The *ton* had noted a singular tendency for Mr Swayne to pay assiduous court to Lady Walford but had dismissed this as a mere smokescreen erected by the gentleman with a view to being regarded as fashionable; none could imagine the undeniably fashionable Lady Walford having any serious interest in a man a good half-head shorter than herself and distinctly less high in social rank to boot. Martin had seen Hedley Swayne at numerous gatherings, but this was the first time the fop had had the temerity to approach Helen.

Long before he reached her side, Martin sensed Helen's unease. Mr Swayne had picked his moment; there were none but the more youthful of her cavaliers at present about her. As he paused to dutifully exchange compliments with an ageing dowager, a friend of his mother's, Martin saw Helen frown.

"I assure you, Mr Swayne, that I am not such a weakling as to need to repair instantly to the terrace immediately a dance is ended." Helen tried not to sound waspish but Hedley Swayne would try the patience of a saint.

"I merely wished to explain—"

"I don't believe I wish to hear any explanation, Mr Swayne." Helen wished it were permissible to glare. She came as close as she could, viewing the pale face and long, pink-tipped nose of the unfortunate Mr Swayne with every evidence of aversion. If the man had any sensibility at all, he would leave. Her court had deserted her, prompted by his declared intention of walking with her on the terrace. As if she would risk a terrace in his company! But she knew from experience that Hedley Swayne was all but irrepressible. She compressed her lips in reluctant resignation as she watched him draw breath to put forward his next suggestion. Why wouldn't he just leave her alone?

"Mr Hedley Swayne, I presume?"

The languid tones surprised Hedley Swayne, making him look rather like a startled rabbit. As his eyes rose to take in the gentleman now by her side, the huge floppy bow at his throat, hallmark of the well-dressed fop, all but quivered in agitation. Swallowing a sudden urge to giggle, Helen turned slightly, putting out her hand to Martin. He took it and tucked it into his arm, but spared only a glance for her before returning his attention to her persecutor.

Under the grey gaze, Hedley Swayne blinked nervously. "Ah—I don't believe we've been introduced, my lord."

Martin noticed he did not say he did not know who he was. He smiled coldly. "Not exactly. Your reputation goes before you, you see. I believe we just missed each other—in Somerset, some weeks ago?"

At the heavy meaning underlying the polite words, Hedley Swayne's pale eyes grew round. He blanched, then flushed. "Er...ah..."

Martin's gaze grew steely. "Just so."

Helen watched in appreciation. It must have been Hedley behind her kidnapping after all. Then the musicians started playing the music for the next dance—a waltz.

Eyes still holding Hedley Swayne's, Martin smiled, letting dire warning show beneath his urbanity. "My dance, I believe, my lady. Mr Swayne." With a nod for the hapless Hedley, Martin drew his future wife firmly into his arms, a little shocked at how intensely possessive he felt.

Slightly surprised at being denied the opportunity to take proper leave of Mr Swayne, irritating though that gentleman was, Helen nevertheless could not find it in her to cavil. Waltzing with Martin was a heavenly delight—she had no intention of losing so much as a moment of her rapture over something as inconsequential as a fop called Hedley Swayne.

"Has he been bothering you?"

Helen glanced up to find a frown gathering in the grey eyes fixed on her face. Bother Hedley! She shrugged. "He's totally innocuous, really."

"Innocuous enough to have you kidnapped."

This time, Helen sighed. "There's no need to worry about him."

"I assure you it's not Hedley Swayne I worry about."

Helen looked up and was trapped in his grey gaze. Suddenly, she felt breathless, her pulse accelerating. "You worry too much, my lord," she whispered, dragging her eyes from his.

At her tone, Martin shut his lips on his retort. He was tempted to order her to avoid Hedley Swayne, but, as yet, his jurisdiction did not stretch that far. He placated his urge to ensure her safety with the reflection that, soon, he would be in a position to make sure she saw nothing more of Mr Swayne.

Despite his not having uttered his decree, Helen got the message quite clearly. She felt thoroughly disgruntled when the music ceased, denying her the chance to dwell further on the peculiarly addictive sensation of drifting, light as air, in Martin's arms. His discussion of Hedley had distracted her and now their waltz—the last one of the night, what was more—was over.

Nevertheless, she made the most of the rest of her evening, going into supper on the Earl of Merton's arm. She had given up trying to tell herself he was not serious. He was perfectly serious when he wished to be and on the subject of her future he was unshake-able. It was simply not possible to mistake the inten-tions of a gentleman who made it patently clear that he attended the *ton* parties purely to dance attendance on one woman. Being that woman made her more ner-vous than she had ever been in her life.

It was the first time she had been in love—the first time she had been the object of love. She comforted herself that it was only the novelty that sent her senses skittering in delicious disarray whenever she heard his voice. Doubtless, the effect would wane with time. A niggling suspicion that it would not, and that she had no real desire that it should, undermined her fragile confidence.

The truth was, she could not quite believe it was all real, that the rainbow that had appeared on her horizon would not simply vanish with the next dawn. Love was something she had convinced herself she would have to do without—to have it served up to her on a gilt-edged, solid-silver platter was well beyond her ex-pectations. Helen Walford had never been so lucky.

Reconciling herself to her sudden change in fates was an uphill battle, her difficulties compounded by his persistent presence and the distraction of his grey eyes. As her carriage wheels rattled over the cobbles, taking her home to her lonely bed, Helen sat back with a sigh and sent a silent prayer winging heavenwards. Please God that this time would be truly different, that this time the fates could find it in them to be kind. That this time her dreams would not turn to dross, that happiness like Dorothea's would at long last be hers.

With a little shiver, Helen closed her eyes. And willed it to be so.

Damian Willesden returned to the capital the next day. Forced by the exigencies of financial commitments to endure a repairing lease with a friend in the country until quarter-day had brought relief, he sauntered into Manton's Shooting Gallery determined to find congenial company with which to make up for lost time. Instead, he found his brother.

The broad shoulders encased in a perfectly cut coat of the best superfine were quite unmistakable. Martin was shooting with a party of his friends.

Beyond informing him that Martin had indeed returned, hale and whole, and was busying himself taking up his inheritance, his mother had been unusually reticent on the subject of the new Earl. Damian had interpreted this as another display of her well-known indifference to Martin and all his exploits. Even more than she, he had lived in the confident expectation that his reckless older brother would have managed to get himself killed, leaving the title to him. Martin's continued existence had been a rude shock. To him and his creditors.

A further surprise had awaited him when he had applied to Martin for assistance. That interview, conducted within days of Martin's return, had left him convinced that he would see little of the Merton revenues while Martin lived. His memories of Martin had been hazy at best; ten years separated them—they had never been close. But he had vaguely supposed that his brother, having spent so many years in the back-waters of the colonies, would be easily enough per-suaded to part with his blunt. Instead, the interview had proved *most* uncomfortable. Pulling the wool over his brother's sharp grey eyes was not something he would try again soon.

He comforted himself with the reflection that a man of Martin's known propensities could be counted on to die young. It could only be a matter of time.

Watching the steadiness of the hand that levelled one of Joseph Manton's famous pistols at the slimmest of wafers propped as target twenty paces down the gallery, Damian reflected that such skills were presum-ably required in order to support the rakehell status his brother enjoyed. The pistol discharged; the smoke cleared. A small charred hole had appeared in the very centre of the wafer. As Manton himself came forward with congratulations, Damian decided that any hope that an indignant husband might put a term to his brother's life was nothing more than wishful thinking.

Turning from Desborough and Fanshawe to lay aside his pistol, Martin saw Damian lounging just in-side the door. He nodded and watched his brother re-luctantly approach. He could not prevent his lips curv-ing in a knowing smile as the fact that it was two days after quarter-day dawned. Damian saw the smile; his expression turned sulky. Martin felt his own expres-sion harden. Studied critically, there was nothing in Damian's dress to disgust one—his coat was well-cut, although not of the finest quality; the same could be said of his breeches and boots. It was his demeanour that raised brows. At twenty-four, he should have attained the age of reason, together with a little maturity. But his petulant attitude coupled with his expectation that his family must necessarily support his wastrel ways convinced Martin that his brother still had considerable maturing to do.

He raised his brows as Damian halted before him. ''Returned to the delights of town?''

Damian shrugged. ''The country's too slow for my taste.'' He considered asking for an advance on his allowance but rejected the idea. He was not that desperate yet. He nodded at the target. ''Pretty shooting. Learned in the colonies, did you?''

Martin laughed. ''No. That was a talent I'd polished long before I departed these shores.'' He paused, then suggested, ''Why not try your luck?''

For an instant, Damian wavered, drawn to the prospect of joining his magnificent brother in such a fashionable pursuit and in such august company. Then his eye fell on the gold signet on Martin's right hand and childish resentment clouded his reason. ''Heaven forbid,'' he said, waving away the pistol Martin held out. ''Not my style. *I* ain't in any danger from irate husbands.''

A little stunned by his own gaucherie, and less than sure what reaction it might provoke, Damian abruptly turned on his heel and walked rapidly from the Gallery.

Tony Fanshawe, standing on Martin's other side, an unintentional auditor to the scene, threw Damian a curious glance. ''That pup wants training,'' he said.

"Deuced bad manners, walking away from an invitation like that."

Martin, his eyes on his brother's retreating back, nodded absent-mindedly. "I'm afraid," he said, "that my brother's manners leave a lot to be desired. In fact, my brother himself falls rather short of the mark." Making a mental note to the effect that some time he was going to have to do something about Damian, Martin turned back to his friends and their game of skills.

He loved her.

That refrain replayed in Helen's head as she revolved about Lady Broxford's ballroom firmly held in Martin Willesden's arms. There was no doubt in her mind of its truth; her heart soared as she finally allowed the prospect of spending the rest of her life under Martin's smoky grey gaze to take definite shape in her mind. The pot of gold at the end of the rainbow was to be hers at last.

She looked up to find the warm grey eyes upon her, a caress in their depths.

"A penny for your thoughts, my lady."

The deep, slightly raspy voice sent a cascade of sensations tingling through her. Suppressing a shiver of pure delight, Helen narrowed her eyes in consideration. "I don't know that telling you my thoughts would be at all wise, my lord. Certainly, all precepts dictate I should stay silent."

"Oh? They can't be that scandalous."

"*They're* not scandalous. You are," Helen retorted. "I'm sure it's written somewhere—in the *Handbook for Young Ladies* under the heading of " 'How to Deal with Rakes' — that it's *most* unwise to do anything to encourage them."

The grey eyes opened wide. "And knowing your thoughts would encourage me?"

Helen tried to return his intent look with one of the greatest blandness. Her partner was undeterred.

"My dear Helen, I suspect your education was somewhat circumscribed. You certainly never finished that chapter, or you would have read that it's even *more* unwise to whet a rake's appetite."

At the unrestrained promise in the gravelly voice, Helen's eyes grew wide. To her relief, they had come to the end of the room and Martin had to give his attention to turning them around. His arm tightened about her, leaving her even more breathless than before. She felt like a lamb about to be devoured by a wolf. For some reason, the idea was quite attractive. Her wits had obviously scattered. With an effort, she sought to collect them.

Martin glanced down at Helen's face. The eau-de-Nil silk sheath she wore moulded to her ample curves, sliding and sussurating against his coat with every gliding step they took. With the shifting silk to distract her further he doubted her ability to reorientate her thoughts from the salacious direction he had given them. Thoroughly satisfied with her state, he forbore to press her to converse, giving his mind instead to the vexed question of when? When should he ask her to marry him?

He had planned to propose as soon as he was sure she had accepted the idea of being the Countess of

Merton and had got over her apparent nervousness regarding a second marriage. His experienced assessment was that any doubts she had harboured were now things of the past. As the last bars of the waltz sounded, he made his decision. There was no reason to wait.

But the ballroom was crowded, the event a "sad crush". The ante-rooms, he knew, would be full of dowagers trying to escape the heat. He would have to reconnoitre.

The music ceased; they whirled to a halt amid the glittering throng. Breathless, wondering what came next, Helen raised her eyes to Martin's face. Their eyes met, their gazes locked, but before either had time to speak Lord Peterborough materialised from the crowd.

"There you are, Helen. I must speak to you about this bad habit of yours—letting this reprobate monopolise your time. Won't do, m'dear—not at all."

"Gerry, how long has it been since someone told you you talk too much?" Martin released Helen to allow her to greet their old friend.

Peterborough slanted a shrewd look at Helen's radiant countenance. "Don't seem to be having much effect in this case." To Helen, he said, "Aside from all the other dangers, I dare swear he's trodden all over your toes—been in the colonies for too long. Come and waltz with a man who knows how."

With a flourish, he presented his arm to Helen. Laughing, she took it, throwing one last smile at Martin before consenting to be led back to the floor.

Free, Martin embarked on a perambulation designed

to explore all potential sites for a declaration among the rooms made available to Lady Broxford's guests.

Helen was glad of the opportunity dancing with her usual court gave her to reassemble her treacherous wits and still the fluttering of her heart. She had lived in anticipation of Martin's declaration for the past week; a sense of acute expectation now had her in its grip. She laughed and smiled, teetering on the brink of the greatest happiness she had yet known.

After Peterborough, she danced with Alvanley, then Desborough and even trod a measure with Hazelmere, spared to her by a radiant Dorothea.

After the first few figures of the cotillion, Hazelmere raised a languid brow. "I take it the pleasures of this Little Season met with your approval?"

Sensing a deeper meaning hidden beneath the urbane drawl, Helen threw him a suspicious glance but answered airily, "Why, yes. It's all been most enjoyable." Nothing could keep the sheer happiness from her voice.

Both black brows rose; the hazel eyes watching her were as sharp as ever. "I wonder why," Hazelmere mused. To Helen's heartfelt relief, her long-time protector forbore to tease her, although his hazel eyes suggested that her joy was transparently obvious.

As he raised her from her final curtsy, Hazelmere said, "I fear I should draw Miss Berry to your notice. She's been trying to attract your attention for some time."

Following his gaze to where small, bird-like Miss Berry perched on a sofa at the side of the room, Helen chuckled. "Poor dear. I dare say she feels she's missing out on things, now she's so deaf."

Hazelmere's lips quirked but he refrained from further comment. He escorted Helen across the room, leaving her ensconced on the sofa, lending a sympathetic ear to Miss Berry.

From the opposite side of the ballroom, partially screened by a potted palm, Damian Willesden eyed the voluptuous figure in eau-de-Nil silk. He frowned, chewing his lip in vexation. He had come to the Broxfords' without an invitation, knowing no hostess would turn him from her door. But doing the pretty by a lot of curst females was hardly his style. He had only come because of what his friend Percy Witherspoon had let fall, of the bets regarding his brother's impending marriage.

He had refused to believe Percy but the entries in Boodle's wagers book had been too numerous to ignore. He stared across the room at Lady Walford; disaster stared back at him. Supremely confident that he would eventually inherit the Merton estates together with the sizeable fortune his mother insisted on tying to the title, sublimely sure that Martin would never trade his free-wheeling rake's existence for one of dull matrimony, he had borrowed until he was ear-deep in debt. Damian swallowed convulsively. It was a wonder the cent percenters were not hounding him already.

No—not yet. They would wait until he was no longer Martin's heir before they moved. Even then, they would start slowly, expecting him to be able to persuade his brother to fish him out of the River Tick. But when they found out Martin had no intention of rescuing him... Never one to dwell on uncomfortable fact, Damian let that thought fade.

He hugged the shadow of the palm and cogitated on his fate—and how to escape it. Ever fertile in subterfuge, his brain fastened on the essential element of his discomfort. It was all quite simple, really. He would just have to see what he could do to prevent this ill-advised marraige.

Having evaded all Miss Berry's leading questions, Helen finally rose, leaving the old lady with a fond smile. She looked about the room, but could not spot Martin's dark head amid the throng. Knowing he would seek her with the Hazelmeres and Fanshawes, in whose company she had come to the ball, she headed in the direction of the chaise on which she had last seen Dorothea.

She had moved but mere feet into the crowd when a hand on her arm halted her.

"Lady Walford?"

Helen turned to see a youth—no, a man, she revised, acknowledging the unformed features that had led her astray. Pale blue eyes returned her regard. There was something vaguely familiar about the gentleman, something about the set and shape of his head, but she was sure she had never met him before. "Sir?"

Damian summoned a smile. "I'm Damian Willesden—Martin's brother."

"Oh." Helen returned his smile readily. "How do you do?" Did Martin know his brother was here?

Damian bowed over her hand. "I haven't seen Martin yet. Is he here?" He knew it was imperative that no hint of the distance between Martin and himself should show.

"I saw him earlier in the evening." Helen raised her head to glance around. "I'm sure he's still about, somewhere, but it's so hard to find anyone in this crush."

Damian fastened on the comment eagerly. "Perhaps we could move to that alcove there." He pointed to where a curved niche in the wall held a statuette. "I'm most curious as to how Martin's been faring, getting back into the swim of things."

Helen took his proffered arm, wondering why he was not addressing such queries to his brother direct.

"I've just returned from the country and haven't had a chance to speak to Martin yet. But," said Damian, striving to infuse his light voice with meaning, "I have heard certain rumours, linking my brother's name with that…of a certain lady."

Helen blushed. "Mr Willesden, I would suggest that rumour is an insubstantial entity and that you might be wise to wait for confirmation before you jump to conclusions."

Damian looked grave, "I can appreciate your feelings, Lady Walford, and if the case were straightforward I would share your reservations. However…" he paused, frowning "…I feel a certain degree of… affection for Martin and would be sorry to see him in difficulties once more."

"Difficulties?" Helen was entirely at sea. What difficulties was Martin's brother alluding to—and why to her? "Sir, I'm afraid you will have to be a great deal more direct if I'm to understand you."

Bowing his head to hide an irrepressible smirk, Damian obliged. But when he spoke again, his voice and features were serious, as befitted his assumed role. ''As you doubtless know, Martin returned from the colonies to take up his inheritance. Naturally, what wealth he now has derives entirely from the Merton estates. And, due to past bad management, the Merton estates are kept afloat by my mother's funds.'' Pausing to let the implications sink in, Damian gave thanks for his eldest brother's failings. Thanks to George's incompetence, he had the perfect threat to remove Lady Walford from Martin's scene. What woman would marry a man forced to hang on his mother's sleeve? A hostile mother, at that. And, once Lady Walford drew back from the well-publicised relationship, other ladies similarly disposed would, with any luck, have second thoughts. ''Unfortunately,'' he continued, ''Martin and the Dowager have never been on good terms. My mother naturally demands that Martin marry as she dictates. Or else...''

Cold fingers had laid hold of Helen's heart, squeezing until it hurt, leaving nothing but numbness behind. But she had to hear all of it, understand the whole story. ''Or else what?''

Damian saw the stricken look in the large green eyes and was momentarily taken aback. Then his own future prospects arose in his mind, stiffening his resolve. ''Or else she'll withdraw her funds. The estate will collapse. Martin will be destitute, unable to support the lifestyle he's accustomed to, the lifestyle expected of the Earl of Merton.''

And he will lose all chance of restoring his home.

Helen recalled all too vividly Martin's face, lit by enthusiasm as he had described the Hermitage and told
her how it would be once he had finished refurbishing
it. As it had been in the days of his father, he had said.
In the past weeks, she had heard even more of his
dreams and had come to realise how important they
were to him. A bridge, a living link to the father he
had lost. The destruction of those dreams was a blow
he would feel most cruelly—if he married against his
mother's wishes.

If he married her.

None knew better than she that few mothers would
approve of an eligible son marrying the widow of a
social outcast—a reprobate who had gone well beyond
the invisible line and had subsequently taken his own
life. She was, she knew, unsuitable.

It had never occurred to her to question Martin's
right to choose his own wife. He had seemed so much
in control, she had never thought of him as being in
any way under another's sway. But his brother's tale
rang chillingly true.

Dull emptiness and the cold taste of despair
swamped her senses.

Chilled to the bone, deaf to the babel about them,
she held out her hand to Martin's brother. "Thank you
for telling me." Her voice didn't sound like her own—
it was cold and distant, as if she were speaking from
a long way away. She put up her chin. "You may be
sure I'll do nothing to encourage Martin to harm his
future."

Her voice threatened to break. She could say nothing more. Withdrawing her hand from Damian's, she

turned and walked into the crowd, all but unaware of her direction, oblivious of the odd looks cast her way.

By the time she found Dorothea, on a chaise by the door, Helen had regained some semblance of composure. If she appeared before Hazelmere, or his equally intelligent wife, with her soul in her eyes, she would never escape explanations. Yet the very thought of Martin and her hopes of happiness, now all gone awry, was enough to bring her to the brink of tears. Resolutely, she shut her mind against the pain and forced herself to act normally.

"Is anything wrong?" was Dorothea's opening gambit.

Helen smiled weakly. "Just a slight headache—no doubt due to all this noise." She sank on to the chaise beside her friend.

"Well," said Dorothea, correctly interpreting Helen's wish to have nothing made of her indisposition, "I've determined to leave soon, so I can take you up with me."

After a fractional hesitation, Helen nodded dully. "Yes, that would be best, I expect." Martin would expect to see her again that evening, but if she escaped with Dorothea, pleading a headache, then he would not worry. He would call at her home tomorrow, and then she would have to explain. But by then she would have had time to get herself in hand, enough, at least, to face him. For, despite the cold fogs shrouding her mind, there was one point that was crystal-clear. She could not, would not, marry Martin Willesden. She could not face the prospect of being the death of his dream. His interest in her was real—that she knew without reservation. His interest in other women of the *ton* was non-existent. If she was out of contention, he would no doubt allow his mother to find him a bride and so would achieve his ambition—an ambition entirely appropriate to his station.

Glumly, Helen stifled a sniff and struggled to force a smile to her lips. She would sit quietly by Dorothea's side until it was time to leave.

Unfortunately for her well-intentioned plans, Martin appeared by her side but minutes later. Helen's heart leapt in her breast at sight of him; she could not keep the welcoming smile from her face. But he instantly noted its tremulous quality. Drawing her to stand close beside him, he bent his dark head close to ask, "What's the matter?"

With a calm she was far from feeling, Helen reiterated her story of a headache.

Martin frowned at the press of bodies about them. "Hardly to be wondered at. Come for a stroll—some fresh air will help clear your head."

Before she had time to protest—not, she suspected, that he would have listened—Helen found herself strolling by Martin's side along a suspiciously deserted corridor. Her heart started to beat rather faster.

Her suspicions were confirmed when they reached the door at the end of the corridor and Martin opened it to reveal a small walled garden, deserted and entirely private.

He led Helen to a stone seat worked into the rockery and waited while she settled her skirts on the thyme-cushion growing over it before sitting beside her. On his knees was the prescribed pose, but, given he was thirty-five and she a widow of twenty-six, he felt he did not need to do such violence to his feelings, or to his satin knee-breeches.

She turned to stare up at him. The moonlight gilded her features, features he had come to know very well over the past week. Her green eyes widened, her lips were slightly parted. Because it seemed the right thing to do, and because he had long ago ceased to stop himself doing whatever he wished to do, Martin drew her smoothly into his arms and kissed her.

Helen tried, really tried to hold firm against that kiss, against the invitation to melt into his arms. She had been gathering her strength to speak—to avert any possible declaration, when his dark head had bent and his lips had slanted over hers. But it was impossible to hold back the tide of longing that swept her. Yielding to the inevitble, she softened against him and felt his arms tighten about her.

It was scandalously wrong to sit in a deserted garden and allow a gentleman she was not going to marry to kiss her. Particularly to kiss her like this.

The touch of his lips on hers was sheer bliss. She let her hands settle against his shoulders and leaned into his warm embrace.

Later. She would have to speak later. But for now she might as well enjoy the delicious sensations he stirred within her. He was unlikely to stop soon and at least while he was thus engaged he could not propose to her. Perhaps he did not intend to propose just yet—was merely indulging in a little dalliance further to enthral her? As the pressure of his lips increased, Helen gave up any attempt at thought.

When he finally raised his head, Martin looked down on glittering green eyes, wide and slightly stunned. She was quite speechless and, if experience was any guide, was probably having difficulty stringing two thoughts together. He smiled. It hardly mattered. She would not need to think to answer his question.

"Will you marry me, my dear?"

Helen's mind fell into place with a thud. She felt her eyes widen even further. She struggled to assemble the right words but none would leap to her tongue. When she saw the grey eyes sharpen and become intent, she swallowed. "No."

It was such a small sound, Martin thought he had misheard. But the expression in her eyes, the wordless pain, convinced him he had not been mistaken. Somehow, he had muffed it. When she drew her hands from his shoulders, he smiled and tried to make light of her problem, hoping to learn what it was. "My dear Helen, I'll have you know it's not done to kiss a man and then refuse his suit."

To his increasing unease, she hung her head. "I know."

Helen found she was wringing her hands, something she had never done in her life. "Truly, my lord, I'm more than honoured by your proposal. But I…" Heavens—what was she to say? "But I've not thought of remarrying."

"Well, try thinking about it." Martin strove to keep the edge from his tone. This was not how this interview was supposed to have gone. In fact, the more he thought of it, the whole business was deucedly odd. What had happened?

"My lord, I must make you understand—"

"No—it's I who must needs make you understand. I love you, Helen. And you love me. What more is there to it than that?"

Helen swallowed and forced her eyes to his. The moon shone from behind him, leaving his features in shadow and her with no real idea of his expression. She imagined it was forbidding. Suppressing a shiver, she tried to speak calmly. "My lord, you know as well as I that there's a great deal more to it than that."

Martin stiffened slightly, then remembered that he was atrociously rich. She must be referring to his past, but he had told her about that. Didn't she believe him? "I'm very much afraid, my dear, that you'll have to be rather more specific if I'm to follow your thread."

Helen's courage was fast deserting her. How to tell a man—an arrogant, proud man—that you knew he was his mother's pensioner? She shifted back on the seat and felt Martin's arms fall from about her. Instead of bringing her relief, the withdrawal of his protection left her feeling more lost than ever. She pressed her hands together and in a very small voice said, "I was thinking of what your mother would say."

His reaction was every bit as violent as she had anticipated.

"My mother?" Martin was dumbfounded. "What the devil do you imagine my mother has to do with this?" He had almost forgotten his mother's plans. Had news of her machinations reached town? "I'll marry who I damn well please! My mother doesn't

have any say in the matter.'' The idea that Helen thought him the sort of man who would allow anyone to interfere in such a matter made his tone even more steely.

Helen had winced at his questions; by the time he had finished his vehement denial she was more than flustered. Her nerves were jittery; she could not think straight. Her head throbbed in earnest. Of course he would deny it. What more could she say? How could she smooth things over and make him understand?

Martin saw her agitation. Immediately, he sought to cut through the morass they had somehow landed in and bring her to peace again. ''Helen, my dear, I love you. Even if my whole estate were in the balance, I'd still want to marry you.''

He spoke simply, from the heart. He was not prepared for her reaction. Wide eyes turned his way; her breath seemed to catch in her throat. Then her full lips trembled and the moonlight glistened on the tears hanging suspended from the tips of her long lashes.

''Oh, *Martin!*''

The whispered words caught on a sob.

Abruptly, Helen looked down, at her fingers tightly twined in her lap. She had never loved anyone as much as she loved him; she could not let him make such a sacrifice.

Becoming more worried with every passing second, every totally confusing minute, Martin frowned at Helen's bent head. He reached for her hand.

The door from the house opened.

''This way, m'dear.''

Helen would have leapt to her feet, but Martin's

hand on hers restrained her. He moved slightly, so that his bulk shielded her from the intruders. As two guests emerged into the small walled court, Martin rose languidly then turned and helped Helen to rise.

"Oh!" said Hedley Swayne. "My goodness! I'm afraid we didn't realise this area was occupied."

One of Martin's brows rose. His gaze went from the frippery sight of Mr Swayne to the slight young thing wavering on his arm. "No matter, I was just about to escort Lady Walford inside."

He turned to offer his arm to Helen. She took it, trying to appear as unaffected as possible, with her nerves in knots and her heart in her shoes.

"Oh, Lady Walford," the slight young thing warbled nervously. "Would you mind if I came inside with you?" Without waiting for assent, the girl turned to Hedley Swayne. "I really don't think I wish to view the gardens just at the moment, Mr Swayne."

She bobbed a curtsy and hurried to Helen's side.

Swallowing his frustration, Martin was forced to escort Helen and her unexpected protégée back to the ballroom. Once under the light of the chandeliers, he saw how badly affected Helen was. Feeling very much as if his world had stopped turning, he resigned himself to letting the matter lapse until a more suitable opportunity to speak privately with her could be arranged. He left her with Dorothea, lifting her hand to his lips with a murmured, "I'll call on you tomorrow," before taking his leave.

Dorothea took one look at Helen's face, then, without comment, called for her carriage.

Dawn was streaking the skies before sleep finally closed Helen's eyes. The pillow beneath her cheek was damp, her lids decidedly puffy. But she had managed to make the decisions that had to be made. There was no hope of explaining things to Martin—he would not accept her refusal any more than she would accept his suit. So she would have to avoid him—make it plain by her behaviour that their association was at an end. It would cause talk, but nothing serious. The *ton* would wonder what she was thinking of, but there were too many waiting in the wings to claim his attention for the gossipmongers to dwell on her peculiar whims for long.

She would have to give him up, even though it would be easier to cut out her heart. Instead, she would have to live with it, a leaden weight in her breast, evermore. He would be hurt by her withdrawal and even more hurt by her lack of explanation. But if she tried to explain, he would refuse to accept her decision. She could not see him readily acquiescing; who knew to what lengths he might go to attain his goals? No—there was only one way forward.

As she snuggled her cheek deeper into the down, she sighed. She should have known how it would end—happiness of that kind was not for her—would never be hers.

The pot of gold at the end of the rainbow had always been beyond her reach.

Chapter Eight

"What will you have?"

Martin waved his hand in the direction of the well-stocked drinks tray reposing on the sideboard in his library.

"If memory serves," said Hazelmere, sinking into the comfort of an armchair, "your father was a particularly fine judge of Madeira."

A grin twisted Martin's lips. "Quite right. And George had no taste for the stuff. Apparently, there's three full racks in the cellar."

He poured two glasses and carried one to his guest before settling in the armchair on the other side of the empty fireplace. A companionable silence fell. Hazelmere, well aware that Martin had asked him to his home for some purpose, was content to wait for his friend to open his budget. Martin, equally well aware of his friend's understanding, was in no hurry to do so.

The matter was a delicate one. He had called on Helen the morning after the débâcle of his first declaration, two nights ago. Hours of intense concentration had yielded no clue as to what it was that had made her balk at his proposal. Nevertheless, he had gone to her small house in Half Moon Street, confident of ironing out whatver wrinkles had insinuated themselves into the fabric of their relationship. That was when he had realised how serious her problem, now their problem, was.

She had refused to see him, sending her maid down with a story of indisposition. For the first time in his life, he had been totally nonplussed. Why?

There had to be a reason—she was not a dim-witted miss, a flibbertigibbet. It had been his avowal of love that had thrown her, though why that should be so he could not imagine. Eventually, he had come to the conclusion that there had to be some hidden bogey in her past that his words, or the meaning behind them, had conjured up.

And the one person who knew enough of Helen's past to be of use was seated in the armchair opposite, a deceptively lazy look in his hazel eyes.

Martin grimaced. ''It's about Helen Walford.''

''Oh?'' A look of reserve veiled Hazelmere's sharp gaze.

''Yes,'' said Martin, ignoring it. ''I want to marry her.''

His friend's features relaxed in warm approval. ''Congratulations.'' Hazelmere raised his glass in the gesture of a toast.

''Premature, I'm afraid. She won't have me.'' Martin bit the words out, then sought solace in a hefty draught of finest quality Madeira.

A puzzled frown settled over Hazelmere's black brows. "Why, for heaven's sake?"

"That's what I want you to tell me." Martin settled back in his chair and looked pointedly at Hazelmere.

Hazelmere frowned back, an exasperated look in his eyes. "She likes you. I know she does."

"So do I—it's not that."

Uncharacteristically at sea, Hazelmere threw Martin a thoroughly bemused look. "What then?"

Martin sighed. "When I told her how much I loved her..." He threw a warning glance at Hazelmere before continuing, "She nearly broke down and wept."

Hazelmere showed no sigh of treating the subject lightly. If anything, his frown deepened. Eventually, he said. "That...is bad. Helen hardly ever cries. I've known her since she was three and she's far more likely to argue than weep."

"Quite." Martin paused, then added diffidently, "I had wondered whether there was anything about her previous marriage that would account for it."

Hazelmere's brows rose. Sitting back, he considered the point, absent-mindedly twirling the stem of his glass between his long fingers. Then, abruptly, as if having reached a decision, he looked at Martin. "As you seem set on marrying her, and, even if *she* doesn't know it yet, *I* know that means she'll be the next Countess of Merton, I'll tell you what I know." At sight of Martin's quick grin, he added, "But I warn you, it's not much."

His features impassive, the expression in his eyes much less so, Martin waited with what patience he could muster while Hazelmere fortified himself with a pensive sip of honey-gold liquor.

"I expect I'd better start at the beginning." Hazelmere settled his shoulders against the back of the chair. "Helen's parents presented her at sixteen—a mistake, for my money. She'd been a tomboy, a hoyden, for years and had yet to grow out of her adventures. But her parents had her life all arranged—a marriage to the son of an old friend, Lord Alfred Walford. The son, Arthur Walford, I think you knew?"

At Hazelmere's questioning glance, Martin nodded curtly. "We met once or twice before I left for the West Indies. Hardly the sort of man careful parents would have in mind for a beautiful and wealthy sixteen-year-old."

A fleeting smile lit Hazelmere's face. "Ah—but you didn't know Helen then. I know it's hard to believe, seeing her now, but, take it from me, at sixteen she was a Long Meg—and a dreadfully scrawny one at that." When Martin looked sceptical, Hazelmere waved the point aside. "Not that it mattered. It wouldn't have made an ounce of difference if she'd been Cleopatra incarnate. The parents, both hers and old Walford, had settled on the alliance long before. It was intended as a dynastic marriage of the most calculated sort. Helen's parents were both ambitious in an odd sort of way. They never mixed much and lived in seclusion in the country, but they were determined to marry their daughter into one of the oldest families about." Hazelmere paused, his gaze far away, remembering. "There were many who tried to dissuade them, my parents among them, but they were fixated on the idea. Walford the elder was keen, because of Helen's dowry. Arthur Walford was amenable for much the same reason. So Helen was married to Walford a bare month after her come-out.''

"A *month?*'' Incredulity sharpened Martin's tone.

"Precisely,'' affirmed Hazelmere, equally sharp. "The newly-weds repaired to Walford Hall. Less than a month after that, Walford reappeared in town. Helen stayed in Oxfordshire. That situation continued, apparently without change, for close on three years. During that time, all the senior players in the drama died — Walford the elder, and both Helen's parents. The crunch came when, against all odds, Walford succeeded in running through his funds. He had lost his own estates and those that had come to him through Helen. Only Walford Hall remained, as it was entailed. He returned there, not to take up residence but to see what more he could wring from the place. By then, Helen was nineteen. She had still not attained the stature she now has, but she had improved considerably on sixteen.''

Hazelmere paused, studying the glass in his hand. "I don't know to this day what actually happened, but the upshot of it was that Walford struck Helen — during an argument, she said. For her part, she promptly broke a pot over his head and left.'' Hazelmere drained his glass before glancing at Martin. "She came to me. She had grown up with my sister Allison and we had always considered her one of the family. I sent her to my estate in Cumbria — well out of Walford's way should he try to find her. The story of his treatment of Helen got out — as such things do. It became something of a *cause célèbre*. The upshot was that Walford was hounded from the *ton* and comprehensively ruined. He took his own life rather than face Newgate.''

Hazelmere paused, considering the past, then shrugged. ''Later, many of those who had won stakes from Walford donated money to set up a fund for Helen. I manage it for her. It pays the rent on her house in Half Moon Street and keeps her in her current style—but little else. None of her estates was salvaged.''

Martin frowned, his chin sunk in one hand, his gaze fixed on the Turkey rug gracing the floor between them. Carefully, choosing his words, he asked, ''Is there anything in what you know of her that would lead you to suppose Helen feels any deep-seated revulsion towards marriage? An aversion to the physical side of matrimony?''

Hazelmere's lips thinned. His eyes on his glass, he shook his head. ''I couldn't say—but, conversely, I would not be at all surprised.'' He lifted his gaze to Martin's face. ''You know what Walford was like.''

Slowly, Martin nodded. ''Could it have scarred her—so that she has difficulty bringing herself to contemplate marriage again?''

Hazelmere shrugged. ''Only Helen could answer that, but I would have thought it a distinct possibility.''

Almost imperceptibly, Martin's expression lightened. His eyes narrowed in consideration.

Hazelmere noticed. ''What is it?''

A crooked grin was Martin's answer. ''I was just thinking—who better to cure such a malady than I?''

He shot Hazelmere a quizzical glance, then sat back, supremely confident, one brow rising arrogantly. "All things considered, I would have to be the perfect candidate for the job of convincing Helen Walford of the earthy benefits of matrimony. If, with my extensive experience, I can't overcome that particular hurdle, I don't deserve the lady."

For a long moment, Hazelmere's hazel eyes remained serious, while their owner pondered what was, after all, a distinctly scandalous threat to a lady whom many, including himself, regarded as under his protection. But, if he read things aright, Helen's future happiness was at stake. She had made her partiality plain. And he trusted Martin Willesden as a brother— Helen would come to no harm at his hands. Slowly, a grin twisted Hazelmere's lips. Inclining his head in tacit approval of Martin's avowed intention, he raised his glass in salute.

"Spoken like a true rake."

Helen settled her skirts and waited for Martin to join her on the box seat of his curricle. The wind whipped loose tendrils of hair about her face and brought colour to her cheeks. As Martin sat beside her and picked up the reins, she flashed a bright smile in answer to his. Then they were off.

With the raucous cries of the Piccadilly street vendors ringing about her, Helen sat, at peace and oddly content, and wondered that it could be so. It was remarkable, she reflected, that, given Martin's painful declaration just over a week before, they should be able to be together like this, companionably setting out for a drive in the Park. For her part, she would not have credited it. But, to her relief, Martin had behaved in the most honourable way.

He had claimed her for a waltz at the Havelocks' rout, the next major function they had both attended. Nothing in his manner had altered; he had behaved every bit as proprietorially as before. Only she had heard his whispered words, "Trust me. Just relax— there's nothing to worry about."

Strangely enough, she had. From beneath her chip bonnet, Helen glanced up at his profile, so harshly handsome. His eyes were fixed on the road ahead, his hands steady on the reins. A smile on her lips, Helen returned her gaze to their surroundings. Relaxing in Martin's company had been made a great deal easier by the fact that he no longer sought to befuddle her senses with his particular brand of wizardry. She was determined to keep her traitorous senses in line; his power over them was just as strong, but, if she was intent on her course, she could not afford to let them gain the upper hand. Thankfully, Martin seemed to understand. It was clear that, now she had brought the matter to his mind, he had, however reluctantly, accepted that, given his circumstances and hers, they could not marry. And, gentleman that he was, he was intent on keeping their situation from the world. All she was called on to do was respond to his lead, to make it appear as if there were no rupture between them. It was, she had realised, the sensible course. Now, as time passed, they would be able to draw apart without either being exposed to the avid interest of the scandalmongers.

The Park was reached without incident. They embarked on a slow circuit about the leafy avenues, stopping time and again to chat with their acquaintances. It was during one of these halts that Ferdie Acheson-Smythe approached. His bland expression totally devoid of guile, he nodded to Martin then reached up to shake hands with Helen.

"Hello, Ferdie. Is that a new coat?" Helen knew any question of fashion was guaranteed to appeal to the immaculate Mr Acheson-Smythe. She had known Ferdie, Hazelmere's cousin, forever and was truly fond of the elegant dandy.

"Yes," replied Ferdie, unwarrantably brief. "But that wasn't what I wanted to tell you." His pale blue eyes flicked to Martin, engrossed with some friends on the other side of the curricle, then returned to her face, a slight frown in their depths. Leaning closer, he said, "I know you've made a damned habit of this, but do you really think it's wise?"

With Ferdie, there was no point in pretending to misunderstand. Helen smiled affectionately at his brother-like concern. She lowered her voice. "You needn't worry. I'm perfectly safe."

"Humph!" Ferdie snorted, his gaze once more on Martin's profile. "That's what I thought about Dorothea and look how wrong I was. Point is, rakes don't change. They're damned dangerous in any circumstances."

Helen laughed. "I assure you this one's tame."

The comment earned her a highly sceptical look, but Ferdie said no more on the matter, turning his attention instead to complimenting her on her new apricot me-

rino pelisse. When a short while later Martin looked
around, ready to move on, Ferdie bowed elegantly and
stood back, contenting himself with a warning look
addressed to Helen's account.

Martin saw it. His brows rose superciliously, but by
then Ferdie Acheson-Smythe was already dwindling
in the distance. Then Martin's sharp ears caught the
muffled giggle as his companion tried to suppress her
reaction. Martin relaxed. "Tell me, fair Juno, am I still
considered 'too dangerous', despite my exemplary behaviour of recent times?"

Helen shot a startled glance up at him. Reassured
by the teasing glint in his grey eyes and the laughter
bubbling through his deep tones, she smiled and gave
due attention to his question. Considering the matter
dispassionately was a decidedly tall order. Eventually,
knowing he was waiting on her answer, she ventured,
"I fear, my lord, that there are some who see your
'exemplary behaviour' as merely the wool beneath
which a wolf is disguised."

Martin's heavy sigh startled her anew.

"And here I was thinking none could discern the
truth."

Helen's eyes flew wide. His tone held equal parts
of dejection and chagrin but the expression in his eyes
was still gently teasing. She tried to read his meaning
in their depths, but the subtle glint defeated her. Was
he warning her that Ferdie was right. Or was he merely
making light conversation, teasing her, knowing she
was easy to twit on that score?

Uncertain, Helen spent the next ten minutes inwardly wrestling with the possibilities while outwardly

playing the social game. They had finished their first circuit when Martin broke into her thoughts.

"I still haven't made the final decisions on the pieces for the parlour."

"Oh?" Helen had heard about the redecoration of his London home, now in its terminal phase, in some detail. Discussions on the relative merits of damasks and chintzes and the impracticality of the current craze for white and gold décor had filled many of their hours together.

Martin was frowning thoughtfully. "There's a piece of furniture on which I would greatly appreciate your opinion. It's at a house not far from here." He glanced at Helen and raised an enquiring brow. "Can you spare me a few moments of your time, my dear?"

Swallowing her instinctive response that such matters should be reserved for the consideration of his bride, Helen smiled her acquiescence. One subject she had no intention of mentioning was matrimony. "I dare say I could manage a moment or two."

Courteously inclining his head in acceptance of her boon, Martin headed his team for the gates, a slow smile of satisfaction curving his lips. They were wending their way through the traffic when Helen asked, "What is this piece?"

"An occasional sofa."

Seeing his attention was fixed on his horses, given to nervously jibbing in the crowded streets, Helen forbore to press him for details. Doubtless she would learn soon enough why there was any question about the suitability of this particular sofa.

To her surprie, Martin drew the horses to a halt in

front of an imposing residence in Grosvenor Square. He turned to smile down at her. "This is it." Relinquishing the reins to Joshua who came running from his perch at the rear, Martin jumped to the pavement and turned to assist Helen. Once on his level, Helen eyed the elegant façade then realised the sofa in question must presently be in the possession of the owner of the mansion.

Surrendering to the subtle pressure of Martin's hand in the small of her back, Helen went up the steps before him. Martin paused before the door and glanced down, his eyes locking with hers, an unfathomable expression in the steely grey. Suddenly, Helen could not breathe. But before she could register more than a flush of unnerving excitement, Martin raised a gloved fist and beat a peremptory tattoo on the polished oak. The door was opened immediately by an imposing if portly butler, who bowed them into a spacious hall.

"M'lord." The butler turned to her. "My lady." He reached for her coat. Uncertain, Helen raised an enquiring brow at Martin. When he nodded, she surrendered her pelisse and bonnet. Clearly, the Earl of Merton was well-known to this household.

"The room at the end of the hall." At Martin's nod, Helen walked forward over the black and white tiles, towards the door that stood open at the far end of the hall. Martin started in her wake, then hesitated and turned back, handing his gloves to the butler. Hearing his footsteps falter, Helen glanced back. Martin smiled his encouragement. Reassured, Helen continued.

As she drew closer to the open door, she noticed a peculiar light glowing from within the room. Almost as if the curtains were drawn and the fire ablaze. Puzzled, Helen gained the threshold and looked in.

"We don't wish to be disturbed, Hillthorpe."

Helen's gasp stuck in her throat. It did not need the butler's deferential "Yes m'lord" to confirm her wild conjecture. The proof that, in the case of Martin Willesden, rake of the highest standing, she had been wrong and Ferdie perfectly right lay before her startled gaze. The heavy velvet curtains were indeed drawn, the fire fully stoked and crackling voraciously. A bottle of wine, uncorked, reposed in a silver bucket of ice on the sideboard. Automatically, irrelevantly, Helen searched the room for the sofa she had come to see—the occasional sofa. At first, she could not find it. Then her eyes widened in shock as they focused on the large piece of furniture standing squarely before the hearth. The most massive daybed she had ever seen.

Flee! was her first thought—immediately followed by, *How?* Martin's footsteps rang on the tiles; he was but feet behind her. If she turned and tried to escape, he would simply pick her up and carry her through the door. Certainly, his butler would be no help.

Helen drew a deep breath. Danger lay across the threshold. She tried to step back into the relative safety of the hall, only to find that she had hesitated too long. Martin, directly behind her, slipped an arm about her waist and she was swept, effortlessly, into the room.

"Martin!" Breathless, Helen swung to face him, to see him shut the door and turn the key. She was only slightly relieved to see that he left the key in the lock. It was him she had to escape; after that, escaping the room would be child's play. Summoning her defences, she took refuge in indignation. Drawing herself to her full height, in this case unfortunately insufficient to allow her to intimidate the reprobate before her, she fixed him with an affronted glare and prayed her voice would not betray her. "You tricked me!"

A slow grin twisted Martin's mobile lips. "'Fraid so." His gaze, heated grey, rested, intent, on her face. Slowly, he moved towards her.

He did not look the least bit contrite.

Helen tried to ignore her skittering pulse and let her temper grow. It was the only thing that might save her. She narrowed her eyes, shutting out as much of the potent male presence approaching slowly but, as far as she was concerned, far too fast, as she could. Forced to tilt her chin up as he drew nearer, she struggled to overcome her suddenly breathless state. "Your behaviour over the past week has all been a sham, hasn't it?" To her horror, it was all she could do not to squeak. What was he about?

Stopping directly in front of her, Martin allowed his grin to develop into the deepest of smiles, a smile of disturbing magnitude and unnerving intent. "You've unmasked me, fair Juno." Eyes glinting, Martin spread his hands in supplication. "What can I say in my defence?"

Transfixed by the warmth in his gaze, Helen struggled to collect enough wit to tell him.

Smoothly, confidently, Martin reached for the comb that held her curls in a knot on the top of her head. With a deft flick, he drew it free, sending golden tresses cascading over her shoulders, down her back.

Helen gasped, instinctively putting up her hands to

stem the tide. But Martin caught them gently in his and drew them down. Glinting, his eyes roamed the tumbled gold. "You've no idea how often I've considered doing that."

The idea that he might have done that in the middle of some fashionable ballroom suspended the few faculties Helen had managed to reassemble. His hands released hers, long fingers rising to slip in among the silken strands. The fingers played, sampling the texture, removing loose pins and dropping them like rain on to the floor, then they firmed about her chin, tilting her head up until her eyes locked with his.

Held mesmerised by the smouldering heat in the cloudy grey gaze, Helen felt all thought slipping from her. Martin's hands left her face; he reached for her and drew her into his arms.

Belatedly, self-preservation jolted Helen back to reality. She braced her hands against Martin's chest. "My lord—Martin!" she amended, accurately reading the comment in his eyes. "This is unseemly. Scandalous—and worse! If you wish to atone for your behaviour—your deceit—you can escort me back to your curricle this instant!"

She tried to sound firm but her tone was weak and wavering, her diaphragm refusing to lend strength to her words. The smile on the dark face hovering closer and closer to hers only deepened. His arms, already about her, tightened.

"I've a much better idea of how to atone for my sins."

Martin kissed her. And kept kissing her until every

vestige of resistance was overcome, overwhelmed, drowned beneath their passion.

Trapped in his embrace, Helen reluctantly admitted that it was *their* passion—not his alone. That was what made Martin so very hard to resist. His scandalous advances drew an equally scandalous response from her. Caught on a crest of burgeoning desire, so sweet in its novelty that she was unable to resist, Helen gave up the unequal fight, softening against him. She felt his arms tighten further, crushing her to him. Then they shifted; his hands moved over her back, moulding her yielding form to his hard frame.

Helen struggled against the insidious invitation of his kiss, a blatant temptation to lose her wits and drown in a sea of sensuous sensation, striving instead against the steadily mounting odds to retain some fragment of lucidity.

Martin raised his head to glance down at her, his eyes glowing. "Relax," he breathed. His lips brushed her forehead. "Don't worry—we'll take it *very slowly*."

As his lips returned to hers, Helen wondered if he intended the deep, gravelly words as a threat or a promise. For a full minute, she considered the implications as her will sank slowly beneath the warm web of sensation evoked by Martin's sure hands. With a mental jerk, she called her wits to order. What was she to do? The way he was progressing, slow or not, she would only have a few more minutes in which to decide.

It was patently obvious to the meanest intelligence that Martin had reverted to form and intended to compromise her beyond all possible doubt, in fact as well as reputation. Helen had not the slightest doubt that he thought thus to force her acquiescence to their marriage, to overcome her refusal to accept his suit. But she was determined to give him his dream—nothing, not even he, could shake her resolution.

However, she admitted, feeling the gentle tug of long fingers at the buttons of her gown, any thought of escape from such a masterful seducer was fantasy. What he had in mind was undeniably scandalous. To her, it was undeniably attractive. If she followed her heart, her truest impulse, she would do as he had said and relax.

Fate had dealt against her, but that did not mean she could not enjoy him, take the moment he offered—this once. This was all the chance she would ever have. Her one touch at happiness—her one chance to touch the pot of gold at the end of the rainbow. She had never been there before, had never known the joy she surmised must exist, wrapped in the clouds of love. Martin's fingers skimmed her shoulders, easing her carriage dress from her. With a little sigh, Helen drew her arms from the long sleeves, letting her dress fall to the floor along with her reservations. Glancing shyly up from beneath her lowered lashes, she lifted her arms and draped them about his neck in tacit acceptance of what was to come. Anticipation throbbing its dizzying pulse through her veins, she waited to see how he would manage her light stays.

Aware, as only one of his extensive experience could be, of the import of Helen's tentative movement, Martin drew a deep breath and fought to shackle a desire so strong, it threatened to addle his wits—a thoroughly undesirable outcome. Juno needed to be wooed slowly, gently, seduced like the veriest virgin, skittish and shy. He applied himself to the task with devotion.

Soon, Helen's mind was whirling, giddy with pleasure. Her past had held no clues to the passion that now engulfed her. Her introduction to wifely duties had been mundane in the extreme; her mother had told her what to expect—she had got that and nothing more. The entire procedure had been so basically boring, she had been only too glad when her husband had returned to his mistresses post haste. But, in the long lonely years since then, she had come to the conclusion that there had to be more to it than that, a positive side to the undertaking she had never experienced— for surely it was that that brought the glow to Dorothea's pale complexion and the stars to her eyes.

She had thought she would never learn what it was. But fate had decided to hand her one chance—a consolation prize in the lottery of life. Who better to teach her of the delights of love then the man in whose strong arms she was trapped?

For he was a trap, to her senses at least. She would do well to acknowledge that, and remember it when the time for explanations arrived. He was going to be angry. Very angry. He would ask her to marry him, confidently expecting her, overwhelmed by his loving, to agree. And when she refused, he was not going to be particularly interested in her reasons. Which was just as well, for she had no idea how to make him understand and was in two minds whether it was safe to do so.

But right now two minds were two minds too many for her wits to cope with. He had stolen them, along with her stays — and she had not even noticed how he had accomplished the deed. All she knew was that she felt more enthralled, more consumed with desire than ever before in her life. Martin filled her mind, overwhelmed her senses — and took control completely.

There was nothing she could do to stem the tide of urgent need welling within and between them, engulfing them both in its heated embrace. Martin stopped and lifted her, carrying her to the daybed and laying her amid the silken covers. He hovered over her, his lips dipping to hers, his hands skilfully weaving webs of delight over her fevered flesh. Then his lips touched her eyelids, placing a kiss on each.

"Keep your eyes shut."

Helen sensed he was about to undress. She wanted to watch. "But—"

"No buts," came the gravelly voice, even deeper and raspier than usual. "Do as I say. Just lie there and relax and everything will be wonderful."

The gentle persuasion in his tone had its effect. Helen lay still, feeling the warmth from the fire flickering over her skin, contrasting with the shimmering touch of the silks and satin on which she lay. Her lips curved slightly at the thought of his lordship's scandalous taste in furniture. The rustle of starched linen came to her ears. The temptation to peek from beneath her lashes grew.

Helen opened her eyes a fraction. A heavily muscled back filled her view. She watched as Martin divested himself of his clothes, staring for as long as she could until, as he joined her on the daybed, she let her lids fall before allowing them to flicker innocently upwards.

Martin smiled gently, encouragingly. His shoulders were angled over her once more, limiting her view of him. He studied her expression but could detect no hint of panic. Yet. "Good girl," he murmured, struggling to harness the passion that vibrated in his voice. He lowered his lips to hers and was relieved when her lids fluttered closed once more. In truth, he had little idea what might scare her but, if she had had a difficult time accommodating Walford, seeing him naked was not going to help.

He released her lips to give more attention to the rest of her, all the while soothing her with comforting, reassuring words. It was not his habit to waste time with talk in such situations but this case was different, unique. He kept watch for any signs of withdrawal or distress, ready to backtrack at the first hint that he was pushing her too fast.

Helen heard his words, letting them wash over her, unable to concentrate on the sentences buried beneath his sensuous rumble. She wished he would stop talking and give all his attention to fulfilling her needs. Her hands itched to explore, but, never having been visited by such a desire before, she was unsure of the etiquette involved. In the end, when, driven by her need, she tentatively spread her hands over the muscles of his back, Martin moved and caught them, trapping them in one of his and drawing them over her head.

"Not yet, sweetheart. We don't want to rush things."

If she had been capable, Helen would have glared. Why not? she wanted to know. She felt as if she wanted to devour him whole and all he would say was "Not yet". Her body felt overheated but all she wanted was more heat.

"Martin—"

"Hush." He silenced her with a kiss. "Trust me. You'll enjoy it. This time will be different, I promise."

Inwardly, Helen frowned. Of course this time would be different—she loved him. She had never loved anyone before. Her inward frown grew. She wished she could shake her head to rid herself of the niggle that there was something here that she was missing, something she did not understand.

"There's nothing to be frightened about. We'll take it slow and easy. No pain at all—only pleasure. Trust me this once and I'll show you how wonderful it can be."

The gentleness in his voice, overlaying the suppressed desire, gave Helen the vital clue. Her eyes flew wide but Martin, busy kissing her, missed the shocked response. Quickly, realising her error, Helen shut her eyes again, willing her body to remain in the languid, floating state he had induced.

He thought she was sexually crippled—or, at least, had a broken bone or two. An aversion to lovemaking of some major degree. If he had not been kissing her, Helen would have shaken her head in amazement.

How had he come to such a crazy conclusion? Arthur had never hurt her—he had simply failed to engage her passions. Now that she knew what passion between a man and woman was, she knew the truth. She was not the least averse to making love with Martin Willesden—but why had he thought she was?

This, however, was no time for imponderables.

Her wits were barely up to recognising facts, let alone dealing with their ramifications. As Martin deepened their kiss, Helen felt her conscious mind melt. Thought, in any form, became all but impossible. Sensation washed through her; joyfully, with abandon, she surrendered to the warm tide.

To Martin's gratification, not the slightest ripple of panic, not the smallest quiver of maidenly nerves, marred the response of the beauty in his arms. Nevertheless, he kept a tight rein on his passions, enforcing ruthless discipline in the face of extreme provocation. It was hard work, seducing a goddess—slowly. Painstakingly, he stoked the fever between them, blowing the embers to flame and pouring desire upon them until the conflagration had her firmly in its grip. It started to singe his control. Still, he held back, ensuring her pleasure beyond all doubt. When he finally brought her to the peak, and held her there for that most fleeting of instants, he felt the most intense surge of satisfaction, before his mind was swamped by his own delight.

The chimes of the elegant French carriage clock sitting on Martin's marble mantelpiece penetrated the pleasured fogs shrouding Helen's mind. Four o'clock.

Four o'clock! With a start, she opened her eyes. An expanse of tanned male chest, liberally sprinkled with curling back hair, met her bemused gaze. Her questing senses detected a heavy, muscled arm lying, relaxed, about her.

Stifling a moan, Helen closed her eyes. What now? Languid pleasure still had her in its grip, drugging her mind and body. It would be easy just to lie here, enjoying the warm intimacy, and let fate take its course. Then he would wake, and ask her to marry him, and she would have to refuse him, while lying naked in his arms.

Helen grimaced. She opened her eyes and slowly raised them to Martin's face. He was still sleeping. With a small sigh of relief, she set about carefully extricating herself from his loose embrace, untangling her legs from the silk sheets he had drawn over them, Luckily, she was lying on the outer edge of the day-bed.

Once free, she dressed quickly. While she wrestled with her stays, she allowed her gaze to roam lovingly over the large frame lying sprawled amid the rumpled sheets. She smiled a trifle mistily. At least she now understood just what it was that lay at the end of the rainbow, what it was that gave rise to the glow of anticipation in Dorothea's eyes whenever she looked at Hazelmere. Martin had transported her to the end of the rainbow, had given her a moment of sheer delight beyond any she had ever experienced. She would hold the memory of that moment, enshrine it in her heart, to light the lonely years ahead.

Stifling a sigh, she stepped into her dress and eased

it up over her petticoat. When he asked for her hand,
how was she to answer him? Despite the passing of a
week since her last attempt, no simple way of explaining her view to him had occurred. In fact, her cogitations had led her to conclude that explaining at all
could itself prove dangerous. Martin was not the sort
of man to accept her sacrifice tamely. He would argue,
threaten, run the gamut of all means available to sway
her. She was not going to be swayed; despite the glory
of the past hours, or, perhaps, because of them, she
was even more firmly determined to give him his
dreams. She loved him—more deeply than she had
realised, more completely than she had understood.
Self-sacrifice was an undertaking of which she had
considerable experience. Her girlish dreams had been
jettisoned for her parents' ambitions, her pride for her
husband's greed. Martin was more worthy of her sacrifice than any other; she would make it willingly, if
sadly.

Calmly determined, Helen allowed her gaze to rest
on the strong features only slightly gentled by sleep.
She would never succeed in making him accept her
view—it would be better not to try. If she offered no
explanation, but simply held firm to her refusal, he
would be exceedingly angry, but impotent to pressure
her to change her mind.

He was not going to like it but it was for his own
good.

The buttons down the back of her gown were prov-
ing refractory. Seeing her soft carriage boots on the
floor, Helen slid her feet into them while glancing
about at the elegantly furnished room. Each piece had

been chosen with a judicious eye. The theme was simplicity of line and form, an austerity which balanced the stark black, blue and gold décor. In truth, the room suited its owner. She could not imagine him in less expensive surrounds; this was his milieu, this was where he rightly belonged. This, she was determined, was where he would stay.

Her eyes went once more to the handsome face. Helen smiled as she recalled his efforts to ease her imagined hurt. Her smile faded. In refusing him, she was going to cause him even more hurt than anger. She was going to land a blow where it would hurt a great deal. Her refusal to succumb to his lovemaking was going to place a very large dent in his rake's pride.

Helen paled and felt suddenly chilled.

At sixteen, she had learned that her life was not destined to be easy. She had borne unhappiness and loneliness and put a brave face on her misery. But what she could not understand was why fate had singled her out for such continually harsh treatment. Why her?

Resolutely, Helen straightened, pushing her depression aside. Her fingers were still fumbling behind her, the small buttons sliding on the silk. Muttering a few choice curses, she attacked them with renewed vigour, only to find them slipping from her grasp.

Exasperated, she glanced up—straight into warm grey eyes, laced with lazy laughter. As she watched, Martin's smile grew.

''You should have woken me.'' His voice was still

several tones deeper than normal, a warm, raspy invitation to illicit delight.

Helen blinked, struggling to focus her wits. She had to keep calm. Trying for her usual brisk tone, she said, "It's late and I need to get home. I suspected waking you before I got dressed would not necessarily be supportive of that aim."

Thoroughly relaxed, Martin chuckled. "You read me so well, fair Juno." He beckoned. "Come here."

Helen eyed him suspiciously. "Martin, I really *do* need to go."

Martin's eyes flicked to the clock. His brows rose in resignation. "I suppose you do." He sighed. "In which case, you had better let me do up your dress." He sat up and swung his leg over the side of the bed, the sheet slipping down to his waist. When he waved her towards him, Helen reluctantly came to stand before him. Martin's strong hands closed about her waist. For one heart-stopping moment, their gazes locked. Mesmerised, her breath trapped in her throat, Helen watched as the slow smile she knew so well twisted his lips. Then he turned her about.

His strong fingers made short work of her buttons. But before she could move away, his hands fastened about her waist and he drew her down to sit on one sheet-swathed knee.

The feel of her warm body between his hands made Martin wish again that she had woken him earlier. He seriously considered pulling her back to the sheets and wrestling her out of her clothes. Who cared what the world thought? With a wry grin, he acknowledged that such wildness would no longer do, not if he intended to assume his social position as the Earl of Merton with his Countess at his side. Speaking of which...

He turned fair Juno about so that he could look into her face. He smiled devilishly, the complete rake. "Did you like it?"

Helen's eyes flew wide. She blushed furiously.

Martin laughed, raising one finger to caress her cheek. "Say you'll marry me and we can enjoy such delights every day—or at least every night." His second proposal, he reflected, but in circumstances much more to his taste. He smiled confidently and waited for fair Juno's assent.

Helen could not meet his eyes. As the silence stretched, she felt Martin tense. Feeling a chill creep over her skin, she tried to ease from his hold. He let her go, his hands falling from her as she stood and moved to the fireplace before turning to face him.

Steeling herself, she raised her eyes to his. Cold grey stone would have held more warmth than the grey gaze steadily regarding her. His features were impassive, set like granite; his hands were fisted on his thighs. The light from the dying fire gilded the heavy musculature of his bare chest. He looked very powerful—and deeply angry.

"Martin, I cannot marry you." Helen forced herself to enunciate the words clearly, calmly. Inside, she felt dead.

"I see." The words came like a whiplash. Helen hung her head. "You'll willingly share my bed but you won't *marry* me." During the pause that ensued, she kept her eyes down, too frightened that she would weaken if she looked up and saw his disillusion.

"Why?"

The confusion and hurt in that single word nearly overset her. She pressed her palms together and forced her head up. "I'm sorry. I can't explain."

"Sorry?" Abruptly, Martin surged to his feet.

Startled, Helen glanced away, colour flaring in her pale cheeks. With a strangled curse, Martin stalked to where a silk robe had been left lying over the back of a chair. He shrugged into it, struggling to bring order to the chaotic and violent emotions seething through his brain. "Let me just get one point clear," he ground out, savagely yanking the sash tight. "You were willing, were you not?"

"Yes." Helen brought her head up, relieved to see him decently garbed. Her admission should have sunk her beyond reproach, shaken her to the core. Yet it was the truth; she admitted it without a blink, all her energies concentrated on the difficult task of persuading him to let her go. "But that alters nothing. It is simply not possible for me to marry you."

"Why?"

This time, the question held more demand. Martin stalked back and forth before her, a wounded beast. Helen stifled the instinctive urge to offer him comfort. She had to hold firm. "I'm sorry, I can't explain."

Eyes narrowed to steely slits, Martin stopped directly in front of her. "Can't explain why you'd make a high-class harlot of yourself rather than marry me? I'm hardly surprised, madam!"

Inwardly flinching, Helen held herself proudly, refusing to quail under the glittering grey gaze. She felt sick. He was not impassive now; hurt pride was clearly etched in his forbidding features. But she could not regret their afternoon of delight; she did not intend to feel guilty over the greatest joy she had ever known.

Martin held her gaze, willing her to back down. When the clear green gaze remained steady, unwavering, he growled and flung away. He felt violent. He wanted to shake her—to take her back to the bed and reduce her to a state where she would do, and say, anything he wished. But that was no real solution. He threw a furious glance her way. She was still standing, with a calm he knew was assumed, before his fireplace—where he wanted to see her, but without the mantle he wished to place on her shoulders. He could push her to become his mistress, and she might just give way. But he wanted her as his wife.

With a growl of frustration, Martin turned and stalked back to her. "If my honest proposal is repugnant to you, my lady, I would suggest you leave. Before my baser instincts drive me to make you a far more insulting offer."

Helen's eyes widened. Martin's fingers closed, vice-like, about her arm. Stifling a gasp, she allowed him to march her, unresisting, to the door. It was better this way. If she had to depart of her own accord, leaving him hurt, wounded and without explanation, she might waver and fail. His furious rejection might break her heart but it might also save his.

In a muddled, befuddled fury, Martin strode into his hall, dragging Helen with him. "Hillthorpe!"

Instantly, his butler emerged from behind the green baize door. At sight of them, his demeanour underwent a subtle change.

Martin ignored the evidence of Hillthorpe's surprise. "Lady Walford is leaving. Get a hackney for her ladyship." He released Helen and, with the curtest of nods, turned on his heel and strode back to the parlour.

When the door slammed behind him, Helen drew a ragged breath. She felt as if her world had crashed about her very ears. Her head was spinning; she felt queasy inside. But there was nothing to do but face the disaster with as much dignity as she could. Her hair was still down, but her pins were irretrievable; she would have to make the best of it. She refused to permit herself to break down and cry, much as she wished to, until she was safe in her chamber. Reaching that sanctuary with all possible haste was her immediate goal.

One glance at Martin's butler showed he was as stunned as she at Martin's rudeness but, unlike her, had no idea from where the uncharacteristic reaction sprang. "If you would get my hat and coat?"

Her quiet question jolted Hillthorpe out of his state of shock. "Yes, of course, my lady." Never in his extensive experience of Mr Martin had Hillthorpe seen him in such a temper. Which, he thought, as he bowed to Lady Walford and hurried to do her bidding, was a damned shame. The servants had been particularly pleased when Mr Martin had inherited. Of the four sons of the house, he had always been their favourite. He was a hard but fair master; they were relieved that the estate was once more in capable hands. Not since the late master, his father, had they felt so secure. And, as servants did, they had kept abreast of his endeavours to secure his Countess. The news that he had chosen Lady Walford for the position had been greeted with considerable relief. Many were the instances when men such as his lordship married youthful misses who led everyone a dance and set the household by the ears. But Lady Walford was well spoken of, kind and generous, a lady in truth.

As he held her ladyship's coat for her, Hillthorpe frowned. She was upset, as she had no doubt every right to be. What was the master thinking of? A hackney? He would summon the unmarked carriage instead. As she turned to face him, buttoning up her coat, he bowed low. "If you'll just take a seat in the drawing-room, ma'am, I'll summon the carriage directly."

Grateful for the man's smooth handling of the matter, Helen followed him, battening down her emotions until it was safe to set them free.

From the bend in the spiral staircase two floors above, Damian Willesden watched her disappear down the hall. His eyes widened in surprise. Slowly, he slumped on to the stairs, the better to consider the implications of what he had just seen.

So—Martin had run true to form and seduced the beautiful Lady Walford? That thought pleased Damian no end. With a little crow of delight, he gave thanks for Martin's rakish tendencies. Lady Walford might be his brother's mistress but she would not be his wife. Her ladyship could be crossed off the list of potential candidates for the position of the Countess of Merton.

Or could she?

Damian sobered and gave the matter due thought. He could not imagine why a man such as his brother would marry a woman he could have as his mistress but the unpalatable truth was, such things had been known to occur. All too often. Particularly with un-married peers.

The front door opened and shut. Lady Walford was gone.

But *he* was not yet safe. Damian frowned and drummed his fingers on his knee. He could not believe that Martin would want to marry the lady now, partic-ularly after that abrupt dismissal, but that did not mean she might not try to entrap him later. Adrift in social straits he normally eschewed with a vengeance, Dam-ian pondered deeply. In the end, he concluded that it would quite obviously be better all round, for Martin as well as for himself, if Lady Walford were not in a position to demand that Martin marry her.

And she could not do that if her reputation was already in shreds.

Aside from anything else, the Dowager would not stand for it. Damian had immense confidence in his mother. And her money.

With a smug smile, Damian rose and sauntered down the stairs. It would be easy, so easy, to ensure his peace of mind. He called for his hat and cane and, once supplied with these necessary items, issued forth from the house of his fathers, determined to make sure that it would one day be his. He turned his footsteps in the direction of St James.

Chapter Nine

The Barham House ball was to be held that night. Wearily, Helen acknowledged that it was impossible for her to miss the event—the Barhams had stood her friends for years. Hopefully, Martin, not so constrained, would not go.

With a dismal sniff, she hauled herself out of the comforting softness of her bed and gave her eyes one last pat with her sodden handkerchief. Janet would have to find some cucumber to take the swelling down. Her bout of tears had done no more than ease her immediate hurt; the deeper pain would linger, undimmed by any show of misery. With an effort, Helen stood and crossed the room to tug the bell-pull. Then she ventured to her wardrobe.

Black was what she felt like wearing, but in the circumstances, dark blue would have to do. The heavy silk was edged with gold ribbons; more ribbon cinched the high waist. In it, she knew she looked austere and a little remote. Perfect for tonight. With any luck, the solid colour would help disguise her paleness.

A bath restored some semblance of vitality. Janet

fussed and fretted and coaxed her to eat some lightly broiled chicken. Her cook had tried, but the food might as well have been ashes.

And then she was in her carriage, bowling along to Barham House. What would she do if Martin did attend? Helen drew a long breath and buried that thought deep. In her present state, it was far too unnerving to contemplate.

The Barhams greeted her warmly. In the ballroom, she found Dorothea and Lady Merion already present. In the comfort of her familiar circle, she relaxed, allowed a mask of calm unconcern to cloak her bruised heart.

Midway through the evening, her mask slipped alarmingly. She was waltzing with Viscount Alvanley when she became aware that Martin had indeed attended the ball. He was standing by the side of the ballroom, powerful shoulders propped against the wall, a look of brooding intensity darkening his features. His gaze was fixed unwaveringly upon her.

Even Alvanley, genial chatterer that he was, noticed her start. "What's up?" he asked, peering at her over the folds of his monstrous neckcloth.

"Er—nothing. What were you saying about Lady Havelock?"

Alvanley frowned at her. "Not Havelock," he said, piqued. "Hatcham."

"Oh, yes," said Helen, praying that he would resume whatever anecdote he had been pouring into her ears. She kept her eyes on the Viscount's face, inwardly struggling to calm her panicky breathing and the erratic pounding of her heart. To her relief, Alvan-ley happily took up his tale.

Helen tried to ignore the grey gaze from across the room, tried to keep her mind engaged with all manner of distractions, afraid that if she allowed herself to meet Martin's eyes her fragile control would break. She could not let that happen—not in the middle of the Barhams' ballroom. Aside from anything else, Martin in his present mood was perfectly capable of taking advantage of such weakness to force her either to explain, or, if she was truly overcome, to accept his suit. Irrelevantly, Helen belatedly recalled Ferdie's warning. Her old friend had been right—rakes were dangerous in any circumstances.

Despite the sea of fashionable heads separating them, Martin's senses, finely tuned where Helen was concerned, detected her unease. Through the veils of rage that still clouded his reason, he realised she did not wish him to approach her. He was tempted to ig-nore her wishes and claim her for a waltz. Only his uncertainty over what might happen if he did, an un-nerving occurrence in itself, kept him from doing so. He was not even sure why he was here, other than that there had been nothing else he had wanted to do. See-ing Helen every evening had become a habit—a habit he was damned if he could break—a habit he had no wish to break. The events of the afternoon had left him more than confused. Anger still rode him, a potent influence, effectively countering all efforts at rational thought. From experience, he knew his mind would not function properly until he had worked it out of his system. How to achieve that laudable goal had him presently at a loss.

He knew his continued staring at Helen was causing comment but he could not stop. His mind was totally consumed by her; his eyes simply followed his thoughts. He saw Hedley Swayne and spared a moment to scowl at him. The fop took fright and disappeared into the crowd.

"Martin! How pleasant to see you again."

Martin looked down as a hand touched his arm. Seeing Serena Monckton—no, she was Lady Rochester now—smiling up at him, he repressed the urge to shake off her hand. He nodded casually and came away from the wall. "Serena."

Lady Rochester preened. It was the first time since he had reappeared as the Earl of Merton that she had managed to get Martin to use her first name. Perhaps there was hope for her yet?

Martin saw her reaction and inwardly cursed. He had studiously kept Serena at a distance, knowing how cloying her attention could be. He also trusted her not at all, a fact he felt was excusable. With his mind engrossed with Helen, he had forgotten to keep his defences up. Now he would have to repair the damage.

"I do *love* waltzing." Coquettishly, Lady Rochester smiled up at him. "So few of the men these days know how to do it properly. But you were with Wellington at Waterloo, weren't you?"

Stifling a curse, Martin reflected that no moss grew on Serena Monckton. She was shameless, propositioning him in such a way. Particularly him. He opened his mouth to put her in her place, when it suddenly occurred to him that perhaps here was an opportunity to demonstate to another shameless woman just what it felt like to be rejected. The very same shameless woman who had spent the afternoon on his daybed and then rejected him. A single glance over the crowd showed that Helen was sitting out the dance, seated on a chaise by Dorothea's side. Martin's eyes dropped to Serena's eager face, his lips curved in a practised smile. "I do believe that's a waltz starting up now. Shall we?"

He did not have to ask twice. But, immediately his feet started to circle, Martin wished he had thought twice. Dancing with Serena felt all wrong; she was not the woman he wanted in his arms. Gripped by a sudden sense of foreboding, Martin glanced over the heads of the dancers. Helen had not seen them yet. But many others had. He had made a habit of dancing with Helen Walford alone; his sudden appearance on the dance-floor with another woman in his arms, Serena Monckton at that, while Helen was in the room and unengaged, was, Martin belatedly realised, a somewhat obvious insult. The full enormity of his mistake hit him when he again looked Helen's way. They were much closer now. She had seen them; the expression in her large green eyes cut him to the core. Abruptly, she looked down and away, saying something to distract Dorothea, who was staring at him in undisguised fury.

Martin felt chilled. He waltzed automatically, paying no attention at all to Serena's chatter. When their revolutions took them past the chaise where Helen had been, he saw that it was empty. The third time around, and Dorothea was back, alone, staring daggers at him.

Helen had left the ball.

Because of him. He had hurt her and she had fled, not something she would readily do, having, as he knew, no liking for appearing in *on-dits*.

An odd numbness had closed about his heart; his mind refused to function at all. As soon as the dance ended, Martin bowed over Serena's hand and, leaving her standing by the side of the room, paid his respects to his by now curious hostess and left.

From the shadows of a potted palm decorating the side of the room, Damian watched Martin depart and rejoiced. Better and better. After that little scene, there was no chance of his brother and Lady Walford patching things up. Particularly not when the story he had spent the evening seeding into fertile soil took root. It would take a day or so, but after that he would be home and hosed, past the post, safe and sound.

He had decided that, in the circumstances, he would do well to attend a few of the *ton* assemblies, just until the danger of Lady Walford was past. Clearly, he would not have to suffer such boring gatherings for much longer. Virtually the entire ballroom had noticed the incident. Inwardly, Damian hugged himself. Whatever had possessed Martin to take such drastic action he could not imagine but he had to admit that, when his brother struck, he was effective. Lady Rochester was still standing a little way away, trying to pretend that Martin had truly been interested in her. Not that anyone would believe that. Feeling in unexpected charity with his brother, Damian decided to do him a favour.

He strolled to her ladyship's side and waited until the ageing roué who was currently bending her ear departed before nodding his greeting. "Helpful of you to give Martin a hand."

Serena scowled. "Whatever do you mean, sir?"

Her peevish tone brought out the devil in Damian. "Oh, I think you know." He watched as Lady Rochester's face purpled. "Who knows?" he continued smoothly before she could explode. "Perhaps Martin might be grateful in a way you'd appreciate, now he's terminated his relationship with Lady Walford and will no longer be availing himself of her charms."

Serena's eyes grew round, and then even rounder as the full implication of what he was saying sank in. "You mean...?" Her voice was an incredulous whisper.

Damian looked surprised. "Didn't you know? I thought everyone did. Ah well." He shrugged. "Just goes to show, don't it?" And with that he moved away, perfectly sure he had warned Lady Rochester off, too. For if Martin could seduce and ruin a woman of Lady Walford's calibre, it stood to reason that he would make short work of such as Lady Rochester.

Left alone, Serena took a long moment to sort out how what she had just heard could be used to greatest effect. She was perfectly well aware that Martin had only waltzed with her to hurt Helen Walford. The fiend had not so much as glanced properly at her—she was finished with trying to attract his notice. But she could not believe he was finished with the beautiful widow. From where she had stood, it had been blatantly obvious that he was still obsessed with Lady Walford. She had no quarrel with Helen Walford, just as long as she did not marry Martin Willesden. She herself held no illusion that she could ever fill that position—not now. But she drew the line at the thought of Martin enjoying his wife. Better anyone than Lady Walford. The rumour Damian was spreading, true or not, would surely cook Lady Walford's goose. And, if Martin was truly enamoured of Helen Walford, as Serena had every reason to suspect, then such an outcome would cause him grief.

Coolly, Lady Rochester smiled. None knew better than she that her long-ago claim of rape had been entirely without foundation. None knew better than she how furious Martin Willesden had made her by denying it and then accepting exile rather than marry her. Time had healed some of the wounds, but she saw no reason not to do what she could to spread Damian's delightful rumour.

Buoyed by a pleasant sense of mischief, she moved into the crowd to see what she could do.

His frown still black, Martin strode into his library. He shut the door with a decided click, then crossed to the sideboard and poured himself a generous quantity of brandy before slumping into the armchair by the fire.

Why? What had possessed him to make such an error of judgement? Never before had he made such a wrong-footed move. He had let his temper take control and it had led him off track. His equilibrium was out of kilter—he was dangerously adrift.

If this was what love did to a man, he was not sure he approved.

With a frustrated groan, he placed his glass on the table beside him and ran his hands over his face. He had hurt her. Dammit—all he wanted to do was make the wretched woman happy. Instead, he had succeeded in making them both miserable. The urge to go around to Half Moon Street and knock on her door until she let him in grew.

Reluctantly, Martin quashed the impulse and reached for his glass.

Enough of histrionics—they had landed him in a worse state than he had been in before. He was more than old enough to know better.

And, speaking of knowing better, did he really want to marry a woman who allowed herself to be seduced while having absolutely no intention of marrying her seducer? A difficult question, given that he had been the seducer and he had not married anyone before. Martin grimaced and took a long sip of brandy. Regardless of present appearance, regardless of her words, he knew, as only a rake could, that Helen Walford was not promiscuous. Why then her refusal?

For a long while, he stared at the fire while the long case clock in the corner ticked on. The sheer fury he had felt when he had understood her intention of refusing him again, when he had realised that the woman he wanted to place before his fireplace was the sort who could walk away from intimacy without a second thought, still seethed, scrambling his wits.

He shook his head in frustration. It was no good. He could not think straight with his mind in such turmoil. Best to get away, to get out of it, until his temper died and he could consider the matter more calmly. Right now, he was not even sure what he wanted any more, let alone how best to achieve it. His agent at Merton had written, begging his attendance. The decorators were there, making his dream a reality; he should see how they were progressing. He would go down for a few days. Perhaps the peace of the Hermitage would help him sort things out, decide where he stood, what he wanted to do.

Decision made, Martin rose and drained his glass. For a long moment, he stood stock-still, staring at the embers dying in the grate. Then, deliberately, he flung the glass into the fireplace. With a brittle tinkle, it shattered, sending crystal shards flying.

His jaw set, Martin swung on his heel and left the room.

The first intimation Helen had that anything at all was wrong came two days later, when she finally stirred herself from her lethargy to go driving in the Park with Cecily Fanshawe. It was her first outing since the disaster of the Barham House ball. Thankfully, Cecily had missed the ball through indisposition. As always bubbling with enthusiasm, she prattled on, giving Helen every opportunity to rest her weary mind.

She was worn out—depressed, hurt and heartweary. The sight of Martin waltzing with Lady Rochester had caused her far more pain than she had been prepared for. She had thought she would be able to weather any such sight, knowing it would come some time. Her nerves had not been up to it that night. His action and her reaction would have caused comment, she knew. Consequently, when she detected the first few whispers, she made nothing of them.

But by the time she and Cecily had gone halfway around the circuit, Helen knew that something more serious was in the wind. There was a coolness in the air. A number of matrons with marriageable daughters drew back from her smile.

It was Ferdie who confirmed her suspicions. He waved to them from the side of the carriageway in the most popular section of the route. When the carriage came to a halt, he opened the door. "Want to talk to you," he said to Helen. He nodded to Cecily, with whom he was well-acquainted, then climbed into the carriage. "Rather think it's time you dropped Helen home. I need to talk to her alone."

Cecily frowned. "But we've only just arrived."

"Never mind. Plenty to keep you busy at home, I dare say."

Cecily glared at Ferdie; Ferdie stared vacantly back. It was Cecily who gave way. "Oh, very well!" she said, and leaned forward to give her coachman directions.

Helen had not thought her heart could have sunk lower than it already had, but, as Ferdie engaged them both in inconsequential patter, she felt the leaden weight in her chest descend to her slippers. But she refused to let herself worry—not until she had heard what Ferdie had to say.

Cecily dropped them off in Half Moon Street, airily

declining an offer of refreshment. "I hope I know when I'm not wanted," she said, looking pointedly at Ferdie.

Ferdie grinned. "Not up to snuff yet, I'm afraid. Being married don't make you older."

Cecily put her nose in the air and, miffed, departed.

Inside her drawing-room, Helen found another visitor waiting. Dorothea was pacing before the unlighted fire. She looked up as they entered. "Thank goodness!" she said. "I hoped you wouldn't be long."

Ferdie entered behind Helen. Dorothea greeted him with relief. "You're just the person we need."

Ferdie took the unusual welcome in his stride. "Got rid of your sister, though. Didn't think she'd take it too well. Never know what she might dash off and do."

"Very true," Dorothea agreed feelingly.

"Do you mind," said Helen, sinking into an armchair, "telling me what all this is about?" She had a nasty suspicion but she wanted to hear it stated plainly.

The simple question succeeded in striking both her visitors dumb. They looked at her, then, rather uncomfortably, at each other.

Helen sighed. "Is it about me and Martin Willesden?"

Dorothea sank on to the chaise. "Yes." She waited while Ferdie drew up another chair and sat down. "There are rumours going the rounds. Perhaps one might expect it, after the Barham ball. But what I've heard this morning seems rather more than can be excused." She raised her large green eyes to Helen's in a gently questioning glance.

Helen held Dorothea's gaze for a moment, then sighed and looked to Ferdie. "You've heard them, too?"

Ferdie, unaccustomedly serious, nodded. "At White's."

Helen closed her eyes. White's. That meant it was all about town.

"The tales suggest," Dorothea began, "that you…have been… Martin Willesden's mistress." She waited, but Helen did not open her eyes. "Is it true?" she asked gently.

"Would it matter?" Helen returned, her weariness very evident in her tone. She opened her eyes, raising her brows in disdain.

It was Ferdie who answered. "'Fraid not." He paused, then continued, "The thing we need to do now is decide how to quash 'em."

"Yes," agreed Dorothea. "And I'm very much afraid, Helen, that you'll have to face it out. Marc's furious. After all, you first met Martin in our house. It was all I could do to persuade him to do nothing until I'd talked to you."

Helen's eyes widened. Hazelmere after Martin? In truth, she could not predict who would be the victor in such a contest—they were both extraordinarily powerful men in every way. But Hazelmere had solid social acceptability on his side—and Dorothea. Abruptly, Helen sat up, reaching across to lay a supplicating hand on Dorothea's sleeve. "You must promise me you'll make Marc promise not to do anything—anything at all—until he hears from me." Helen stared at Dorothea earnestly. "Promise?"

A worried frown in her eyes, Dorothea grimaced. "I promise to *try*. But you know as well as I that on some issues Marc won't be led."

That was indisputably true. Helen nodded her acceptance of Dorothea's limited offer. She sank back into her chair. "I need to think."

"Best thing to do is to carry on as usual," said Ferdie. "Merton'll have to play his part. If neither of you gets the wind up, it'll all blow over."

Dully, Helen nodded. "Yes. I suppose that's true." With a visible effort, she put aside her depression to smile at her guests. "With friends like you, I'm sure we'll get by."

Dorothea rose, shaking out her skirts. "I'll leave you to your thoughts. If you need any additional support, you know you can call on us for whatever you need. Meanwhile, we'll do what we can to dampen the interest."

Helen nodded her thanks.

Ferdie rose, too. "I'll come with you," he said to Dorothea. "Might help if I saw Hazelmere."

Both Dorothea and Helen welcomed this magnanimous offer.

After seeing her guests out, Helen returned to her small drawing-room to slump, even more weary than before, into her armchair. She struggled to make sense of what had happened. How had the story of her afternoon with Martin got out? No one had seen her leave Martin's house—his careful butler had seen to that. And, against Martin's orders, he had sent her home in one of the Merton coaches, but an unmarked one, with no crest on the door to give her away.

Had Martin spread the tale—to hurt her? Given the fact that he had deliberately and so very publicly flayed her feelings by waltzing with Lady Rochester—of all women—under her nose, she felt reasonably sure that he was capable of anything. Knowing that her standing in society was one of the few assets she had left, had he set out to strip her of that, too? Helen bit her lip. A sickening sense of betrayal threatened to engulf her. Determined to see things clearly, she forced herself to think long and hard but, in the end, could not believe it of him. He might strike out at her in anger, as he had done at the Barhams', but to seek to pull her down by making public what they had shared that afternoon was not the action of a gentleman. And, beneath his rakehell exterior, Martin Willesden was every inch a gentleman.

The only proof she needed of that was her memory. He had taken great pains to keep her safe, from himself as well as all others, on their unorthodox journey to London. An unscrupulous rake would have taken advantage; she blushed as she recalled their night at Cholderton—he had certainly had opportunity enough.

No—whoever had spread the tale of their afternoon together, it was not, could not be, Martin. Nevertheless, the uncertainty added yet another bruise to her already battered heart.

After half an hour's painful cogitation, she succeeded in convincing herself that she would have to see Martin, to discuss what they should do. He must have heard the rumours by now.

Reluctantly, Helen rose and crossed to the small escritoire which stood before the window. She sat and pulled a blank sheet of paper towards her. After mending her quill, she spent fifteen minutes staring fruitlessly into space. In the end, she shook herself in disgust. Without allowing herself any time to think further, she dashed off a note to the Earl of Merton.

The answer came back two hours later. The Earl of Merton, wrote his secretary, was presently in the country. It was not known when he would be back but her letter would be shown to him instantly on his return.

Helen stared at the plain note, reading the two sentences over and over. Ten minutes passed, then twenty. Finally, as the light started to wane, she stirred. Crumpling the note into a ball, she dropped it into the grate. Then, slowly, she went to the door and climbed the stairs to her chamber.

She lay on her bed and stared at the ceiling. She was alone. Not an unusual occurrence in her life, but it felt much worse this time. Insensibly, Martin had been with her ever since their first meeting in the woods. Now he had withdrawn, at the very moment when she most needed his strength.

What was she to do? That refrain played over and over in her head. The shadows lengthened. Outside, darkness fell. Inside her chamber, the outlook was bleak. In Martin's absence, she could not readily face down the rumours, scotch the scandal by simply denying its truth. Together, they could have pulled it off easily enough, even though, given their present situation, the effort would have cost both of them dearly. Without Martin, she did not have the strength to hold her head high until his return. Who knew when he might come back?

What were the alternatives? Helen bit her lower lip and frowned. If she retired from town for the rest of the Season, there was every likelihood that some other scandal would blow up to eclipse hers. Hazelmere, she knew, would not support such a course, tacitly admitting as it did that there was some substance to the rumours. But she was not a green girl. She was a widow of twenty-six. The *ton* was inclined to turn a blind eye to such matters, as long as the affair was not paraded before their collective eyes. As theirs had been. The cheapest price to secure her future acceptance seemed to be a sojourn in the country. She had little doubt that next year she would be able to return to town and join in the Season as if nothing untoward had occurred.

So the country it would be. But where? Unseeing, Helen stared into the gathering gloom. Hazelmere's estates were always open to her but, given that her absence from town would be against his wishes, she did not feel at ease with such a solution. There was Heliotrope Cottage, of course—her only remaining land, all five acres of it, in west Cornwall. The cottage was a tiny place, just big enough for Janet and herself. Hazelmere had always been against her staying there, on the grounds that she would be without male protection.

But Cornwall was a long way from London. Perhaps, in the isolation of the country, her broken heart would mend faster?

With a sigh, Helen sat up and swung her feet to the floor. There was no sense in thinking further—there was nowhere else to think of. Heliotrope Cottage it would have to be. She rose and crossed to the bell-pull. If Janet packed tonight, she could close the house in the morning and hire a chaise to take them down. Three days would see her far from the capital, far from the grey eyes that haunted her dreams.

Late that night, with all her plans made and her orders given, Helen sank into her bed and closed her eyes. She had decided not to tell anyone of her decision. They would only argue and, at the moment, she was not up to arguing back. No one would worry, however, for, with the knocker off the door and Janet gone, they would know she had shut up her house and gone away. Her dearest friends, those whose approval she valued, were all close enough to respect her wish for privacy. After Christmas, perhaps, she could visit Dorothea once her friend had returned to Hazelmere.

With a little sigh, Helen tried to relax, waiting for sleep to claim her, wondering irrelevantly how long it would be before slumber ceased to bring the image of grey eyes in its train.

Chapter Ten

Hammering still echoed throughout the ground floor of the Hermitage. Martin paced around the new conservatory, added at the back of the ballroom, admiring his new domain. It was all coming together much as he had planned.

The decorators would take another week to complete their work; the carpenters were expected to leave tomorrow. The sharp tang of new wood mixed with the smell of freshly mown grass. Not to be outdone by their house-bound rivals, the small army of gardeners he had hired to transform the wilderness back into landscaped grounds had taken full advantage of the fine weather. He had noticed the change immediately he had arrived. The drive had been cleared and newly gravelled, the huge wrought-iron gates that had hung for centuries at the main entrance to the estate had been cleaned and rehung. At the sight, Joshua's grumbles, all but constant since London, had abruptly ceased.

Martin leaned both hands on the sill of an open window and breathed deeply. Everywhere he looked, the evidence of his success leaped forward to greet him. Soon, his dream would be a reality; the Hermitage would be fit to take its rightful place as a centre of fashionable living once more, a suitable home for him—and his family.

At the thought, his mood clouded.

His success on one front had not been mirrored on the other. And now he was no longer sure which was the more important. Before he had met Helen Walford, restoring the Hermitage had been his principal goal. Now, with that goal in sight, he was looking far further ahead, beyond having his house, to fulfilling what he recognised as an even more basic need. He would soon have his house—he needed a family to fill it.

And, try as he might, there was only one woman he could picture in that all-important position before his fireplace. His mind was not capable of letting go of the image of Helen Walford, the flames gilding her glorious hair, with his son balanced on her hip.

From being merely an aim, marrying Helen Walford had become an obsession. He knew himself well enough to accept that if he did not marry her he would marry no one. His dream of a family inhabiting his home would never materialise.

He was determined that it would—every bit as determined as she seemed to be to fight shy of marrying him.

She was in for a shock.

He was not giving up.

Martin smiled a twisted smile. The life of a rake, a rich, well-born rake, was hardly conducive to teaching one self-sacrifice. He had no intention of giving up his dream. But how to convince Helen to go along with it was more than he had yet worked out.

Noticing the shadows lengthening, he shook free of his reverie. He would think more on the matter later. Right now, he was due for some light entertainment.

Quickly crossing the conservatory and striding through the refurbished ballroom, he paused to cast a critical eye over the now elegant dining-room before taking the stairs two at a time. He strode towards his mother's rooms, noting with deep satisfaction how different the atmosphere in the long corridors now was. Gone was the must and the damp. Newly painted woodwork gleamed, and the floor was well-buffed and covered with bright runners. Windows, long stuck, had been repaired and the fresh autumn air danced in. Slim tables stood along the walls, some overhung by paintings, others sporting vases filled with bright flowers. Martin stopped by one such and chose a pink for his buttonhole.

Tucking it into position, he fronted his mother's door. He knocked. When she called to him to enter, he grinned in wicked anticipation and obeyed.

Catherine Willesden looked up as he entered, unsurprised, for she knew his knock by now. To her amazement, Martin had taken to dropping by her room in the late afternoons, not to cause any furore but merely to chat. At first she had been stunned, then disarmed. He had a sharp eye and a ready wit, very reminiscent of his father. She had enjoyed his company far more than she would ever admit.

Regally, she nodded and watched as he appropriated

one of her gnarled hands and bent to kiss it. Then he placed a dutiful kiss on her cheek and stood back.

"I've a surprise for you." Martin smiled down at her.

Lady Catherine struggled to remain immune. "Oh? What?"

"I can't possibly tell you, or it wouldn't be a surprise." Martin watched his mother's eyes narrow.

"My dear sir, if you think I'm about to play guessing games with you, you're mistaken."

"Naturally not," Martin replied. He found his mother's acerbity refreshing and took the greatest delight in teasing her. "I would never presume to play games with you, ma'am."

"Huh!" was his mother's instant response.

"But you're distracting me from your surprise. You'll have to come downstairs to get it."

Lady Catherine frowned at her son. "I've not been downstairs for well nigh ten years—as you well know."

"I know nothing of the sort. If you were well enough to look about the place six weeks ago, you must be well enough to see my surprise." Martin watched as his mother's crabbed fingers picked at the edge of her shawl.

"Oh," said the Dowager. "You heard about that."

"Yes," Martin said, his tone several shades more gentle. "But there was no need for you to see it like that." He had learned that, when he'd left so abruptly after his first visit, she had insisted on being carried down to view the state she had by then guessed the house had disintegrated into.

"It was awful." Lady Catherine shuddered. "I couldn't even recognise some of the rooms."

Her grief for her lost dreams, the images she had carried for so many years destroyed when she had seen the decay of her home, shadowed her voice.

"Enough of the past. It's all gone." Martin stooped and scooped her into his arms. Lady Catherine bit back a squeal and clutched at him, then glared when he smiled at her. Reflecting that Helen was at least twice his mother's weight, Martin swung towards the door. His eyes fell on Melissa's bent head. "Melissa—are you coming? Dinner will be downstairs tonight—come with us by all means, if you've a mind to see the workings, or come to the drawing-room at six."

Melissa gawked at him. Dismissing her from his mind, Martin strode towards the door.

"Downstairs?" Lady Catherine finally found her tongue. "I have my dinner up here. On a tray."

Martin shook his head. "Not any more. Now that we have a habitable dining-room, while I'm in residence, you'll take your proper place at the end of my table." He made his voice sound stern, as if he was issuing an order.

He glanced sidelong at his mother. She did not know what to say. On the one hand, she did not like to accept what might just be his charity; on the other, she longed to be seated at her table again. Martin grinned and strode along the corridor to the stairs.

Catherine Willesden barely noticed the bright new furnishings through the veil of tears clouding her eyes. She had never, ever valued Martin and his arrogant, impulsive ways as he deserved. She knew quite well that it was because he had never been tractable, as his brothers had always been. But, while George had brought the place to ruin, Martin had set it to rights. Her heart had been broken when she had finally understood the full sum of the mess—Mr Matthews had been distressingly blunt when she had asked. Now it was as if a magic wand had been waved—it was even better than she recalled.

Not that she could tell Martin that—the rogue would be insufferable. As they reached the bottom of the stairs, she blinked rapidly. Martin eased her into a chair which had been set waiting. She settled her skirts as he stood back.

Suddenly, the chair started to move.

"Martin!" The Dowager awkwardly grabbed at the arms of the chair.

Her reprobate son chuckled—actually chuckled!

"It's all right. I've got hold of it." Martin pushed the chair slowly forward. "It's a wheelchair. Set on wheels so you can be moved about easily. See?" He stopped and showed her the wheels. "I saw it in London. I thought you might find it useful."

"I dare say," said his mother, vainly trying to sound as forbidding as usual.

She failed. Martin pushed her on to the drawing-room, a smile of satisfaction on his face.

He took her through all the main rooms, explaining how those yet unfinished were to be decorated. To his surprise, she made no demur at any of his choices, going so far as to add some suggestions of her own. At five o'clock, totally in charity one with the other, they parted to dress for dinner.

The meal was the first they had shared in over thirteen years. Despite that fact, there was no constraint, beyond that provided by Melissa, who sat, dumb, throughout. Martin tried to include her in their conversation; in the end, his mother grimaced at him and shook her head.

But at the end of the evening, after tea taken in the comfort of the fashionable blue and white drawing-room, his mother declined his offer to carry her upstairs.

"Melissa can go," she said, waving her ineffectual daughter-in-law away. She turned to look at Martin. "Are you going to sit in the library?"

Martin eyed her suspiciously. "Yes."

"Good! You can wheel me in there. I want to talk to you."

Reflecting that his mother had not changed all that much in thirteen years, Martin complied, a rueful smile hovering about his lips.

The library had been the first room rendered habitable by the efforts of his decorators. It had always been the room in which his father had sat. Simple but elegant furniture in the classic style Martin favoured was scattered in a deceptively ad hoc manner throughout the long room; warm wooden bookshelves, ceiling high, were packed with leather-bound tomes. Martin dutifully wheeled his mother in, wondering just what she had on her mind. But, when he had settled her before the fireplace, she did not seem to know where to begin.

The Dowager Countess tried to remind herself she was just that, and the mother of the gentleman lounging at his ease in the latest style of wing chair opposite her. She eyed the elegant figure, clad in a simple yet exquisitely tailored blue coat and black knee-breeches, with some hesitation. What she felt she had to say was sensitive—or at least likely to be, given her relationship with this unpredictable son. She drew a careful breath and began. "As you know, I have always been kept informed of happenings in town by my friends. They write to me, telling me all the latest news and *on-dits*."

Martin suppressed the impulse to put an immediate halt to the conversation. Instead, he raised one brow coldly. "Indeed?"

The Dowager stiffened. "You needn't be so defensive," she said. Really, he was his father all over again. One only had to mention something he did not want to discuss and he withdrew. "I merely wished to tell you," she went on before he had a chance to hinder her, "that it has come to my notice that you appear to have a great interest in Helen Walford. To wit, everyone expects you to offer for her. As you never were witless, I assume that means you do intend to marry her. My only aim in mentioning the matter is to assure you that I will not raise any objection— even though I'm perfectly aware you wouldn't pay any attention if I did," she added ascerbically. "I recall Lady Walford's story and was a little acquainted with her parents. From everything I've heard, she's eminently suitable to be your countess."

To Martin's astonishment, Lady Catherine paused, frowning, then added, "I must say, I couldn't imagine you taking a bright little deb to wife—you'd probably strangle her before the honeymoon was over. Or, more likely, dump her on me.''

The Dowager raised her eyes to her son's, and beheld the amusement therein. Her eyes narrowed. ''Which brings me to my point. I don't know what state the Dower House is in, but if you would make arrangements to have it refurbished by this firm you're dealing with I'd be obliged.''

When Martin made no immediate comment, she added, ''I'll stand the nonsense, naturally.''

''Naturally be damned.'' Martin put his glass of port down on a table beside his chair and leaned forward so that his mother could see his face clearly. ''You've lived in those rooms above stairs for...oh, yes—the past ten years. You've lived in this house for close on fifty. Neither I nor my wife would wish to see you leave.''

For a moment, his mother stared at him, wanting to accept his decree yet unwilling to be suffered out of pity.

''Don't be daft,'' the Dowager eventally returned, although the phrase lacked strength. ''Your wife will hardly want me and Melissa cluttering up her house.''

Martin laughed and leaned back in his chair. ''I'd forgotten Melissa,'' he admitted, his eyes twinkling. ''Who knows?'' he said, his smile twisting. ''Perhaps Fair Juno will be able to get her to speak.''

''Who?''

With a quick smile for his parent's confusion, he brushed the question aside. ''Regardless of all else, I can assure you Helen will expect you to continue here. I suspect you'll deal famously. Aside from anything

else, I imagine I'll be facing an unholy alliance every time I want to do anything the least unconventional. You never know, she might need your support."
When the Dowager still looked unconvinced, he added pensively, "And then there's always the children to be looked after."

"Children?" His mother's stunned expression suggested she had leaped rather further than he had intended.

Martin grinned. "Not yet. Rake though I am, I suspect that they had better come after we are wed."

His mother looked decidedly relieved.

"And now, if I've put all your worries to rest, I'll take you upstairs." Martin rose. He scooped his mother, thoughtful and silent, into his arms. They were on the stairs when she asked, "So you are going to marry Helen Walford?"

"Indubitably," Martin replied. "As the sun rises in the east, as one day follows another—you may count on it."

Later, when he had returned to the library and his port, his words echoed in his mind. He had spoken the truth. The only question remaining was how to get his prospective bride to agree.

He lounged in his chair, stretching his long legs before him. Why she insisted on refusing his suit was still a mystery. But he felt certain, now, that he had misunderstood the nature of the hurdle which stood in his path. It was clearly not physical—which was something of a relief. Her reticence had to stem from some more simple problem—possibly a reluctance to place any faith in a man's avowed devotion? Martin raised his brows. Given her first husband's reputation, that was not hard to believe. Whatever the problem, he was confident of finding the answer. His anger at her apparent promiscuity had receded, draining away even as his need for her grew more acute. Rational thought now prevailed; he knew she was not promiscuous; her acts were driven by some deeper motive. He still faced a problem but it was not insurmountable. But he needed to solve it soon. With every passing day, he missed her more. There was nothing—*nothing*—that was more important to him.

With a gesture of decision, Martin drained his glass. There were no objections to be considered, no ramifications to be weighed. Tomorrow, he would return to town and see her.

He would woo her—he would win her. And then he would bring her home.

Two days later, at the fashionable hour of noon, Martin turned his bays into the familiar precinct of Half Moon Street. He drew them smartly to the kerb before Helen's narrow-fronted house. Joshua jumped down and ran to their heads. Martin threw him the reins. "I don't know how long I'll be. Walk 'em if necessary."

Martin strode purposefully up the steps. She was going to say yes this time. He was not going to leave until she did. He raised his hand to the knocker—and froze.

The knocker was off the door.

He stared at the empty hinge from which it normally

hung—a small brass weight in the shape of a bell. Only its outline remained.

Helen had gone out of town.

Abruptly, Martin turned on his heel and strode back to his curricle. Surprised by his master's sudden return, Joshua glanced up and opened his mouth, then shut it again. Silently, he handed his master the reins and scrambled up behind. From long experience, he knew better than to ask questions when Mr Martin looked like thunder.

Heading his team back into the traffic, Martin considered the Park, then decided against it. The last thing he needed was inconsequential chatter. He turned his horses towards Grosvenor Square mews. Soon, he was striding back and forth before the fireplace in his library, feeling caged and impotent.

Why? Why had she left?

The talk after the Barhams' ball could not have been that bad. He might have committed a blunder under stress but he knew his London. The tattlemongers would have twittered over it for all of twenty-four hours, then forgotten it entirely.

So why had she gone?

To avoid him?

Martin thrust the thought aside, then, when no other explanation offered, reluctantly brought it back for examination. Too restless to sit, he prowled the room. Could she have thought he would repeat his performance—with Selina or whoever—and make her life a misery? With a frustrated growl, he shook his head. No—no he could not believe she would imagine he would hurt her—well, not more than the Barham effort. Given that they had developed a degree of understanding through the long hours they had spent together, she would know he would calm down after that—after he had seen her distress. Hell, he wanted to marry the woman—she could not believe he would hurt her. Could she?

Sunk in semi-guilt, Martin prowled the room.

A sudden realisation brought him to a halt. He raised his head and stared, unseeing, at his own reflection in the mirror above the mantelpiece. She could not have gone off to escape him—because he had taken himself off. With a sigh of relief, he sank into a chair. She would have realised within a day or so that he had left the capital. He doubted her friends would have sanctioned a withdrawal before that. So...

So why had she left? Perhaps the reason had nothing to do with their relationship? She had no immediate family; her friends were a select few, all of whom were presently residing in London. Perhaps Dorothea had taken ill and retired to the country? Recalling the last sight he had had of Hazelmere's lovely bride, Martin rejected that idea as unlikely.

Had Helen been forced to leave by something else entirely? The thought jerked Martin upright. After a moment's cogitation, he rose and tugged the bell-pull, insensibly relieved to have something concrete to do.

When Hillthorpe answered, he asked for Joshua.

Moments later, "You wanted me, guv'nor?" broke across Martin's thoughts. He raised his head and beckoned Joshua closer.

"That gentleman I had you watch—Hedley

Swayne. You mentioned you'd struck up a relationship with his man?''

Joshua wriggled his shoulders. ''Not so much a re- lationship as a drinking partnership, if you take my meaning?''

Martin did. He smiled, a touch grimly. ''That will do admirably. I want you to get over there now and find out what you can of Mr Swayne's recent exploits. Particularly, if he's had any unusual visitors—or if he's dressed down to attend any meeting. I expect that's something his man would notice.''

''Oh, he'd notice right enough. Went on a treat over the gent's new coloured silk neckerchiefs last time I saw him. The way he tells it, the swell only thinks of the rags on his back.''

Martin raised a brow. ''That's certainly the way he appears—but I know for certain there's at least one other thing Hedley Swayne exercises his wits over.'' He fixed Joshua with a commanding eye. ''I want to know what Hedley Swayne's been up to this week— and I want to know as soon as possible.''

''Right-ho, guv'nor.''

With a cheery half-salute, Joshua left.

He was back far faster than Martin had anticipated.

''He's gone—bolted.''

''What?'' Martin exploded out of the chair he had slumped into. ''When?''

''Seems like the gentleman's taken hisself and his man and his usual escort—whatever that might mean—off to his estates. In Cornwall, they be, so the housekeeper said. They left two days ago.''

"Two days," Martin mused, pacing back and forth on the hearthrug. "Any reason given?"

Joshua shook his head. He watched his master stalk the room, then, when no further orders came his way, he asked, "D'ye want me to keep watch—to see when he returns?"

Martin stopped his pacing. He looked at Joshua, then slowly shook his head. "I've a nasty suspicion that when he returns it'll be too late." With a nod, he dismissed Joshua and renewed his striding. It helped him to think.

There was no necessary connection between Helen's leaving town and Hedley Swayne's departure. That did not mean there wasn't one. Martin swore. He wished he had followed up the peculiar Mr Swayne's abduction attempt. His preoccupation with making Helen Walford his wife—and thus safe from such as Hedley Swayne—had pushed that little incident to the back of his mind. His memories of it had been overlaid by far more interesting recollections of Helen herself.

Shaking such recollections aside, Martin acknowledged his worries. He wanted answers and the only way of finding them was to ask questions—of the right people. And, in this instance, the right people were undoubtedly the Hazelmeres.

When a rapid reconnoitre of the gentlemen's clubs drew a blank, Martin presented himself at Hazelmere House. To his surprise, although Mytton was as gracious as ever and went immediately to inform his master, ensconced in his library, of his arrival, he was kept kicking his heels in the black-and white-tiled hall for what seemed like an age. Eventually, the library door opened.

Dorothea emerged, the heir in her arms.

If she had looked daggers at him at the Barhams', this afternoon she had added spears and crossbows to her armoury. Bemused, Martin reflected that he should, by all accounts, be dead.

With a decidedly cool nod, Dorothea turned on her heel and climbed the stairs. The stiffness of her spine bespoke her disapproval.

Martin raised his brows slightly at the sight. He was not overly surprised that she should still be so starchy—he had yet to make his peace with Helen and Dorothea was, after all, Helen's closest friend. But there was a haughtiness in her disapproval that evoked memories of how the matrons had looked at him thirteen years earlier.

Mytton approached. "His lordship will see you now, my lord."

There was nothing, of course, to be learned from Mytton's impassive countenance. Martin followed him to the library.

Inside, he discovered that his pricking thumbs were justified. Hazelmere was standing by the long French windows, open to the afternoon breeze. His stance, rigid and unyielding, warned Martin that something indeed was up, even before he drew close enough to see the stony hazel gaze.

Martin stopped by a chair, laying one hand on its back. He raised a laconic brow and sighed. "What am I supposed to have done now?"

There was an infinitesimal pause while Hazelmere

assimilated the information underlying that question. Then his features eased. "Don't you know?" he asked, his voice slightly strangled.

"Other than losing my head at the Barhams' the other night, I'm not aware that I've transgressed any of the immutable laws."

"Not even *before* the Barhams' ball?"

At the quiet question, Martin's gaze locked with his friend's. After a long moment, Martin moved around the chair in front of him and slowly sank into it. "Oh."

"Precisely." Slowly, Hazelmere came forward to sit in the chair facing his guest. "I take it I don't need to ask if it's true?"

Martin threw him a grimace. "I did say I was going to cure her, didn't I?"

Hazelmere acknowledged that with a resigned nod. "I hadn't, however, imagined you would allow such an item to become public property."

"Public property?" Martin was on his feet and pacing. "Bloody hell!" he growled. "How the hell did that get out?"

Hazelmere viewed his friend's agitation with transparent satisfaction. "I didn't think you knew anything about it."

He spoke softly, but Martin caught the quiet comment. He swung about, brows knit in a furious frown. "Of course I knew nothing of it! Why on earth...?" He stopped, struck, his face drained of expression. Slowly, he sank back into the chair. "Dorothea—and everyone else—thinks I let the information slip?"

Succinctly, Hazelmere nodded. "To Lady Rochester,'' he added. ''She was spreading the tale shortly after you danced so briefly with her at the Barhams.''

Martin groaned and sank his head into his hands. How had Serena found out? A more worrying thought surfaced. He looked up. ''Helen can't believe that surely?''

A frown had invaded Hazelmere's face ''To be perfectly honest, I don't know what Helen thinks—I haven't had a chance to ask her. She's disappeared—gone out of town. I'd hoped you might know where she was, but obviously that's not the case.''

''I came to ask if you knew where she was.'' Martin straightened, his worry overcoming his frown. ''I left town early on the morning after the ball. What exactly happened?''

Hazelmere told him, briefly, concisely. ''So Dorothea and Ferdie left her to think things through. The next morning, she left.''

''Damn!'' Martin stood again, automatically falling to pacing before the hearth. With an effort, he forced himself to evaluate the situation coolly. ''Luckily, the position's not irretrievable. Once we marry, it'll cease to be news.''

Hazelmere inclined his head in agreement. ''True. But, if you don't mind my curiosity, when, exactly, is the wedding?''

The glance Martin shot him contained equal parts of frustration and sheer exasperation. ''The witless wanton wouldn't accept.''

For once, the hazel eyes opened wide in honest surprise. Black brows rising, Hazelmere considered his wayward charge. "What on earth is she about?" he eventually asked.

"Damned if I know," Martin muttered. "But if I can lay hands on her, you can rely on me to shake some sense into her." Tired of pacing, he returned to his chair. "Have you any idea where she might have gone?"

Hazelmere frowned. "There aren't all that many options. I know she hasn't gone to one of my estates—I'd have heard by now. I can't imagine her going to an inn or any such."

Martin shook his head. "Too risky by half."

Nodding sagely, Hazelmere continued, "Which leaves Heliotrope Cottage."

Martin looked his question.

"As I recall, I told you that none of Helen's properties was saved from the collapse of the Walford estates?" At Martin's nod, Hazelmere said, "As far as substance goes, that's true. But Heliotrope Cottage was considered beneath the dignity of any gambler. Consequently, it's the one part of Helen's patrimony that remains hers. It's a tiny place on barely five acres. In Cornwall."

"Cornwall?"

At Martin's incredulous exclamation, Hazelmere blinked. "Yes. Cornwall. You know—it's that bit beyond Devon."

Martin brushed his levity aside. "I know where the damned place is but, what's more to the point, so does Hedley Swayne. His estates are there, too."

Hazelmere's hazel gaze was confused. "Quite a few people have estates in Cornwall."

"But," said Martin grimly, getting to his feet once more, "none of the others has tried to kidnap Helen."

Hazelmere blinked. "I beg your pardon?"

Pacing again, Martin threw his explanation over his shoulder. "I first met Helen not here but in a wood in Somerset, not far from Ilchester. She'd been grabbed from a ball by two ruffians. They were waiting with her for their client to arrive. From everything I've learned, that client was Hedley Swayne. Helen thought it was at the time."

Hazelmere met his glance, then fell to considering the facts. "It doesn't make sense," he eventually said.

"I know it doesn't make sense," Martin growled.

"We've all seen Swayne dancing about Helen's skirts, but I wouldn't have thought he'd have any real inclination in that direction."

Martin shook his head. "He's definitely not one of us." A moment later, he added, "There must be some reason that we can't see. But whatever it is I'd much rather Helen was safe before I shake the answer from Hedley Swayne."

With that, Hazelmere was in complete agreement. "Will you go down or will I?"

"Oh, I'll go, if you'll give me her direction. I intend having a very long talk with your wife's dearest friend. After that, I rather think we'll return by way of Merton." At the thought of taking Helen to the Hermitage, Martin's features eased for the first time that day.

Hazelmere nodded and stood. "I'll write the route down—it's not exactly straightforward."

Armed with a complicated set of directions which Hazelmere assured him would take him to the door of

Heliotrope Cottage, Martin departed from Hazelmere House, pausing at the last to request Hazelmere to speak to his wife regarding her killing glances.

As soon as he crossed his threshold in Grosvenor Square, Martin issued a stream of orders, which culminated in his sending Joshua scurrying to harness the bays while he strode upstairs to throw a selection of clothes into a bag. Laying shirts and a supply of freshly laundered cravats in the base of the bag, Martin grimaced. He would have to get a valet if he was set on observing all the niceties. Men such as he were expected to have one, but he had managed well enough without throughout his eventful life. Nevertheless, if he was to settle down to socially acceptable wedded bliss, a valet seemed inevitable. The idea of marriage halted him mid-stride.

Who knew what situation he would face in Cornwall? Who knew to what lengths he might have to go to convince Helen to say yes? All in all, the insurance of being able to secure his prize the very instant she agreed to his proposal seemed advisable.

A wry grin twisted Martin's lips. He resumed his packing, mentally rehearsing his plea to the Bishop of Winchester, a connection of his father's who would doubtless be only too pleased to do what he could to entangle a rake past redemption in the sacred toils of matrimony.

The bed at the Four Swans was lumpy. Ruefully reflecting that easy living had exacted a toll from his tolerance, Martin stretched out and closed his eyes. The day had been unwarrantedly full.

First, his arrival in London, full of his plans for fair Juno, plans which were dashed by her absence. Then his interview with Hazelmere, and his preparations for his journey. As it had been his secretary's day off, he had decided to go through the pile of mail placed waiting on his desk before quitting his house for an indeterminate time. He had found Helen's brief note in the pile, with a scrawled message from his secretary appended. Initially, he had been downcast that she had appealed for his help and he had not been there to assist her. Then the implication of her appeal had struck him.

Despite the hurt he had inflicted, she had not balked from summoning him; she had clearly envisaged being able to play a part, with him by her side to conceal their illicit liaison. All in all, it would not have been hard, together. They would simply have pretended nothing was amiss—none, he was sure, would have pressed the point.

But the important feature of her call for help was that she had been prepared to see him again, to speak with him again. That was, Martin felt, definitely encouraging.

He sighed and settled his shoulders. Things were looking up. The drive from London to Winchester had been accomplished in time for him to be invited to sup at his Grace's board. His ageing relative had proved much as he had imagined, but more curious than censorious. A special licence had been duly provided. Thus armed, he was looking forward to the second day after the next with keen anticipation.

Even if he left early the next morning, it would still

take him more than two days to reach Heliotrope Cottage. Two more days in which to polish his apologies and frame his proposal while keeping his cattle on the road. He had nearly landed them in a ditch this evening. He would have to make sure he kept sufficient wits functioning to drive; he could not bear any further delay.

He still could not fathom how the fact of their afternoon together had been broadcast to the *ton*. However, rake that he was, he recognised the added weapon the potential scandal gave him. It would have to be wielded with care, of course, and only if Helen still showed reluctance. No woman liked to feel jockeyed into any decision; none knew that better than he. Somehow, he would have to ensure that the idea of marrying him as the most socially acceptable course was subtly conveyed to his love.

No light had yet glowed on her reasons for refusing him; in truth, if she was simply too wary to try marriage again, the only way he could think of to convince her was to marry her and consequently demonstrate how wrong she was. A little gentle persuasion was surely excusable in such circumstances?

With a slight frown, Martin shook aside such quibbles and let his usual positive attitude resurface. He wanted Helen Walford to wife, therefore, however it came about, she would marry him. It was in her own best interests, after all.

The moonlight streamed in through the open window, a slight breeze wafted the net curtains. Martin felt sleep take hold. His dreams would doubtless be of the last inn bed he had slept in—and his fair companion in dreams.

Chapter Eleven

Was it two spoons of milk or only one? Helen rubbed a floury hand across her brow and struggled to remember Janet's instructions. She had sent her maid to the mill just outside the tiny village half a mile away, to buy more flour. Meanwhile, she had decided to use what was left and make some bread.

She had never cooked anything before—other than the pancakes she had assisted with during that night in the old barn. Even then, *he* had actually done the cooking. At the thought of him, whom she refused to acknowledge by name in the vain hope that that would assist her mind in forgetting him, Helen's eyes filled. Annoyed, she blinked rapidly. She sniffed. Damn! She had never been the sniffy sort but, ever since leaving London, she had hovered on the brink of tears. It would not do—she had to pull herself together and get on with her life. No matter how lacking in all enticement that life now seemed. For a while, he had filled her with hopes for the future. They had come to nought, but her life was not, in truth, any more drab than it had been before. She tried to reason with her emotions, to no avail. All they seemed capable of dwelling on was her misery at losing him.

Helen gritted her teeth and plunged both hands into her dough. Her sudden urge to action was simply an attempt to get some purpose, however inconsequential, into her life. The past five days had disappeared in a dull daze, the fine weather outside clouded by her misery. Heliotrope Cottage was comfortable enough but, without menservants, Janet had to do everything. Helen poked at the dough disparagingly and reflected that she would have to see about hiring a young girl to come in and help with the cleaning and cooking, and maybe find a gardener as well.

The kitchen was a sunny nook, part of the large room that made up the ground floor of the cottage. A window beside the table at which she stood looked out over the small kitchen garden. The plot was currently overgrown, choked with a full season's weeds, but reddish earth showed in one corner where Janet had made a start on clearing it. Helen breathed deeply of the tangy breeze wafting in through the open door of the cottage, to play with her curls before whisking out again through the back door. With a grimace, she regarded the floury mass in the copper basin. It must have been two spoonfuls.

She was replacing the milk jug on the dresser when the sound of horses' hooves and the sliding thump of heavy carriage wheels rolling down the rutted lane came to her ear. Helen froze. Then her heart started to pound, faster and faster as anticipation rose.

The cottage stood at the end of the lane; there was

no passing traffic. Who was it who had come to visit her?

The likely answer addled her wits.

Then she heard a voice, a light voice, giving instructions, and knew it was not the Earl of Merton who had called.

Disappointment sent her back to despair.

Consequently, when a sharp rap came on the doorframe, she made no move to take her hands from the copper basin, but called out, "Come in!" in as interested a tone as she could manage.

To her surprise, it was Hedley Swayne's slight figure that appeared in the doorway. "Lady Walford?"

Helen stifled her sigh. Country hospitality demanded that she at least invite him in for refreshment. "Come in, Mr Swayne." She waited until her unexpected visitor had mincingly picked his way across her small front room, his features registering disapproval of her rustic surrounds, before commenting, "I had hardly looked to see anyone from London hereabouts. To what do I owe the pleasure of your visit?"

"Dear lady." Hedley Swayne bowed effusively. "Just a neighbourly visit." When Helen looked her confusion, he added, "I own Creachley Manor."

Creachley Manor? Helen blinked. If that was so, Hedley was, in fact, her nearest neighbour. The lands attached to the Manor all but enclosed hers; it was the largest single holding in the immediate area.

"I see," she said. "How very thoughtful of you." She waved a whitened hand at a nearby chair and watched as Hedley disposed himself upon it, fussing about the arrangement of his coat-tails. Dismay was her predominant reaction—to his visit and to the news that he was so closely situated. She did not trust his airy excuse one bit. "But how did you know I was here?"

For an instant, Hedley's pale eyes went perfectly blank. "Er...ah, that is to say...heard about it. On the village grapevine, if you know what I mean."

Helen inclined her head civilly. Having lived in the country for most of her life, she knew perfectly well what he meant, but, although it often amazed her with its speed, no village grapevine worked that fast. She and Janet had arrived late in the evening; their post-chaise and post-boys had immediately returned to the road for London. Today was the first day anyone in the village could know of their arrival and that only through Janet's appearance at the mill. Hedley Swayne was lying, but to what purpose?

"Could I offer you some tea, sir?"

Hedley looked slightly perturbed at the suggestion. His roving gaze alighted on a small decanter on the sideboard. Helen saw it and correctly divined that the fastidious Mr Swayne did not partake of tea. "Or perhaps some cowslip wine would be more to your taste?"

To this, Hedley Swayne agreed readily. Sending silent thanks to her cook in London, who had slipped a bottle of her delicious wine into the provisions Janet had packed, Helen lifted her hands from her basin and looked in consternation at the gooey mess covering her fingers.

"Er...perhaps if you'd just tell me where the glasses are?"

Appeased by this show of neighbourly good sense, Helen directed Hedley to the cupboard beneath the sideboard. She watched as her visitor arose and helped himself, her brow creasing as she struggled to understand just what he was about this time. His visit was not driven by pure neighbourly concern, of that she was sure. But what did he hope to achieve? His dress was as finicky as ever, better suited to the Grand Strut than a small cottage in deepest Cornwall. The coat of puce cloth was offset by yellow pantaloons; a wide floppy yellow neckerchief tied in a bow proclaimed his allegiance to fashionable fripperies. As with most of the fops, he disdained the highly polished Hessians of the Corinthians, opting instead for heeled shoes, in this case sporting gold buckles. There was a gold pin in the neckerchief and a huge fob watch vied with a range of seals for prominence against a perfectly hideous purple embossed silk waistcoat. Considering the spectacle, Helen reflected that it was almost as if Hedley had dressed to impress. Unfortunately, in his present surroundings, he only succeeded in looking woefully out of place.

Her own dull olive gown, with its round neck and simple sleeves, was far more in keeping with the country atmosphere. Its colour did nothing for her complexion, drawn and sallow after days of weeping. Not that she cared. There was no reason to make the most of herself; she did not desire to impress her neighbours—not even be they Hedley Swayne.

Pouring himself a generous measure of cowslip wine, Hedley returned to his chair. ''I must say, dear

Lady Walford, that it's a pleasure to see a woman such as yourself engaged in such a womanly pursuit.''

Helen eyed his smile warily. His attitude was one of a man well-pleased, almost smug, as if he had solved some fiendishly difficult problem and was looking forward to claiming his prize. Helen's unease grew, but she merely nodded, wondering what to say next. Luckily, Hedley had an inexhaustible flow of patter. He rambled on, and, at first, she thought his direction aimless. Then, as she followed his recitation of *ton* events, she started to perceive a pattern to his revelations. They were all concerned with recent scandals and how these had adversely affected the women involved. In particular, how the unfortunate proceedings had affected the subsequent marriageability of the women involved. She made the right noises at the right places, which was all Hedley required to keep him going while she wondered if she dared guess at his summation.

It was as she had suspected.

''Actually,'' he said pausing to take a sip of his wine, ''I left the capital six days ago. So ennervating—the Season—don't you think?''

Helen murmured appropriately.

''And then, too,'' said Hedley, examining his fingernails, ''there was a distressing rumour going the rounds.''

And that, thought Helen, is enough. ''Indeed?'' She infused the single word with arctic iciness. To her dismay, the effect was not at all what she had hoped.

''My dear, dear Lady Walford!'' Hedley Swayne was on his feet and approaching.

Helen's eyes grew round as she saw him place his glass on the table. She stood rooted to the spot in surprise as he advanced on her, arms spread wide as if intending to scoop her ample charms into his embrace. When one arm slipped about her, Helen came to her senses with a jolt. "Mr Swayne!" She brought up her hands to ward him off. To her surprise, he jumped back, as if she had threatened him with a burning brand. Then she focused on her fingers and realised they were still liberally coated with dough.

When Hedley stared, nonplussed, at the threat to his immaculate suiting, Helen struggled to swallow her giggles. Determinedly, she replaced her hands in the dough. As long as her fingers constituted such deadly weapons, she was safe. "Mr Swayne," she reiterated, striving for calm. "I have no idea what rumours you have heard, but I assure you I do not wish to discuss them."

Hedley Swayne frowned, clearly piqued at having his orchestrated performance cut short. "All very well for you to say, m'dear lady," he said peevishly. "But people will talk, y'know."

"I dare say," Helen replied discouragingly. "But whatever they might say is of no concern to me. Rumour is rumour and nothing more."

"Ah, yes. But this rumour is rather more specific than usual," Hedley continued, then, when he glanced up at his hostess and saw the wrath gathering in her clear eyes, he hurriedly expostulated, "But that wasn't what I came here to say—dear me, no!"

"Mr Swayne," said Helen, suddenly very weary of his company, "I really don't think that you could have anything to say, on that subject or any other, that I wish to hear.''

"Now don't be too hasty, dear lady.'' Hedley Swayne took a step back and, to Helen's wary gaze, seemed to reorganise his forces. "I suggest you listen to my reasoning before you make any intemperate judgements.''

Helen's lips thinned. Her gaze as bleak as she could make it, she steeled herself to hear him out.

Encouraged by her silence, Hedley Swayne drew a portentous breath. "I regret the need to speak plainly, m'dear lady, but your recent indiscretion with a peer—who shall remain nameless—is the talk of the town. We all understand, of course,'' he went on, "that this association is at an end.'' He took several paces towards the door, then turned to look sternly at Helen. "Naturally, the entire episode, and the consequent publicity, has left you in an unenviable position. That being so,'' he stated, pacing back towards her again, "you must be glad of any offer that will reinstate you in the eyes of society—the censorious eyes of society.''

Helen had no difficulty restraining her laughter at his measured periods; she could see where his arguments were headed.

"Thus, my dear Lady Walford, you see me here in the guise of a knight in shining armour. I am come to offer you the protection of my name.''

There was no help for it but to make her refusal as gracious as she could. Helen suspected his motives were not nearly as pure as he made out, but had no wish to antagonise the man unnecessarily, a neighbour at that. "Mr Swayne, I do most sincerely value your proposal but I'm afraid I have no intention of marrying again."

"Oh, there's no need to fear I'll claim any rights over the marriage dear lady. A marriage in name only is what I propose. Why, you're a widow and I—I'm a man about town. I'm sure we'll deal famously. No need for you to entertain any worries on that head."

Unbeknown to Hedley Swayne, his declaration, far from easing Helen's fears, only added to the deadening misery threatening to pull her down. Martin had offered her so much more—and she had had to refuse him. How cruel of fate to send Hedley Swayne with his mockery of a proposal in the Earl of Merton's place. "Mr Swayne, I truly—"

"No, no! Don't be hasty. Just think of the advantages. Why, it'll put paid to all the rumours—you'll be able to return to London immediately, rather than languish in this backwater."

"I enjoy the country."

"Ah...yes." For a moment, Hedley's lights dimmed. Then he brightened. "Well if that's the case, you can take up residence at Creachley. No problem there. Can't abide the place myself, but there's no need for you to come back to town if you don't favour it."

Helen drew herself up haughtily. "Mr Swayne, I cannot—will not—accept your proposal. Please," she said, holding up one dough-encased hand to halt his reaction, "say no more on the matter. I have no intention of remarrying. My decision is final."

Hedley's weak-featured face turned sulky. "But you must marry me—stands to reason. Merton won't marry you. He's ruined you and now there's nothing left for it but that you must marry. You should marry me, indeed you should.''

What little reserve was left to Helen evaporated at his petulant tone. ''Mr Swayne, I am not constrained to marry anyone!''

Hedley returned her glare belligerently.

Just how long they would have remained so, locked in a contest of wills, Helen was destined never to learn, for at that moment the sounds of an arrival reached them. Another carriage, wonder of wonders. Her breathing oddly suspended, Helen waited, eyes glued to the door, to see who it was this time.

When a large, well-remembered broad-shouldered figure blocked out the light, she was not sure whether to feel relieved or apprehensive. She might have guessed Martin would come to find her.

The cool gaze swept the room, alighting on the occupants frozen in a most peculiar tableau. Martin instantly realised he had walked in on an altercation of sorts. As if on a stage, Helen stared at him from the other side of a deal table, her hands sunk in a copper basin, her golden curls rioting about her face. One glance was enough to tell him that she had not been taking care of herself as she should. Annoyance at her unwise bolt from the capital, which had developed over the long miles from London, grew. But his immediate concern was to relieve her of the obviously unwelcome presence of Hedley Swayne.

Martin nodded coolly to Helen and strolled into the room. Then he turned his attention to Hedley Swayne. ''Swayne.'' With the curtest of nods, Martin acknowledged Hedley Swayne's flustered bow. The man's face was evidence enough that he had heard the rumours. Had he had the temerity to approach Helen with them? Martin decided that the sooner Hedley Swayne left, the safer it would be—for Hedley Swayne. "But I believe you were about to leave, Mr Swayne?"

Hedley Swayne swallowed. He glanced nervously at Helen.

Helen sensed his glance but did not return it, too busy drinking in a sight she had convinced herself she would never see again. It meant that she would have to argue with him again, but, right now, she did not care. Just the sound of his deep, raspy voice had sent tingles down her spine. She was alive again. Her eyes roamed the large figure, noting the broad shoulders stretching the blue material of his coat, and the long sweep of muscled thighs encased in buckskin breeches. One lock of thick dark hair had fallen across his brow. She had forgotten the excitement his mere presence generated; for a moment, at least, she would bask in the warmth.

"Actually—no."

The tentative response concentrated Martin's attention firmly on the flustered fop. "What do you mean, no?"

Sheer aggression vibrated in Martin's growl. Helen blinked and realised the danger. Good God—the last thing she needed was to have to save Hedley Swayne from annihilation by throwing herself into the breach! Knowing Martin, that was what it would take, once he got started.

"What I mean, my lord," said Hedley, screwing his

courage to its highest pitch, "is that before you inter-
rupted, her ladyship and I were engaged in a delicate
negotiation and I really don't think it would be at all
considerate of me to leave before we've come to an
agreement on the matter."

A black scowl had invaded Martin's face. When the
stormy grey gaze flicked her way, Helen was no longer
sure which of her suitors it was safest to encourage.
Martin radiated menace. He also looked very determined. His jaw was set, his eyes were cold. Just how
far he would go to gain her consent to their marriage
she did not feel qualified to judge. Hedley she was
sure she could manage; Martin she was sure she could
not.

Martin stalked the few paces to the other side of the
table. "Just what sort of 'delicate negotiation' were
you discussing?"

Helen wished she could have kicked Hedley but he
was too far away. Predictably, the fool thrust his chin
in the air and stated. "As a matter of fact, we were
discussing a topic I doubt you have any interest in,
my lord. We were discussing marriage."

Martin's black brows flew. "I see. Whose?"

Helen closed her eyes.

Hedley blinked. "Why—ours, naturally." He bri-
dled, but before he could say more Martin's deep
voice, carefully controlled, cut him off.

"Contrary to your suppositions, I rather suspect I'm
close to becoming an expert on marriage proposals."

His grey gaze flicked Helen's way. Opening her
eyes in time to catch it, she suppressed a wince.

"As it happens, I've already proposed to Lady Walford. I'm here to repeat that proposal and ask for her ladyship's...final answer.''

Hedley Swayne's jaw dropped.

Helen resisted the impulse to close her eyes and fake a faint. The subtle emphasis on the last two words did not escape her. Martin was telling her this was the last time—the last chance she would have to grab happiness. He had turned until he was facing her. The grey eyes were watchful, sharply acute. Then, as she watched, a slight smile twisted his long lips.

''Well, my dear?'' The grey gaze became slightly mocking, distinctly untrustworthy. ''Now that our liaison is public property, it would seem the only respectable solution for you is marriage. It seems you have a choice. The Countess of Merton or Mrs Swayne. Which is it to be?''

Helen only just managed to swallow her gasp. *Outrageous!* He had jockeyed her into the position of accepting one of them, or appearing a reckless wanton, blind to society's rules. Her instinctive response to his manipulation was to reject them both summarily. Martin, at least, knew she did not have to marry. He, damn his grey eyes, was merely using the situation to further his ends. She opened her mouth but was forestalled by his deep, gravelly voice.

''Think carefully, my dear, before you choose.''

The look in his eyes warned her that flat rejection of them both would not work. Helen drew a tortured breath and struggled to think. Hedley Swayne was looking at her in fascinated wonder. The fact that she had not immediately leaped to accept Martin's proposal no doubt gave him heart. If she refused them both, then she would face continued pressure, not just from one, but from both. Martin might say it was her final chance—she did not believe him. He was determined and she suspected few had successfully gainsaid him—not in the past thirteen years. Hedley, on the other hand, would hold out hope undiminished if she rejected Martin. He, too, would persist—he had for the past twelve months, with even less encouragement.

Her gaze locked with the grey eyes across the table, Helen felt all her strength drain. Frowning, she dragged her eyes from Martin's and, automatically, put up her hand to push back her curls. Both men moved to stop her. Startled, she remembered the state of her hands and, just in time, used her wrist instead. "Give me a moment to think," she pleaded.

Her tone twisted through Martin. He frowned. What the devil did she have to think about? He loved her, she loved him—there was no reason to cogitate. She looked so weary, he was tempted to pick her up and put her to bed—to sleep. Which said a great deal about the state to which love had reduced him. Right now, all he wanted was a yes to his proposal, and after that Helen badly needed looking after—all else took second place. The presence of Hedley Swayne was a bonus. He knew Helen's instinctive dislike of the man—nothing overly strong but simply the natural antipathy of a beautiful woman for a man who had no use for beautiful women. It was, he suspected, just the situation to break down her barriers. He needed her to say yes—after that, he was prepared to devote his life to ensuring that she never regretted it—in fact, to ensuring that she enjoyed her second marriage as completely as she had disliked her first. He waited for her answer, supremely confident as to what it would be.

Helen wished the ground would open up and swallow her, that Janet would arrive and break the deadlock, anything at all to get out of making her choice. She did not want to marry Hedley Swayne. But, with every passing minute, that fate took firmer shape.

She had not expected to see Martin again, not after his brutal dismissal of her and his slap in the face at the Barhams' ball. That had all been reaction, of course, natural, no doubt, in a man of his temperament. But she had imagined that that would be the end of it; why, then, was he here? The answer was staring her in the face, stated plainly in his words. Her heart contracted painfully. He had come because of the scandal.

How could she have forgotten? Agonised as she imagined what his feelings must be, finding himself once more forced to make an offer by the weight of the *ton's* displeasure, she pressed her hands tightly together inside her dough. He was now the Earl of Merton and would be expected to play by society's rules. Thus, he would be expected to offer for her. But if she accepted, his mother would, she felt sure, have no compunction in disinheriting him. He would lose his dream. She could save him from both fates—social ignominy and maternal retribution—by the simple expedient of marrying Hedley Swayne. If she were already engaged to marry Hedley, Martin would be absolved from offering her his name in place of her reputation. He would then be free to marry a lady of whom his mother approved, and thus gain his most desired objective.

Martin shifted his weight. Helen noticed; her time was running out. She glanced up and met his gaze. Something of her decision must have shown in her eyes, for, as she watched, his brows descended and his eyes grew stormy.

"I've made up my mind," she announced, afraid that if she did not get it out quickly her courage would fail her. Her eyes remained on Martin's face an instant longer before she turned to Hedley Swayne. "Mr Swayne, I accept your proposal."

Hedley Swayne gawked at her. "Oh. I mean—yes, of course! Delighted, m'dear."

The silence from across the table was awful. Helen forced herself to look. Stunned astonishment held Martin's features immobile for a fleeting moment, then the hurt she had expected showed for the briefest of instants before a mask of impassivity put an end to all revelations. With dreadful civility, he bowed, his natural grace so much more polished than Hedley's flamboyant rendition.

"You've made your choice—I wish you happy, my dear." He glanced up and met her gaze. His eyes were cold and stony, grey upon grey, his face a mask. "I pray you'll not regret the bargain you've made this day."

His eyes held hers for one last, agonised minute, then he turned on his heel and left.

Helen stood by the table, slowly extricating her hands from the mess of her dough. She was deaf to Hedley's garrulous self-congratulations, her ears straining to catch the sound of Martin's retreating carriage. When the rumble had finally died in the distance, she moved slowly to the chair by the end of the table and sank into it. Then, as the full measure of what she had lost, of what she had committed herself to, became clear, she leaned her arms on the table and, laying her forehead upon them, gave way to her tears.

The crackle of flames came from behind him but, although he felt chilled to the bone, Martin made no move to turn his chair to the fire. If he did, he would see the mantelpiece. Which in turn would remind him of the woman he had left to her fate that morning in Cornwall.

He could not believe she had accepted Hedley Swayne over him. His frown turned to a scowl. He took a long swig of the amber fluid in his glass. The most damning thought of all was the certain knowledge that by forcing his unholy ultimatum upon her he had driven her into Hedley Swayne's arms. That thought threatened to drive him mad. He felt like howling with rage. Instead, he drained his glass and reached for the decanter on the small table at his elbow.

Outside the uncurtained windows, the stars shone in a black sky. It had been full dark before he had reached the Hermitage, even driving in a frenzy as he had been. Joshua had been silent the entire way, a sure sign of dire disapproval. How long he had sat in the darkened library, drowning his sorrows in the time-honoured way, he did not know. Pentley, his new butler, had entered to suggest dinner but he had ordered him out. All he wanted to do was wallow in his misery—and drink himself into a stupor sufficiently deep to let him sleep.

He had lost her—irretrievably; nothing else mattered any more.

The doors to the hall opened. Martin glowered through the dark, preparing an acid rebuke for whoever had dared to disturb his despair. His eyes, adjusted to the gloom, detected no one until, awkwardly, a chair came hesitantly into the room. It stopped just inside the doors, then they shut behind it.

Stifling a curse, Martin rose to his feet. His mother had come down to him. Who the hell had told her he had arrived?

Drawing on considerable experience, he summoned the skills required to cross the long room to his mother's side. He kissed her hand, then her cheek. "Mama. There was no need for you to come down—I would have called on you at a more fitting hour tomorrow."

"Yes, I dare say you would prefer me to leave you in peace to drink yourself into oblivion, but, before you've entirely lost your wits, there's something I have to tell you."

Through the dark, Martin frowned. "I'm not in the mood to listen to homilies or any such, ma'am."

Catherine Willesden's lips twisted. "This is more in the nature of information. Information I think you would wish to hear sooner rather than later." When her aggravating son made no effort to move, she grimaced. "Do come to, Martin! You can't be *that* addled yet. Light a candle for goodness' sake; I'm not particularly fond of the dark. And, if you please, you can push me nearer the fire.''

With a deep sigh, Martin accepted the inevitable and did as he was told. He could not imagine what she had to tell him, but in his present befuddled state, he was not up to arguing with her. But once he had lighted a single candle and placed the candlestick on a table beside her chair, drawn up before the fire as requested, he retreated to his own chair, still engulfed in shadows, moving it back so that he could see his mother but still be largely screened from the mantelpiece.

As he sat, he noticed that her face was more drawn and pinched than he recalled. ''Have you been well?''

With a little start, she raised her eyes to his face. ''Oh, yes. Quite well. But,'' she temporised, ''I've had rather a lot on my mind, of late.''

''Such as?''

She threw him a darkling glance. ''For a start, I suppose I should tell you that, as far as the question of Serena Monckton goes, I've known for some considerable time that her charge was without foundation.''

Silence stretched, then, ''Did my father know?''

Catherine Willesden shook her head. ''No, I only learned the truth from Damian some years after John died. But I gather most people now suspect the truth.''

For a long moment, she kept her gaze on her interlaced fingers, then, when no comment came, she glanced up through the shadows.

Martin shrugged. ''It doesn't matter any more. That's all history.''

Slowly, his mother nodded. "I did consider sending for you, but, from everything I'd heard, it seemed you were enjoying yourself hugely and, very likely, wouldn't have heeded the summons anyway."

A bark of laughter answered her. "Very true." Martin reached for his glass.

The Dowager caught the flash of the flames on the cut crystal and decided she would do well to make a long story short. "Ever since you've returned and rejoined society, I've heard tell of you, from my friends' letters. What worried me was that, despite the fact he's been on the town for close to four years, I've never heard anything of Damian. That led me to ask some questions of my closest acquaintances. The answers were hardly conducive to a mother's peace of mind." She paused to stare through the shadows at Martin. "Is it true Damian is one of the louts who frequent such places as Tothill Fields, drinking gin and getting up to all manner of disgraceful exploits?"

There was a long pause before Martin answered. "As far as I know, that's true."

Catherine Willesden looked down at her hands and sighed. "I suppose that explains some of what's happened. I just couldn't credit it that a son of mine could have behaved as he has, but clearly he's been off the tracks for some time."

"In my esteemed brother's defence, I feel compelled to point out that he's had precious little guidance from any source. But what's he done now?"

The question flustered the Dowager. In her lap, her stiff fingers laced and unlaced awkwardly. "I'm very much afraid that something I said put the whole business into his mind. You mustn't blame him entirely.''

Slowly, Martin sat up. "Blame him for what?''

The Dowager winced at his tone. But she stuck to her guns, determined to present the matter in the most accurate way. If Martin wished to disown them all after hearing it, so be it. "As you know,'' she began, "Damian was always my favourite—more than anything else because he was the last of you and so much younger. Also,'' she added, determined to be truthful, "because he was more ingratiating than the rest of you. You, certainly.''

"I know all this.''

"Yes, well what you may not know is that Damian has long imagined that he would eventually succeed to the title. If not to George, then to you. The catalogue of your past exploits reads like a deathwish. Furthermore, you'd shown not the smallest desire to wed. Naturally, Damian thought that, in time, the Hermitage would be his.'' The Dowager paused to assemble her thoughts, then hurried on. "However, more importantly, Damian has been in the habit of coming to see me on flying visits, and when he has done anything he feels is particularly clever he tells me about it.''

"Boasts about it, I suppose.''

The Dowager nodded. "Yes. I must confess that, when I was making plans for you, before you arrived, I mentioned them to Damian.'' She paused, then looked up. "I dare say you recall what those plans were?''

"Marrying me to some dull frump, as I recall.''

"Yes. And forcing you to it with the threat of dis-inheritance."

Martin nodded. "So?"

The Dowager drew breath. "So, when Damian saw you getting too close to Helen Walford, he repeated my threat against you to her. He didn't know it wasn't the truth." She glanced up and swallowed. Martin was no longer lounging in his chair. The shadowy figure was tense and intent.

"Are you telling me that Damian led Helen to believe that if she married me I'd lose all my supposed wealth?"

The suppressed energy vibrating beneath the slowly enunciated words all but paralysed the Dowager. Feeling very like prey in the presence of an enraged predator, she nodded.

"Aaaaaagh!" Martin sprang from his chair and strode about the room, all feeling of indolence vanquished. Halfway down the room, he abruptly turned and came back to stand in front of his mother. "Was Damian the agent who spread the tale of Helen's spending the afternoon at Merton House?"

The Dowager looked up into eyes like flint. All inclination to defend her wretched fourth son evaporated. She nodded. "Yes, he admitted that, too. However, it seems as if he believed he was doing you a favour at the time."

Martin paused in his pacing to throw an incredulous glance her way. *"Favour?"*

"I gather he was certain you'd broken off with Lady Walford. He thought to protect you from any claim made by her ladyship by ensuring that her reputation was already destroyed.''

When Martin simply stared at her, Catherine Willesden nodded. ''I know. He's not really very clever at all. He doesn't seem to understand how people should behave.''

Martin groaned. ''Where is he?''

''At the Bascombes', near Dunster. He said he'd be back in a few days.''

Martin nodded. ''I'll deal with him later.''

For five minutes, he paced the room, his brow furrowed as he pieced together the tangled web of his proposals and Helen's refusals. The damn woman had put him through hell, believing she was saving him from financial ruin. With an inward groan, he recalled his comment of not caring for his fortune, only for her. He had tripped himself up with his passionate avowal. But he had it all clear at last. Damian, of course, would have to be licked into shape, but first he had to extricate Helen from the mess her penchant for self-sacrifice had landed her in. Now he understood her steadfast refusals. She had decided to save him and nothing he had been able to say had swayed her. Gratifying, that, even if it had proved frustrating.

With an exasperated snort, Martin halted before the mantelpiece. His raving about his plans for the Hermitage and Merton House had doubtless played their part—he had gone out of his way to share his dreams with her, to make her see she was part of his life. Couldn't she see that his dreams would not be complete without her, here, where she belonged, in front of his hearth? How could she have believed he would value a house more than her—more than their love? Clearly, fair Juno required intense instruction on the whys and wherefores of a love match.

Glancing up, Martin noticed his mother's grey eyes, watching him in open concern. He smiled, for the first time that day. Going to her, he turned her chair from the fire. "Thank you for your information, Mama. I'll take you to your rooms."

"And then?" His mother twisted her head to look up at him.

"And then I'm for bed. At first light, I'm heading for Cornwall."

"Cornwall?"

"Cornwall. I've a goddess to rescue from a fate worse than death."

When his mother looked her question, Martin added, "Being married to a fop."

Chapter Twelve

Wisps of fog wreathed outside the leaded panes of Helen's bedchamber window. She stood before it, listlessly brushing her hair, at one with the dismal chill of early morning. If she had had any sense, she would have stayed in bed. But she could not sleep; there had been no point in lying there, imagining what might have been. Trying to block out the future.

There was no escape. By her own choice, she had cast the die. Now she had to pay the price. She just had not expected the account to be presented quite so soon.

Hedley had a special licence. The man was a bundle of contradictions but could, apparently, organise himself well enough when sufficiently moved. And he had certainly been moved last night.

Helen bit her lip, her eyes fixed, unseeing, on the gloom outside. She had indulged in a rare exhibition of tears after Martin had left, sobbing for what had seemed like hours. Janet had returned and held her, rocking her like a child, soothing her with comforting nonsenses until, finally, she had been numb enough inside to stop. Only then had she become aware that Hedley Swayne was still there.

When he had explained the arrangements he had made, she had realised that he had left, but had returned to tell her of their wedding. The next day.

Today. This morning, in fact.

With a deep sigh, Helen moved listlessly to the window-seat and sank on to the simple cushions. She had spent half an hour arguing with Hedley, why she could not now recall. Martin was gone; it did not really matter when she married Hedley. In fact, for her purposes, perhaps sooner was best, as he had said? Once the knot was tied, Martin would be forever safe.

Again, Helen sighed. She could barely summon the energy to stand, let alone think. Thinking was too painful. If permitted to roam, her errant thoughts showed a depressing tendency to dwell on the bounty she would have reaped as Martin's wife, throwing into stark contrast the dismal prospect of marriage to Hedley. He had made it plain, in a burst of quite remarkable candour, that he considered theirs to be a marriage of convenience, nothing more. She was coming to understand that he was truly indifferent to her but, for some unfathomable reason, was equally steadfast in his desire to marry her.

Shaking her head, she raised her brush once more to her tresses, which were tangling about her shoulders. Hedley was beyond her understanding. More definitely within her grasp was the realisation that, in just a few hours, she would say the words which would condemn her to purgatory a second time around. Like a wet grey cloak, despair sat her shoulders, dragging her down. She would have to put on a brave face at the church, although she doubted there would be many there. Janet, of course, and Hedley's servants, but she did not know anyone else in the village. She did not even know the vicar.

Her brush stilled. Tears filled her eyes, then slowly welled over to course down her cheeks and fall, un-heeded, into her lap.

Minutes ticked by and the fog lifted, yet still the cloud of cold despair shrouded her heart.

Eventually, Janet came to her rescue. The maid fussed and prodded and poked and cajoled and at last she was ready—or as ready as she would ever be. Her bronze silk dress was the only one she had brought with her that was halfway suitable for the occasion, and even that was stretching tolerance a bit far. The low neckline and clinging skirts were intended for *ton* parties, not religious ceremonies. She had no bouquet but chose a small beaded purse to clutch. Her curls were set in the simple knot she preferred; she waved away the rouge pot, dismissing Janet's criticisms of her wan complexion.

Hedley had sent a carriage. Resigned to her fate, Helen allowed herself to be helped aboard.

The short journey to the village was accomplished far too fast. Descending before the lych-gate, Helen was surprised to find a small crowd gathered, country folk all, eager to view the unexpected happenings. She plastered a smile to her lips. As things were shaping, these people might well be her neighbours for the rest of her life.

Buxom farmers' wives bobbed their round faces in

smiling greeting; their husbands, broad and brawny, grinned. Between the adults, children swarmed in a continuous stream. Suddenly, a freckle-faced miss bobbed up in Helen's path. Bright eyes, glowing with delight, looked up into Helen's face. A small hand held out a tightly packed bunch of flowers—daisies, lilies and assorted hedgerow blooms.

For an instant, Helen's determination faltered. She swayed slightly, but the necessity of taking the offering and suitably thanking the child took her past the dangerous moment. She would *not* think of what might have been—she could not afford his dreams and hers, too.

Relief swept through her when the cool dimness of the church porch engulfed her. Dragging in a deep breath, Helen saw that the tiny church was packed with locals, most likely Hedley's people from Creachley Manor, for they did not have the look of farmers, like those outside. Everyone had noticed her arrival. As she stood, frozen, at the entrance to the short nave, all heads turned slowly to view her.

With a last, desperate breath, Helen raised her head and walked forward.

Martin cracked his whip above the bays' ears, more to relieve his frustrations than to exhort his cattle to move faster. They were already rocketing along, the well-sprung curricle swaying dangerously. Joshua had been silent ever since they had passed out of the gates of the Hermitage just before sunrise.

Squinting against the glare, Martin took a blind curve at full speed. Six hours of sleep had cleared his

head; the brandy he had consumed the evening before
had been enough to ensure his slumber free from
worry. But immediately the effects had worn off, he
had woken—to a full realisation of the potential for
disaster. Just because he now knew Helen's reasons
for refusing him, it did not mean that he could afford
to sit back in comfort and plan how to best reassure
her of his wealth and the lack of necessity for her
sacrifice. Not when he had left her primed to make
that sacrifice. Doubtless if he had been less experienced in the ways of the world, he would accept the
widsom that, having got Helen's agreement to marriage, Hedley Swayne was unlikely to rush her to the
altar. But he had not amassed a sizeable fortune in
commodities by taking unnecessary risks—why
should he take risks with his future?

Aside from anything else, a species of sheer terror
rode him. What if he had misjudged Hedley Swayne?
What if the fop really did desire Helen. What if he
forced her to marry him forthwith? What if, given she
was promised to him, the blackguard sought a down
payment on his husbandly rights?

The whip cracked again; Martin gritted his teeth.
Reason told him that, although pre-empting the marriage ceremony was precisely the sort of behaviour he
would contemplate without a flicker of conscience,
Hedley Swayne was not of that ilk. Reason was not
enough. He wanted to make sure of Helen without
delay.

As he checked his team for the turn into the nar-
rower road leading to the village of St Agnes, Martin
reviewed his options for getting rid of the redundant

Mr Swayne. If necessary, he would buy him off. At the thought, Martin's lips twitched in a self-deprecatory smile. His father had paid a small fortune to extricate him from Serena Monckton's clutches. Now he was prepared to pay an even larger fortune to release Helen from her misguided promise to Hedley Swayne. Doubtless, as fair Juno herself had once observed, there was a moral in this somewhere.

It was market day at St Agnes, which proved a severe trial to Martin's temper. He carefully edged the curricle and his high-bred horses through the mêlée, muttering curses at the delay. Then they were through and heading out of the village to the hamlet of Kelporth, beyond which Helen's little cottage lay.

Joshua had not thought it possible to be glad to see such an out-of-the-way place as Kelporth again. Yet, when they gained the crest of the small hill before the village and went smartly down the lane towards it, he heaved a decidedly heartfelt sigh of relief. He glanced about at the neat little cottages, set back from the road with their neat little gardens, tinged with autumn's colours, before them. Ahead, to their left, a gaggle of children were playing about the back of a carriage drawn up to the side of the road. As they drew nearer, Joshua made out the dark mass of a lych-gate and surmised that a church must lie beyond. He paled, then looked at the straight back of his master, presently fully occupied with his fretting horses. Joshua coughed. "Master, I don't rightly know as how this is important but take a look to the left."

"What now?" Martin snapped but did as directed. The horses plunged, hauled to a halt so abrupt that the curricle rocked perilously, nearly flinging Joshua from his perch. He hung on grimly, then, as soon as it was safe, jumped to the ground and ran as fast as his stiff legs would allow to the horses' head. His master had already sprung down, throwing the reins haphazardly towards him.

As Martin stared at the children playing in the dust behind the carriage decked with white ribbons, his blood ran cold. Slowly, he dragged his eyes from the horrifying sight and raised them to the church door, just visible through the lych-gate. What if she had married him already?

The thought jerked him into action. He ran up the path to the church, all but skidding to a halt in the stone-flagged porch. A few of the heads near the door turned his way, but he ignored them, his eyes going to the sight which held most of the congregation spellbound.

Was he too late? His heart was pounding so hard he could not hear. Martin clenched his fists and forced himself to calm down. Gradually, his hearing returning. He frowned. As he was not familiar with the words of the marriage ceremony, it was an agonising three minutes before he realised he had one last chance remaining. Hard on the heels of relief came the vicar's sonorous tones, ''Therefore if any man can show any just cause, why they may not lawfully be joined together, let him now speak, or else hereafter forever hold his peace—''

Martin waited for no further invitation. ''Yes!'' he declared, adding, ''I do,'' just in case the vicar had misunderstood. He strode forward, his boots echoing on the flags, his gaze fixed on the object of his desire.

At the totally unexpected sound of that deep voice, a voice she had convinced herself she would never hear again, Helen froze. Abruptly, she lost all feeling, all sense of time and place. Her breathing suspended, her eyes had grown round with disbelief even before she turned to find Martin all but upon her, his grey eyes clear and bright and burning with determination.

To her amazement, he took her arm in a vice-like grip.

"I want to talk to you."

He would have drawn her out of the church then and there but for the combined expostulations of the vicar and the putative groom.

"I say, Merton, she agreed to marry me, y'know!"

"What *is* the meaning of this, sir?"

Martin looked at the vicar, a frown rapidly developing.

But the vicar, secure in his own house and thoroughly disapproving, was not readily cowed. "This is a marriage ceremony. How dare you interrupt?"

Glancing up into Martin's arrogantly handsome face, Helen saw the cynical gleam in his eyes. Her heart sank. Oh, God! He was going to be outrageous.

"But you asked for objectors to speak up," Martin replied reasonably. "I'm merely obliging."

For one instant, as the truth dawned, the vicar looked blank. Then he looked thunderstruck. "You're *objecting?*" His gaze took in Martin's austerely expensive dress, and his commanding visage. Then the vicar turned to gaze at Hedley Swayne. "I knew I should never have agreed to such a hubble-bubble af-fair,'' he said snapping his bible shut.

''No such thing!'' Hedley had turned several shades of puce and was all but flapping in agitation. ''Ask him what his objection is—this is nothing more than some lark because he knows she agreed to marry *me!*''

Hedley glared at Martin. Helen felt ready to sink. But the grip on her arm eased not one whit.

The vicar glanced uneasily from Hedley to Martin. ''If you could, perhaps, tell me what your objection is?''

Without a blink, Martin said, ''Lady Walford agreed to marry me.''

Hedley gasped at what was, quite obviously, a bra-zen lie. Helen decided it was time for her to take a hand. Despite all, Martin could not be allowed to give up his dreams—not after all the mental agony she had been through to save them for him. ''I did not, nor have I ever, agreed to marry you, my lord.''

Martin looked down at her. As she watched, a glow of warm appreciation filled his eyes, shaking the grip she was endeavouring to keep on her senses. Her eyes widened as that look was superseded by an expression she could only describe as unholy. ''You did, you know,'' he said with a slow smile. ''When you were in bed with me that afternoon.''

Helen felt her mouth fall open. Her cheeks were aflame. How *dared* he say such a thing? In church, with the entire congregation for witness?

The vicar threw up his hands in scandalised horror. ''I should have known better than to have anything to do with fashionable folk. London folk,'' he added, glowering at Hedley. "In the circumstances, I must ask you—all *three* of you—to leave the church immediately! And I most seriously advise you to look to your souls." And with that parting shot the vicar turned and marched into the sacristy.

The congregation erupted. Under cover of the ensuing uproar, Martin dragged Helen through a side-door and into the graveyard. They were midway across the grassed expanse, dotted with worn headstones, before Helen found the strength to haul back, bringing them to a halt.

"My lord! This is ridic—"

The rest of her words disintegrated under the force of his kiss. Fiery passion seared her lips, then, when they surrendered, threatened to cinder what was left of her wits. She struggled, trying to escape a too well-desired fate, trying to deny the hunger that rose up to overwhelm her reason. In response to her ineffectual wriggling, Martin's arms tightened about her, pressing her more fully against his hard chest, until, at last, she admitted defeat and melted against him.

Only when all trace of resistance had been vanquished did Martin risk releasing her lips. She was a stubborn goddess, as he had every reason to know.

"Don't talk," he said, laying one finger across her reddened lips to enjoin her obedience. "Just listen." Gazing down into her wide green orbs, he smiled and enunciated clearly, "My fortune is mine. Not my mother's, not even vaguely dependent on her whim. I'm excessively wealthy in my own right and have every intention of choosing my own bride. Do you understand?"

The wide eyes widened even further. Helen could barely find the breath to speak. "But your brother said..." was all she could manage.

"Regrettably," said Martin, his jaw hardening, "Damian was labouring under a misapprehension."

Helen detected his anger but knew it was not directed at her. "Oh," she said, struggling to decide what it all meant.

"Which means I'm going to marry you."

The decisive statement brought Helen's eyes up to Martin's grey ones. His stern, not to say forbidding expression gave her pause. "Oh," was all it seemed safe to say.

"Yes, 'Oh'," Martin repeated. "I've asked you three times already, which is more than enough. I've given up proposing. You're going to marry me regardless."

Helen simply stared, too enthralled by the vision of the rainbow rising once more on her horizon.

When she said nothing, Martin went on, entirely serious, "If necessary, I'm prepared to lock you in my apartments at the Hermitage and keep you there until you agree." He paused, brows rising. "In fact, that's a damned good idea—far more appealing than proposing."

Helen blushed and looked down. Things were moving so fast; her head was spinning, her heart was beating an insistent but happy tattoo. She could barely formulate a thought, with her mind whirling with the giddy promise of happiness his words had implied. Could it really be true?

Martin examined her flushed countenance, conscious of a medley of emotions coursing his veins. Relief that she was once more in his arms was slowly giving way to pride that she had loved him so much she had been willing to accede to another meaningless marriage to save his dreams. An urgency to secure her hand, beyond all possible loss, was slowly growing. He was about to speak, to assure her that he now understood her odd behaviour, before showing her that he appreciated it as he should, when, from the corner of his eye, he saw Hedley Swayne, also leaving the church by the side-door. The fop saw them and turned away, disgruntlement visible in the slump of his shoulders as he made his way jerkily through the headstones.

Reluctantly, Martin released Helen. "Wait here. And don't move!" He enforced his command with a meaningful look, then strode after Hedley Swayne.

Mr Hedley Swayne had tried very hard to get Helen to marry him—why? Martin held no fears for his future wife—he intended to keep her safe from all danger. But the stone of Hedley Swayne's interest was too intriguing to leave unturned.

Hedley heard him and stopped, all but sulking with disappointment. "What do you want now?" he asked as Martin drew near.

"One simple answer," Martin said, coming to a halt directly before the slighter man. "Why did you want to marry Lady Walford?"

Hedley scowled, then, after a pregnant pause, gave a petulant shrug. "Oh, very well. You're bound to learn of it sooner than late, what with your business connections." He eyed Martin with resignation. "That little cottage of hers is on land bordering my estate. I own many of the tin mines around here. But the purest deposit my people have ever found lies under those five acres. Can't be accessed by any other route.''

For one long moment, Martin stared at the fop, now seen in a new light. Abruptly, he made up his mind. "Here," he said, pulling out his note-case, and extracting a card. "Come and see me when we get back to town. We can discuss a lease then."

"A lease?" Hedley took the card, speculation dawning in his pale eyes.

Martin shrugged. A crooked smile twisted his lips. "I warn you you'll have to wait a few months but by then I think it very likely that both Helen and I will feel somewhat in your debt."

With a nod, he left Hedley Swayne pondering over that cryptic utterance.

Helen was seated on the marble coping of a grave, trying to see her way forward. Could she safely agree to all Martin said—or was he making their situation appear more rosy than it, in reality, was? He wanted to marry her—that was beyond question. He was ruthless and determined and very used to getting his own way. Was it really in his best interests to marry her? And, most importantly, how could she find out? She looked up as he approached, a frown nagging at her fine brows.

Martin ignored it, holding out his hands to her. Dutifully, Helen put her hands in his and he pulled her to his feet. "And now, fair Juno, it's time for us to depart."

"But Martin—"

"I'll leave Joshua here to collect your maid and baggage. We can send a carriage for them from the Hermitage." Martin paused to glance at her dress. "Where's your coat?"

"In the carriage. But Martin—"

"Good. If we leave straight away, we should be able to reach the Hermitage by nightfall." He guided her down the shallow steps to the roadway and fetched her coat from Hedley's carriage.

Taking her arm, Martin led her to his curricle. Beside him, Helen allowed her eyes to seek the heavens for one brief instant. If this was how he was going to behave, she would never learn anything to her purpose. With her own determination growing, she put her hands on his arms as he reached for her waist. "My lord, I cannot simply go with you like this."

Martin sighed. "You can, you know. It's quite simple. But if it's all the same to you, my dear, while I'm perfectly ready to discuss our future together in whatever detail you desire, I'd rather not do so in such a public location."

He stood back to allow Helen a clear view of the churchyard, now filled with a sea of curious faces. Her eyes grew round. "Oh," she said. She held her peace while Martin lifted her to the box seat, shifting across to give him room. He paused to give directions to his groom, before mounting beside her. Within two minutes, they had left Kelporth, and her past, behind them.

Helen took a moment to savour the fresh tang of the breeze on her face, to allow the feeling of having escaped a dismal prospect sink in. Ahead, the future

beckoned, exciting and beguiling. But largely unknown. Drawing a deep breath, she turned to view the
man beside her, noting the strong hands on the reins,
the slight frown—was it of concentration?—tugging at
the black brows. "My lord—" she began.

"Martin," promptly came back.

Despite her determination, Helen's lips twitched.
"Martin, then." She raised her eyes to his face. "Is it
really true that marrying me will not alter your state?"

The smile Martin turned on her was dazzling. "I
very much hope it will alter my state." At her confusion, his smile grew. "But if you mean will it affect
my financial state—no. Other than making suitable
settlements on you, marriage to you will not seriously
erode my fortune." When she remained silent, he
added, "I did say so, you know."

"You also said I'd agreed to marry you!" Helen
countered, indignation at the way he had said it returning.

His grin was unrepentant. "Ah, well. Needs must
when the devil drives, I'm afraid."

Helen swallowed a snort and looked away. He was
impossible and, she was quite sure, would remain so,
behaving outrageously whenever it suited him, making
amends with a wicked smile in the sure expectation of
being excused. For the space of a few miles, she let
the steady swaying of the carriage soothe her ruffled
sensibilites. "I didn't want you to lose your home,"
she eventually said, her voice rather small. Without
that information, she was not sure what he might make
of her own behaviour.

"My home—and my dreams of restoring it?" Martin asked gently.

Wordlessly, Helen nodded.

"Finally, despite the dust you and fate seemed intent on throwing into my eyes, I figured that much out. You'll be pleased to know that my dreams are all but reality, as far as the Hermitage goes. However, there's an even more important dream that I'm very keen to see transmuted to reality—one you can help me with."

"Oh?" Helen glanced up at him, not sure any longer if he was serious or just trying to cheer her up. But the grey eyes were perfectly clear and intent, holding an expression which made her feel quite breathless.

"Yes," said Martin, slowly smiling before giving his attention to the road again. "It'll take some time to achieve, this dearest dream of mine, but I'm more than prepared to devote myself assiduously to its achievement."

Helen puzzled for a moment before asking, "What is this dream of yours?"

Martin considered long and hard before shaking his head. "I don't think I should tell you just yet. Not until we're wed. In fact, possibly not even then."

"How am I supposed to help you attain it if I don't know what it is?" Helen threw him an exasperated look, wondering again if he was merely trying to distract her. But his face remained serious.

"If I tell you what I want," said Martin, frowning in earnest as he tried to unravel the tangle of his thoughts, "then, with your propensity for giving me what I wish regardless of your own feelings in the matter, how will I ever know if you're helping me because you really wish to, rather than because you want to give me my heart's desire?''

Helen stared at him in total confusion. What on earth was this latest dream of his?

Seeing her confusion, Martin laughed. ''I promise to tell you if I need your—er—active assistance.'' With an effort, he kept his face straight, despite the wild scenes his rampant imagination was fabricating. Thankfully, his horses gave him excuse enough to keep his eyes on the road.

As the miles fell beneath the powerful hooves, Helen brooded over Martin's disclosures, but could make all too little of them. His assurance about his home had relieved her mind of its most persistent worry, but there still remained one potential cloud hovering over his rainbow. ''Tell me about your mother,'' she said. ''She lives at the Hermitage, doesn't she?''

Martin was only too ready to supply his bride-to-be with information on that subject, eliciting her ready sympathy for his ailing parent. ''And regardless of anything Damian may have said, she most definitely approves of my offering for you. In fact, it was she who told me of Damian's interference. Although she didn't say so, I have reason to suspect she was somewhat disappointed that I didn't leave to come after you last night.''

Privately, Helen considered that a reasonable reaction. Her thoughts must have shown in her eyes, for, when she glanced up and found Martin's gaze upon her, he smiled and added, "I didn't because, quite apart from the state of the roads, I was—er...somewhat under the hatches. Your fault, I might add."

Understanding this to mean he had been drinking rather more than usual because of her, Helen felt an odd inner glow warm her. As the curricle shot past a farmer's cart, she reflected that it was just as well Martin was not drunk now, for he was driving at a shocking pace.

Martin kept his horses well up to their bits, only easing them when absolutely necessary. They were a strong pair of Welsh thoroughbreds and made short work of the relatively level roads. Lunch was a hasty affair—some bread and cheese washed down with ale, taken in a small inn at Wadebridge. Even so, by the time they left Barnstaple, and Martin headed the horses on to the road to South Molton, the sun was sinking in the west, the way ahead lit by its slanting rays. Realising that they would not reach the Hermitage, just north of Wiveliscombe, until evening, Martin bethought himself of a pertinent point he would do well to inform fair Juno upon.

"We'll be married tomorrow."

The bald statement jerked Helen's slumbering wits to life. Tomorrow? She looked up in time to catch Martin's glance. He was deadly serious. As she watched, one dark brow rose arrogantly. "I've a special licence, supplied by the Bishop of Winchester."

Helen straightened in her seat. "Don't you think...?" she began lamely.

"No," said Martin. "I want to marry you as soon as possible and that's tomorrow."

Seeing his jaw firm and the line of his lips narrow, Helen resigned herself to walking up the aisle at the earliest possible hour the next morning. But she was beginning to feel that her overbearing suitor was having things a great deal too much his own way. Consequently, she composed her features to calm and stated, "That's as maybe. However, despite whatever outrageous claims you may choose to make to the contrary, I have not yet agreed to marry you, Martin."

A worried frown, tending black, was thrown at her. For a moment, he said nothing. Then, "All you have to do is say yes."

The low growl suggested that was her only option. Helen put her head on one side, to consider his point. "I would really feel much happier waiting until after I've met your mother."

"You can meet her tonight and spend all tomorrow morning with her. We can be married in the afternoon."

"But I've nothing to wear," Helen said, appalled as she realised this was true. She had not thought anything of marrying Hedley Swayne in whatever was to hand, but the idea of becoming the Countess of Merton in a worn ballgown was too hideous to contemplate. "No, Martin," she said, her voice increasing in firmness. "I'm very much afraid you'll have to wait at least until I get a suitable gown. I will not marry you otherwise."

A groan of surpassing frustration fell on her ears.

The horses were hauled to a halt; she was hauled into Martin's arms and ruthlessly kissed.

"Woman!" he growled when he eventually raised his head. "What further tortures do you have planned for me?"

With an enormous effort, Helen focused her faculties. Heaven preserve her, but if he realised she lost her wits every time he kissed her she would be in serious trouble. "Is it torture?" she asked, quite fascinated.

That question got her kissed again. "Dammit—I want you, don't you know that?"

She did, but Helen also wanted a wedding to remember. Her first, she had spent years trying to forget. And, despite the facts, a rushed wedding would be food for the gossip mills. Suppressing the shiver of delight that Martin's gravelly tone sent coursing through her, she set herself to the task of winning him over. "It'll only take a few days—a week at the outside," she offered.

Martin snorted disgustedly and released her. Helen watched as he took up the reins again and set the horses forward. The cast of his features suggested, at the least, disenchantment, at the worst, downright aggravation. She cast about for some gesture, some facet she could add to her plan, which would make the delay more appealing to him. Then she remembered his home and his hopes for it. She sat up straighter. "You said your father used to entertain a great deal at the Hermitage and that you wanted to do the same."

Martin shot her a glance from under lowered brows. "So?"

"So why not make our marriage the first occasion you throw open your refurbished house?"

For a few moments, the horses' hoofbeats and the regular rattle of the wheels were the only sounds about them. Then Helen saw Martin purse his lips in consideration. When she saw his dejection lift, she inwardly hugged herself.

"Not a bad idea," he eventually conceded. He glanced down at her. "We could invite the Hazelmeres and Fanshawes and Acheson-Smythe and a few of the others."

Helen smiled brilliantly, and slipped a small hand through his arm. "I'm sure they'll come."

The grey eyes glinted down at her. Then Martin humphed and gave his attention to the road. "Just as long as you say yes at the appropriate time."

Chapter Thirteen

The Hermitage was much bigger than Helen had expected. Even allowing for the deceptive perspective of twilight, the many-windowed two wings stretched deep into the formal gardens. They approached the house from the rear, Martin having driven the curricle around to the stables. The formal front façade, holding court before the sweep of manicured lawns leading to a lake on one side and a stand of majestic horse chestnuts on the other, had been impressive. The back of the mansion was even more appealing, with the pergola-like glassed conservatory positioned at the end of the ballroom in the centre of the main block. The conservatory steps led to a small fountain, centrepiece of the formal gardens enclosed within the wings. Beyond, Helen could just make out the outliers of a wood and the mellow brick wall of the kitchen garden.

Her hand firmly trapped on Martin's sleeve, she was led to a door at the end of one of the wings.

"I suppose I should take you around to the front door, but it's quite a long way." Glancing down into her upturned face, Martin forbore to add that she was looking tired, which she was. Hardly surprising, for she had had a long day. But at least she was smiling and her eyes were alight. He patted her hand. "You'll want to freshen up before we have dinner."

Helen came to an abrupt halt, her eyes widening as she realised what he intended. Then her eyes went to her creased and crumpled bronze silk gown. "Oh, Martin!" she all but wailed.

Swiftly, Martin pulled her to him and kissed her soundly. "My mother would welcome you if you were dressed in rags. Now don't fret." He smiled down into her anguished eyes. "I'll take you to Bender, my housekeeper. I'm sure she'll be able to help."

Twenty minutes later, Helen gave thanks for Bender. The large, round-faced woman, in country plaid rather than the regulation bombazine, had immediately understood her wordless plea. While she washed her face and hands and brushed her hair free of the dust of the road, her dress was ruthlessly shaken, then quickly pressed. It would never be the same again, of course, but at least it looked halfway respectable. When Martin tapped on the door of the pleasant bedchamber Bender had taken her to, Helen was ready to face what she privately considered her final hurdle—the final hurdle before she could reach for her rainbow.

Martin's presence by her side, large and infinitely reassuring, helped her hold her head high as she crossed the threshold of the drawing-room, her eyes opening wide as she beheld quite the most elegant room she had entered in years. At the sudden thought that, if the fates were at last disposed to be kind, she would soon be mistress here, Helen's confidence faltered. But then Martin was speaking, introducing her. Helen looked down into the grey eyes watching her, and blinked in surprise.

How alike they were, was her first thought, superseded almost immediately by the recognition of subtle differences. Martin's mother's dark brows were much finer than her son's, though her features were equally arrogant in cast. Her chin and lips were much softer in line, and the grey eyes, so startlingly similar, lacked the wicked glint often lurking in her son's. Helen realised she was staring. With a little start, she bobbed a curtsy.

''I'm most honoured to meet you, ma'am.''

Catherine Willesden eyed the golden-haired beauty before her and was not displeased with what she saw. An unusually tall woman and well-built with it—she could readily see just what in Helen Walford had excited her son's interest. And she looked the sort who could carry children well and would enjoy doing so, even more to the point. But what decided the Dowager in Helen's favour, beyond the slightest qualms, was the look of untold pride that lit her son's grey eyes whenever, as now, they rested on his bride-to-be. That, thought the Dowager, was what counted above all.

''Believe me when I say that it is I who am most thoroughly pleased to see you, my dear.'' The Dowager threw a meaningful look at her son before, with an effort, she raised her hands to grasp Helen's cold fingers.

Realising the Dowager's difficulty, Helen immediately took hold of the frail claws and readily bent to place a kiss on the older woman's lined cheek.

From then on, it was fair weather and plain sailing between the Dowager and the soon-to-be Countess. Pleased with their ready acceptance of each other and not a little entertained, Martin drew back, leaving the two women to find their own way about each other. But when, after they had left the dining-table for the comfort of the drawing-room, and spent half an hour discussing the details of the wedding and planning the week-long house party, they turned their attention to the wedding feast, he had had enough.

"Mama, it's late. I'll take you upstairs."

His mother's eyes widened. She opened her mouth to protest, then, catching his eye, closed it again. "Very well," she agreed. She turned to Helen, holding out one frail hand. "Sleep well, my child."

Martin wheeled his mother out before she could think of any more witticisms. He returned from the Dowager's rooms to find Helen wandering the hall, examining the landscapes on the wall.

"Come for a stroll. The light's not yet gone."

Helen smiled and calmly placed her hand on his proffered sleeve. Inside, she felt anything but calm. Her heart was leaping about, turning cartwheels and somersaults with sheer happiness. The Dowager was no dragon and clearly well-disposed. The house— Martin's home—pleased her beyond her wildest dreams. She already felt drawn to it, at home within its spell, though whether the feeling owed anything to the house itself, rather than being a reflection of her all-encompassing love for Martin, she could not have said.

As they stepped from the terrace to stroll, arm in arm, along a gravelled path into a landscaped shrubbery, she felt contentment such as she had never known lay its hand upon her.

"We can send letters to the Hazelmeres and the rest tomorrow."

Martin's murmur wafted the curls by her ear. Helen turned to smile her acquiescence, then, fleetingly, pressed her temple against his shoulder. With no need for words, they wended their way about the low clipped hedges of a miniature maze, to stand by the small fountain at its centre. Smoothly, Martin drew her around, so that the back of her shoulders brushed his chest. His arms slipped about her waist, steel bands holding her against him. He bent his head and his lips grazed her bare shoulder. Helen felt a giggle bubble in her throat. Only a very accomplished rake, she felt sure, would choose the middle of a maze to play at seduction. However, she was not in the mood to deny him. Obligingly, she tilted her head away, giving him access to the long column of her throat. She did not try to stifle the shiver of pure delight that ran through her at the intimate caress.

A crackling twig brought Martin's head up. His eyes scanned the bushes, then the grassed path leading around to the stables. Just discernible in the gloom was the figure of a man, temporarily immobile. With an oath, Martin released Helen and gave chase, leaping over the low hedges, making directly for the man who, after an instant's hesitation, had taken to his heels.

Martin's long legs gave him a telling advantage. He caught up with Damian before he had reached the wood. Catching hold of one padded shoulder, Martin spun his brother about before sending him to grass with a punishing right cross.

For an instant, Damian simply lay, eyes closed, stretched out on the turf. Then he groaned. Perfectly certain that he had not hit his brother with sufficeint force to do permanent injury, Martin stood over him, hands on hips, and waited for him to get up. When it became clear that Damian was not going to get up without assistance, Martin's jaw hardened. He was reaching for his brother's coat when Helen erupted out of the darkness behind him and caught hold of his arm.

One glance at Damian, cringing on the ground, confirmed Helen's guess. "Don't kill him," she pleaded, gasping to catch her breath. Abruptly deserted by the fountain, she had spent no more than a minute staring in amazement. Then she had followed. But her escape from the maze had been a great deal slower than Martin's. She could not leap over the low hedges in her gown and, without Martin's asistance, she had not known how to get out of the maze. In the end, glancing about through the gathering gloom and deciding that the gardeners would long since have gone home, she had hiked her skirts to her thighs and clambered over the bushes.

Now, finding Martin looking as if he was preparing to thrash the life out of his brother, her only thought was to stop him.

To her relief, Martin promptly drew back, his hands coming to hold hers, his eyes searching her face in the last of the twilight, a curious expression in their grey depths. ''I wasn't about to,'' he replied mildly. ''But I shouldn't have thought that, in the circumstances, you would mind.''

Still out of breath, Helen shook her head. She had learned the full sum of Damian's iniquity from the Dowager. ''If it were that simple, you could have at him with my goodwill. But if you kill him, you'll be tried for murder and where would that leave my rainbow?''

''Your what?'' Martin's smile gleamed white in the dark.

Helen felt her cheeks burn with embarrassment.

Still smiling, Martin patted her hand. ''Never mind. You can explain it to me later.'' He slipped an arm about his bride-to-be's waist and drew her to his side. Then he looked down at his brother, still sprawled at his feet. He shook his head. ''For God's sake, get up! I'm not going to hit you again, though, as God is my witness, you deserve to be horse-whipped.''

Damian half rose, but at the strengthening of his brother's tone he froze.

Martin looked down at him in exasperation. ''You may thank your soon-to-be sister-in-law for deliverance from any punishment I might otherwise have been inclined to mete out.'' When Damian said nothing but simply stared, Martin snorted in disgust and turned away. ''Get to your room. I'll see you tomorrow.''

Drawing Helen with him, Martin started back towards the house, then bethought himself of one last warning. He turned to find Damian weaving on his feet. "In case you're planning a sudden departure, I should warn you I've already given orders that, once here, you are not to be permitted to leave again. Not until tomorrow, when you'll depart under escort for Plymouth."

"Plymouth?" Damian all but shuddered. "I won't go," he said, but to Helen his tone lacked strength.

"I rather think you will." Martin's tone, on the other hand, radiated strength. "Mama and I have decided a sojourn in the Indies might well be of as much benefit to you as it was to me." He paused, then added in a more pensive tone, "I rather think you'll find it a tad difficult, living in London, once it becomes known that both Mama and I have withdrawn our support."

Even in the dim light, Helen could see how Damian paled. Obviously, Martin's threat was well-aimed. Martin did not wait to see how his brother reacted. He turned once more in the direction of the house, tucking her hand into the crook of his arm. Obediently, Helen paced by his side.

There was a storm brewing. Large ruffled clouds of deepest grey were blowing up from the west. After a few minutes, Helen glanced up to find that Martin's forbidding expression had disappeared. In its place was a pensive look she rather thought she should distrust.

"Now, where were we?" he murmured, before flashing her a devilish smile. "Wherever, I rather think we had better go indoors. The evening grows cold and you're without a shawl."

Forbearing to point out that her lack of a shawl was

entirely his fault, Helen happily permitted him to escort her within doors. He led her upstairs, picking up a candelabra from the table in the hall to light their way. In the long gallery, he showed her the portraits of past Willesdens, hanging between the long velvet-curtained windows.

Picking the most scandalous of the family's tales of yore as the most suitable for his purpose, Martin had Helen in stitches as they moved on through the long corridor that led to the west wing. Embellishing freely, he ensured that she was completely enthralled long enough for them to reach the door at the end of the wing.

It was only then that Helen, catching a sudden gleam in Martin's mesmerising grey eyes, looked about her and realised she was lost—in company with a thoroughly untrustworthy host. Far from feeling threatened, she revelled in the delicious anticipation that stirred in her breast. She looked at the door before her—a very large, well-polished oak door—and then looked at Martin, one brow rising in question.

All he did was smile, successfully scattering her wits, then leaned forward to set the door wide.

Feeling very much as if she was taking some irretrievable step, Helen crossed the threshold. The room was huge—and so was the four-poster bed that stood against the wall, long windows flanking it open to the balcony, their fine lace curtains streaming in with the freshening breeze. She watched as Martin closed the shutters. The only light came from the candelabra, which he had placed on a table by the bed. The glow centred on the bed, drawing Helen's awareness with it. A heavy silk counterpane, embossed with what she recognised as the Willesden arms, covered the expanse in deep blue-grey. Silken tassels of the same colour hung from the cord holding the bed curtains back. The oak headboard was heavily carved, again incorporating the family arms, meshed within twining vine leaves.

Nervousness crept up on her, but then Martin was there, drawing her firmly into his arms. Before he could kiss her, and render her witless, Helen placed her hands on his shoulders and smiled up into the stormy grey eyes. "Is this where I say yes?" she asked, and was surprised at the husky quality of her own voice.

Martin smiled slowly, so slowly that Helen had plenty of time to feel her heart somersault and her stomach contract.

"Actually," he said, "given the difficulty you seem to have with that word, I've decided some practice would not go astray."

His tone feathered over her stretched senses, teasing and tantalising. Helen opened her eyes wide. "Practice?" she asked in as innocent a voice as she could muster.

"Mmm," Martin murmured, bending his head to brush his lips across hers. "I'd rather thought to make you say it a great...many...times." His last words were punctuated by light kisses, firm enough to whet her appetite, insubstantial enough to leave her hungry.

Helen felt her will slowly seep from her but she retained sufficient curiosity to ask. "How will you make me do that?"

Martin did not answer.

Instead, he showed her.

Much later, Martin reached out with one hand and snuffed the candles by the bed. His other arm was occupied, cradling Helen's warm body by his side. She was asleep, thoroughly exhausted, having said the word he had wanted to hear a great many times indeed. Martin smiled into the dark. She still needed more practice—he was quite certain he would be able to convince her of that later. With her head once more on his shoulder, her soft curls like silk at his throat, he listened to the storm passing overhead. Wind lashed the trees in the Home Wood, rain pelted down on the gravel walks. Helen had not even noticed the tempest without, being too much caught up in the tempest they had created within.

With a deep sigh, Martin closed his eyes. Contentment coursed his veins like a drug, bringing peace and satisfaction in its wake. His house was in order, fair Juno safe by his side. Tonight, with any luck, he would get some sleep. Maybe not much, but some. And, unlike the last stormy night he had spent with fair Juno, the torture between times would be much more to his taste. He closed his hand over one full breast. And fell asleep.

Helen awoke to rub her nose, then realised that the curly black hair tickling it was attached to Martin's chest. She stifled a giggle and pushed it aside, then glanced up to find lazy eyes watching her, a suspicious twinkle in their depths.

With a smile, Helen stretched, cat-like, and watched the twinkle intensify to a satisfying gleam. As she felt the arm about her tighten, she pressed her hands against his chest. Heavens! She needed at least two minutes to think! "What is your latest dream, my lord?" she purred, hoping to distract him and appease her curiosity in one stroke.

Martin relaxed and laughed, the warmth in his eyes spreading like a languorous flame over her skin. "Should I tell you?" he asked rhetorically. Then, "Perhaps I should." His eyes held hers, mock-serious. "I don't think it'll be too hard for you to handle." His smile grew. "Well within your capacity, so to speak."

Feeling the rumble of his laughter, Helen scowled. "Martin!"

"Ah—yes. Well, having had an opportunity to assess your abilities, my love, and having ascertained that you really do enjoy our recent activities for their own delight, as it were, I feel secure in the knowledge that, once you hear of my dream, you'll not be called on to sacrifice any feelings of your own in its accomplishment."

Helen glared at him. "Martin! What is it?"

Martin eyed her a little warily. "Promise not to laugh?"

Puzzled, Helen's glare turned to a stare. "Why should I laugh?" she asked. When he said nothing further, she grimaced. "All right. I promise not to laugh. Now, what is this dream of yours?"

"I have this vision of you standing before the mantelpiece—I think the one in the library at Merton

House..." Martin paused, then went on in a rush, "With my son balanced on your hip."

Helen blinked. "Oh," she said, her voice non-committal. But she could not stop the smile that curved her lips, then deepened to light her eyes. Gazing deep into the grey eyes that held hers, and seeing the hesitant expression that lingered there, Helen decided that she had clearly reached the end of her rainbow and found her pot of gold. Rapidly blinking to clear her eyes of the tears of happiness that threatened, she swallowed and said, "Oh, Martin!" before throwing her arms about his neck and burying her face in his shoulder.

His arms came up to close about her, holding her close. "I take it that means you approve?"

A mumble which was clearly an assent answered him. Martin grinned and hugged her more tightly, conscious of the dampness of tears on his shoulder.

Once she had regained her composure, Helen could not resist asking, "Is that a typical dream for a rake?"

"I assure you it's this rake's dream." Martin moved to glance down at her. He smiled slowly. "Now come and do your bit to make it real."

Helen's smile answered him. "Gladly, my lord."

She reached up and drew his lips down to hers and, in truth, there was no dream in her mind beyond the attainment of his.

* * * * *

Also by Stephanie Laurens

AN UNWILLING CONQUEST
ISBN 978-0-7278-8728-3

Successful horse breeder and self-proclaimed rake Harry Lester has no
intention of falling for a woman again after having his heart trampled on.
Escaping London for Newmarket, Harry encounters Lucinda Babbacombe
– a beautiful, intelligent widow. Will Harry let himself be taken prisoner in
this most passionate of traps?

A LADY OF EXPECTATIONS
ISBN 978-0-7278-8551-7

Jack Lester is ready to marry, but he knows that if London society discov-
ers his hidden wealth, he'll never find the right woman. Jack's heart races
when he first lays eyes on Sophie Winterton. She is everything he desires,
but he is caught in his own ...

More romance titles from Severn House

BABY, COME BACK
ISBN 978-0-7278-8628-6

The very handsome man sitting on Alice Dougherty's sofa and asking
for her advice was none other than Hayes Bradford – the widowed father
she'd once come so close to marrying. It seemed like yesterday that Hayes
had broken her heart, yet it had been twelve years. Suddenly Alice found
herself in the middle of the family she still wanted to call hers.

WHITE LIES
ISBN 978-0-7278-8723-8

Jay Granger is summoned by the FBI to identify her gravely injured
ex-husband, Steve Crossfield. He's not at all like the man she remembered,
and she's drawn to him more than ever. Could this be a new start? Can the
new Steve ever share her cherished memories?